FARSCAPE™

SHIP OF GHOSTS

Farscape™ Novels
available from Tor Books

House of Cards
by Keith R.A. DeCandido

Dark Side of the Sun
by Andrew Dymond

Ship of Ghosts
by David Bischoff

FARSCAPE™

SHIP OF GHOSTS

David Bischoff

TOR®

A TOM DOHERTY ASSOCIATES BOOK
NEW YORK

Dedicated to all those responsible for good
sci-fi TV shows.

This is a work of fiction. All the characters and events portrayed in this
book are either products of the author's imagination or are used
fictitiously.

FARSCAPE: SHIP OF GHOSTS

A Tor Book
Published by Tom Doherty Associates, LLC
175 Fifth Avenue
New York, NY 10010

www.tor.com

Tor® is a registered trademark of Tom Doherty Associates, LLC.

ISBN: 0-765-34002-X

First Tor edition: January 2002

Printed in the United States of America

0 9 8 7 6 5 4 3 2 1

ACKNOWLEDGEMENTS

I would like to thank Guillaume Mustaars and
Greg Cox for their patience and their exciting editing.

I would also like to acknowledge
Martha Bayless as co-author of this book.

AUTHOR'S NOTE: "Ship of Ghosts" takes place during the first season of *Farscape*, not long after Crichton's voyage away from Earth in *Farscape I*, his trip through the wormhole, and his arrival on board Moya.

PROLOGUE

The figure standing on the vessel's bridge was as hard and unyielding as an ice planet: frozen on the surface, molten at the core.

"Fire!" he snarled.

"Captain!" exclaimed a WeaponTech, looking up startled from the blinking nubs and pressors of his command array. "I told you, sir, we haven't reached full energy capacity."

"There's no time! Can't you see?" The dark figure's forefinger shot up at the vu-screens hovering before them. "The damned Leviathan has seen us! She refuses to respond to comm efforts. She's going to StarBurst at any moment, and then she'll be out of our grasp!"

"We had to use a lot of power to keep up forcefield through that asteroid field, Commander Crais," said a young female adjutant at the side of the bridge. She adjusted her speaker-wire and looked up at Crais, worry in her blue eyes. "We haven't got full power, sir. If we fire now, we could threaten the hyperflux homeostasis—it could break apart our ship as well as theirs. We used up part of our reserves when we lowered the shields and destroyed that asteroid."

A smile crept across the commander's face, the smile of a Sebacean closing in on his quarry. "Lowering the shields and blasting the asteroid was the master stroke," he said, the gleam in his dark eyes triumphant. "The Leviathan was cowering behind that asteroid. I told them I would find them, and I told them I would wipe them from the face of the universe!" Crais watched as the huge ship floated above him in the screens, now exposed and vulnerable with the asteroid that had shielded it pulverized into a million spinning fragments. Crais's eyes narrowed and he raised his chin as he studied the ship on the vu-screen for one final moment. He did not see it as a Leviathan, a huge living cargo ship transformed from its use as a floating prison. No, he saw it as his nemesis—and the bearer of the creature who had killed his brother.

John Crichton was aboard that ship.

The Leviathan was an immense ovoid, with sleek curves like a sea-creature gliding through space. Even now Crais could see evanescent energies tremble along the tail and flicker up along the mottled edges of the cargo transport: the clear beginnings of StarBurst, the hyperspace jump that could take it across the wide gulfs of space in a flash. The damned thing didn't even have weapons. This whole business should be like shooting a fish in a barrel. The only problem was that this fish could jump—and its barrel was the whole of the universe.

Crais would have preferred to recapture the Leviathan, to imprison again the creatures who had stolen it and the traitorous Peacekeeper who had joined their crew. Most of all, though, he would have liked to have Crichton . . . alive. Alive for a time, at least. However, if that could not be—then they all must be destroyed.

His crew looked at him, waiting—waiting for the ship to regain full power, while the Leviathan readied itself to slip away.

"You're all afraid I'll break the ship up?" Crais cried. "If we wait for the power to rebuild, they'll be halfway across the galaxy! Is no one on this ship brave enough to wage war?" He erupted into action. The tails of his uniform ballooned as he leaped over the battlestation. With a powerful arm he swept the WeaponTech aside. His eyes took in the monitors with one glance and his gloved fingers fell upon the nubs of the controls. Crais knew every fibre of the *LightMessenger*: its speed, its agility and its powers of destruction. He was a TechGenius, and could not abide the weak wills of this new crop of Peacekeeper space-sailors. Better to take matters into his own hands—and savor the satisfaction of destroying the enemy himself. "I am a Peacekeeper," he said with a hard smile. "And now I shall keep the peace!" He thumbed up the power to full threshold, sighted and slammed a fist down on the engager.

"Kill!" he commanded.

The *LightMessenger* thrummed and throbbed as every bit of power was tapped. A penumbra of roiling energy formed in the screens. The Peacekeeper techs had to lower their visors to shield their eyes. Even with his special contact lenses, Commander Crais himself had to hold up a hand against the brilliance.

A single bolt of energy sliced through space toward the Leviathan.

"Yes!" said Crais. The shot was true. He could feel it deep in his guts. True!

But even as the crackling aurora speared toward the enemy vessel, the Leviathan's energies altered. Instead of continuing its StarBurst, it engaged its rockets and pulsed itself away from the strike of the energy missile. It rocked in the wake of the *LightMessenger*'s shot, but when the missile had passed it remained, as intact and as infuriating as ever.

Livid, Commander Crais pulled at the controls for another blast.

"Sir!" cried the female adjutant. "Another blast would weaken the colloidal suspension—the ship will break up!"

"Damn their eyes!" cried Crais, ignoring the adjutant. Still coaxing any energies he could from the control helm, Crais snapped orders to the comm officer. "Raise the *DarkWind*!"

The *DarkWind* was the *LightMessenger*'s companion vessel. Smaller, fleeter, it had managed to skirt the asteroid field and had been hovering well away from danger, its captain, Sha Sutt, awaiting her commander's orders. Crais had been so intent on personally finding and capturing—or, if capture was impossible, obliterating—the escaped Leviathan and his intended victims that he had scarcely thought it necessary to give orders to a lesser ship. But if he had to summon help to destroy his target, he was not above letting lesser captains in on the kill.

"Yes, sir," said the comm officer, and tapped the commands in.

After a screech of opening sig-frequencies, a familiar female voice fell from the ceiling: "*DarkWind*, at your command!"

"Sutt. Get into position and fire upon the Leviathan!"

There was a pause while the tech made distance calculations, even as the images in the vu-screens showed the Leviathan hovering, the shimmer along its tail clearer now.

"They are out of our range, sir. We are approaching. Forty-six seconds until they're within target range."

"Maximum speed!" roared Crais. Fury raged in him. The huge Leviathan was well within striking distance of his own ship, but now there was insufficient power. Or so his adjutant claimed. Crais fingered another switch. Yes! That was it!

"Commander! Cease conduction-energy flow to aft panel seven. Cut off fields and support for aft portion seven point two."

"But, sir! Those are where the prison cells are! Sir, you will remember that we're carrying a load of captured Jardagians from the Starside battle."

"I hereby declare them free beings once more," said Crais, "or as free as they'll ever be. Now do it!"

The commander ran his fingers over the controls and slapped a blinking override button with the palm of his hand. Energy was re-routed and the prisoners were freed—of light, warmth, atmosphere—of life. Immediately, the energy reserves powered up, the lights on the console shone a steady white, and the hum of the ship returned to its normal strength. A spark of dark hope glimmered in Crais's eye as he pressed down again upon the firing mechanism.

"Sir! No!" cried the commander.

The vortex of energies warped and wrenched into existence, a power blast of diminished proportions compared to the last, but enough to destroy a small moon—or a Leviathan. It drove through the blackness of space. However, so quickly had Crais fired the blast that the *LightMessenger*'s sensors had not been able to factor in the complex strategies to avoid obstruction. Drifting debris caught the brunt of the blast. When the glare of the explosion faded, the Leviathan still floated above them on the vu-screen. As the debris of the blast drifted away, the shimmer of imminent StarBurst began once again along the Leviathan's tail.

Crais yelped in frustration.

"*DarkWind*. Sha Sutt. You are the last hope," Crais cried. "Destroy them!"

"Maneuvering with all possible speed toward quarry!" came the voice of the commander of the *DarkWind* through the comm-link. "Debris and asteroids everywhere. Even in range it will take some doing to get a clear shot."

"Closer, then. Dammit, ram them if you must!"

The techs on the bridge of the *LightMessenger* were working madly. The lights had dimmed. Crais could smell burned insulation. He knew he had damaged this ship, but ships could easily be repaired—the Peacekeepers had nothing if not many ships and many minions.

What Crais needed now was vengeance—and damn the cost.

"We'll do whatever we have to, sir," replied the commander of the *DarkWind*.

"Do your duty!" said Crais. "That is all I ask."

Even now, he could see the *DarkWind* maneuvering through the asteroid field like a needle threading through a fabric of chaos. It shone in the energy flares, a silver fish in the ether.

But then Crais could see the energies gathering strength on a much bigger fish: the Leviathan. She was seconds away from StarBurst, he could tell it. Even as he noted this, another voice filtered through the commchannel, breaking up but still comprehensible.

"Nice try, Crais," said the voice of John Crichton. "But we're out of here. I don't suppose it will help to tell you again—I didn't mean to kill your brother. It was an accident. Is there any chance you can understand that?"

"You!" said Crais.

"One of these days maybe we'll have the chance for a neutral parley," said the voice of the human. "Until then, my friends and I agree that we should be departing this area with maximum speed. StarBurst speed, as a matter of fact."

The *DarkWind* was racing toward them. Crais could see it on the vu-screen, a quick, dark ship weaving between the asteroids. They would be within range in moments.

Crais watched helplessly as the telltale glowings of StarBurst fluttered around the huge expanse of the Leviathan. Within seconds the ship would be enveloped in unimaginable energies that would transport it to a part of the universe far, far from this sector—a place beyond the authority of the Peacekeepers.

"Maneuvering around asteroids. Clear shot in nineteen seconds," said the *DarkWind* commander. "However, I calculate that Moya will be long gone by then."

Crais clenched his jaw. He had promised Crichton that he would confront him and personally destroy him, avenge the death of his brother at last. However, Crais prided himself on being a practical Sebacean. This universe would be a better one without the Earth creature called John Crichton to stink it up. Ultimately it did not matter whether Crichton was killed by his hand or by another's. Crais was too great, and too ruthless, to be petty about vengeance. Anybody who killed John Crichton would be serving the cause of justice—and revenge.

Crais nodded to himself and calmly opened the comm.

"Captain . . ." he said to the commander of the *DarkWind*.

Crais knew what he had to do. Captain Sha Sutt would do anything for him—he knew she venerated him, even though they never quite had that closer relationship he had dangled before her. He could hear that veneration even in the clipped voice that came across the comm. Moreover, he well knew that the one person she despised most was aboard that Leviathan: Aeryn Sun. It was a desperate maneuver, but it was his only hope now of destroying that damned ship, and Crichton in it.

"Sutt," snarled Crais. "Too late for conventional weapons. Use the hellhound—and send Crichton to hell."

CHAPTER 1

The sound reverberated through the living ship like claws on a blackboard. Crichton looked up from the scope he had been studying. The huge vu-screen, spanning one entire side of the chamber, showed a dark immensity of space scattered with stars. Crichton glanced over at Aeryn, who was also studying the vu-screen, her brow furrowed.

"A distress signal," said Aeryn. "As loud and obnoxious as a two-headed Tronkan shrill-singer!" She looked at Crichton, her chin held high. She had intense eyes, hair as black as the chasms between the galaxies, a physique that was slim and strong, and a temperament that varied between sensitive and merciless.

Zhaan moved to the front of the bridge in her usual regal style, her turquoise-blue robes swirling out behind her as she walked. "Without question it's some sort of cry for help," she said. Her head, a serene blue like the rest of her, was as smooth and dappled as the bottom of a shallow stream. Crichton liked Zhaan and, what's more, trusted her, but when he looked into her startling eyes all he saw was the light-years that separated their minds. "I can hear it on deeper frequencies as well," she said.

"Peacekeeper trick!" cried Ka D'Argo, his braids whipping as he turned to the screens. The great ridges above his eyes seemed to stand out with a warlike fury, and his voice, which always seemed as if he were used to barking orders to cowards, took on a harsher tone. "Turn Moya around. Head the opposite direction. We can't take the chance!"

Crichton could not blame the guy. When they'd StarBursted out of the asteroid field and into who-knew-where, they'd only escaped Crais and his minions by the skin of their teeth. Supposedly they were now well beyond Peacekeeper space. However, the suspicious and the cautious always tended to live longer.

The distress signal paused for a moment and then resumed its distant shrieking.

"Depart in the opposite direction? Are you addled?" said Rygel XVI, all awobble in his ThroneSled, the device in which he preferred to move his little body about. Of all the Leviathan's crew, Rygel conformed most to the image of the kind of aliens that Crichton had actually imagined inhabiting outer space: bizarre, and yet somehow familiar. Rygel sometimes seemed more like a fungoid growth than a person, a growth with eyes and tiny little hands, and a funny face tucked under shrubby white brows and packed with more expressions than any earthly primate. He looked like the result of some mad scientist's experiments in melding a baboon, a terrier and a large frog. He was vainglorious, disgusting, arrogant and nasty. Fortunately, in an animated blob less than three feet tall, these traits could occasionally come off as endearing. As long as he didn't bite people too often.

"Are you truly sure we want to avoid that thing?" asked Rygel. "They may have something good to eat!"

"Is that all you think of?" said D'Argo, his deep voice throbbing, his eyes shining with a warrior's indignation. "Your black hole of a stomach? We must survive! We must find our way to our homes!"

"You think I am not concerned that my people regain their Prized One?" said Rygel, his expressive eyebrows rising as high and as regal as his ego. His empire had been usurped. He wanted it back. In the meantime he acted as if he already had it back. "But I must regain my true majesty with the right delicacies, properly prepared and—"

D'Argo roared and struck at the minuscule monarch, who sped away on his ThroneSled.

Crichton looked around him, assessing the expressions of his companions. Together by no choice of their own, Crichton and the other inhabitants of Moya—a sleek living ship shaped something like a horseshoe crab spangled with lights—could be called a "crew" only by default. Far, far from home, with no captain, no chain of command, and no reason to stay together other than a common enemy pursuing them, they were forced to trust one another. Not long ago, Crichton had reflected that misery loved company, and so it was with this odd bunch. Usually, though, it was only calamity that bred cohesion . . . if you could call what they had cohesion.

"Shipmates, shipmates!" cried Zhaan above the blended din of the alarms and the shrieks. "Lives may be at stake!"

Aeryn shook her long, dark locks and bent over to tune down the onboard sensors once more. "The lives I'm concerned about are ours." She tilted toward her comm. "Pilot! First could you get that wretched noise down to something below screech level? And then could you tell us what Moya thinks is putting out that hellish whine?"

"Yes," Zhaan assented. "We should at least get an idea of what it is before we make any mistakes."

"Mistakes," said D'Argo, "are best made at discretionary distances." He moved out from behind his console to look at the vu-screen, his fiery hair and the quilted blood-red tunic making him look, to Crichton's eyes, like a Mongol warrior about to launch a spear at an oncoming horde.

"And you call yourself a man of war," Rygel taunted, making his own violations of good manners at a discreet distance, Crichton noted. Rygel's ThroneSled was hovering at the edge of the bridge, under the arc of one of Moya's metallic ribs, far from the consoles where the rest of the crew stood trying to punch up information. Rygel smoothed one of the long whiskers trailing from his cheek and fingered his royal-purple collar. "Why, in my army," he said importantly, "you would be lucky to scrub the Nebari latrines!"

D'Argo had regained his composure. "Retreat, escape and survival are no shame to a warrior!" he intoned.

"Pilot, have you found the source of that noise?"

"Still checking," responded Pilot, or rather Pilot's hologram, clasped between two clamshell-shaped halves like Pilot on the halfshell. Pilot's actual self—four-armed, carapaced and seemingly always on the alert—stayed in Moya's innermost chamber, where, living in symbiosis, he had become a part of her neural network.

He looked down, studying Moya's interfaces. "Moya too is concerned for your safety, and of course her own."

"And yours, Pilot?" said Aeryn, gritting her teeth less as the blasting signal eased.

"I live to serve, and I serve most humbly," Pilot replied mildly. As the interface between the crew and the huge and splendid living starship, Pilot's entire existence revolved around his starship. This particular starship, Moya, was a Leviathan, a species of ship normally used for peaceful purposes. She had been quite a prize for the Peacekeepers, who had fitted her with a control collar and then managed to modify her. Like the others, Pilot and Moya had been prisoners. But not only had Moya been a prisoner, she had been a prison. When Rygel, Zhaan and D'Argo had escaped the clutches of the so-called Peacekeepers, they'd also liberated Pilot and Moya. Not many escapees took their prison with them. Actually operating her was a different story entirely. Sometimes it felt to Crichton as though Moya were operating them.

As a boy, John Crichton had often gazed up at the stars with his father, the famous twentieth-century Earth astronaut Jack Crichton. Looking up at the inky blackness his father had travelled in, he had been filled with wonder. How could he have guessed that there'd be much more terror up here than wonder!

The distinction of being a second-generation astronaut was, for Crichton, double-edged. After earning his doctorate in theoretical sciences, Crichton spent his time as a scientist/astronaut in his famous father's shadow, always trying to impress and please the Great Jack Crichton, Mister Extremely Right Stuff. However, John Crichton was never forced to scrabble to make a name for himself, since he was born into a legacy that seemed destined for space travel. When his experimental mission aboard the *Farscape I* module had shot him through a wormhole, Crichton found he was definitely not in Kansas any more. Here at last he was forced to call upon the courage and determination he'd inherited from his dad but never needed to use. Sometimes he remembered those days with a wistful nostalgia, back when travelling through Earth's solar system had seemed like the biggest adventure possible.

"Registering incoming transitional feedback," Pilot said. "Analyzing. Processing. Reflecting . . ."

"Pilot," said Aeryn. "Just tell us what the frell that thing is."

"I sincerely wish that I could, Aeryn," replied Pilot.

"Sometimes I yearn for the days before control interfaces talked!" said Rygel. "Ah well. I shall amuse myself by twiddling my toes."

"Pilot, Moya must be able to find something!" said D'Argo, pacing from the empty vu-screen to the console and back again.

Pilot peered down at a screen. "Yes, Moya has found

it." As he spoke, they could feel the great ship beginning to veer around. "And I can now classify it, as well.
Our databanks indicate that the vessel resembles a Nokmadi Navigator, legendarily lethal to foes—"

"And just plain legendary!" said Zhaan. "Pilot, the
Nokmadi are mythical creatures, surely. How can we—?"

"Fabled, perhaps. Mythical, apparently not." Crichton
could see Pilot's appendages dance and sway over the
controls. "Databanks do contain information on the
Nokmadi as a space-faring people. I am trying to retrieve that information now."

Rygel's eyebrows were nearly on the ceiling. "I with-
draw my suggestion! I advocate doing what this group
does best—run!"

"Wait a moment," said Zhaan, ever the calm voice at
times such as these. "Nokmadi—Navigator." She
breathed in, breathed out. Her eyes closed. Her smooth
head seemed to radiate intelligence. She was the image
of concentration.

Suddenly those large alien eyes were open again.

"Navigation! Of course. Our Delvian myths say the
Nokmadi were a race that set out to map the galaxies!"

"Navigation?" said D'Argo, suddenly interested.
"Maps, you say? Such vessels would surely be equipped
with databases. Old perhaps, but—"

Crichton could feel his adrenaline surge. "Yes!" he
cried, pumping his arm in the air. "A motherlode of
maps!"

The others looked askance at Crichton and he winced.
He had to remember to limit his Earth gestures. Even
the translator microbe injection in his parietal cortex,

which made communication possible with aliens, couldn't always handle those references.

"I mean," he explained, "that sounds like the navigational material we need to find our homes."

D'Argo's deep voice rumbled. "Crichton's summation, however bizarrely expressed, is correct. We may have the opportunity here to obtain the information we need." His eyes grew soft. "I will hazard risk if it brings me closer to a reunion with my son."

A rapid jumble of images swept through Crichton's mind. Adventure in space was exciting, sure—especially if the length of your lifespan wasn't much of a concern. And he had always looked out at the great inky expanse of space, deeper than night, with eagerness about what new discoveries might turn up under the light of those flaming stars. But now it had been months since he had had his feet firm on the soil of Mother Earth, had felt the warmth of the sun on his face, had read a newspaper or seen a movie or gorged on waffles and coffee late on a Sunday morning. Space was big, and there was a lot of room to be far from home.

He looked around at the others and nodded. "I agree. I don't know about you guys, but I can't help but notice that this part of the universe is nothing but trouble. We might as well get some trouble that might help our ultimate goal."

The silence between them was thick. Emotions raced through eyes as they looked at one another. The flashing lights of the distress signal, registered on the bridge, formed a backdrop to their indecision. Crichton could feel the worry and the desperation, but he could also sense the hope and longing and need. He didn't need a translator for that.

"Pilot, I command you to depart at full possible speed!" Rygel pronounced imperiously.

"Fool!" cried D'Argo. He grabbed the diminutive alien by his bulging neck and started throttling. Rygel's gray skin turned even grayer than before and his face went through ineffectual gnashing contortions that suggested he was trying to sink his teeth into D'Argo's arm.

"Pilot," said Zhaan. "Disregard that order. We have not yet decided—"

"I'm getting a reading on the screens," announced Aeryn. "Are those measurements I'm getting correct? Those specs are quite large for a travelling ship—"

"I'm trying to countermand, but Moya is startled," said Pilot. "StarBurst is engaging—"

"No!" said D'Argo, dropping Rygel, who began to sputter. "We can't—"

"We're giving her too many orders!" said Aeryn, flinging back her hair and punching in rapid overrides as her console began to light up in red. "The power can't be switched back and forth like that—something's going to fry down there!"

Oh God, thought Crichton. He had always known that being an astronaut might be a rollercoaster ride, but he hadn't expected a galactic amusement park.

Moya resumed her turn toward the sound, and the gleaming floor of the bridge began to tilt slightly as they wheeled around. Abruptly the vu-scopes on the walls held a larger, darker object. Some sort of raging, wavering beam emerged from it like a streak of yellow crayon in the hands of an angry kid god. It roiled through the ether, sparking with violent energies. Before Moya could even think about engaging StarBurst engines and thus warping space into a jump across light-years, the beam enveloped her.

"A tractor beam!" cried D'Argo. "By J'Anra's dewlaps, I've never seen one bigger than—"

Even as Zhaan and Aeryn worked madly at the controls to yank some kind of counter-maneuver from the ship, the vivid yellow spread over the screens. The bridge shook.

Crichton grabbed hold of his station-stalk and held on for dear life. Ripples of kinetic energy passed through the bridge's ceiling and floor. Rygel's Throne-Sled hopped around like a Mexican jumping bean, throwing him on his small posterior. The DRD units scurried over to prevent him from rolling around.

"Indecision!" roared D'Argo, struggling up from the floor. "It could be the death of us. And perhaps it already is."

"Pilot," said Zhaan. "Status report."

The holographic image flickered. "Moya is surrounded by some sort of containment field linked to a nexus fulcrum anchored to a remarkable counterforce of indeterminate origin," said Pilot.

"As I said," D'Argo said. "A tractor beam."

"It looks as though we're going to help whatever broadcast that distress signal, whether we like it or not," Zhaan said, yanking herself up to her station.

"This is not Peacekeeper tech," said Aeryn. "This is not anybody I recognize."

"Silver linings are good," said Crichton. "Everything's remarkably intact for such an onslaught of ener—"

The beam flared to orange and Moya was shaken again. Crichton was ripped from his place and staggered toward the wall. His head slammed against a bulkhead, and blackness came down like an anvil.

CHAPTER 2

 ohn?"
J   He was sitting at a table in a conference room. In
front of him was a large coffee mug with a cartoon by
Gary Larson. He must be back on Earth, then. Somehow
it didn't surprise him. He took a gulp of coffee, strong
and hot, set the mug back on the table, and studied the
cartoon. In it, aliens were descending the ramp of a
flying saucer: one of the bug-eyes had fallen down and
was now a jumbled pile of tentacles and eyestalks in
front of clueless Earth people. "Oh," says the alien captain sarcastically, "that will fill the Earthlings with a
sense of awe and wonder."
   "John?"
   Beyond the table was a huge window of special
shock-resistant Plexiglas, looking out on the Atlantic
Ocean and giant towers of scaffolding holding a Titan
rocket topped with a space shuttle. A flock of seabirds

were flying through, flecks of white against blue. He could almost smell the sea breeze whispering through the long grass on the marsh banks and the fuel on the tarmac, taste the salt of the sea and the—

"John?"

He recognized the voice—it rang with authority, yet it also had that devil-may-care Chuck Yeager the-plane's-going-down-in-flames-but-we're-having-a-barbecue-in-the-cockpit twang. Astronauts and airline pilots had perfected that twang to its present twenty-first-century state and Crichton himself could do it in his sleep, with Industrial Light and Magic special effects.

It was his father. Commander Jack.

Crichton turned. Through a haze made up of the scents of coffee and fresh carpet, he saw the Old Man rearing up before him.

"John?"

"Dad?"

"John, we've got to talk."

The Old Man was in his Air Force uniform, complete with medals and epaulets. He moved until he stood just on the other side of the table, but to Crichton he felt a million miles away.

Crichton had always been thankful for his own good looks. Even during the usual nervous adolescence, he'd always found it easy to talk to girls, and they seemed to find him attractive, thanks to his symmetrical features, sea-blue eyes and brown hair, straight and bushy when short but with a hint of a curl when it got longer. There were times, though, when he stared into the mirror and hated his face, because he knew that in thirty years it was going to look a lot like the Old Man's. Jack Crichton looked as though he'd been chiselled on Mount Rushmore out of Right Stuff granite, come alive and stumped over to fly Apollo missions. He had a face of mythic proportions. The same kind of steely gray eyes had looked out over the prairie and said, "Yup." Those wrinkles had been beaten out by Western skies in lawless towns when men were men and whiskey was inner hurt's only salve. He was the kind of guy who had built America into the can-do empire it had become.

Too bad about the sons who had been neglected along the way to glory.

"Talk, Dad? Sure. Let's have a good father-son talk. A real one, like I've always wanted. What's going on?" said Crichton.

"This mission of yours," said Jack Crichton. He smelled of Old Spice after-shave. "I'm proud of you and everything, but really—faster-than-light travel? That's a big stretch. I just don't want you to get your hopes up too high." The big twinkling smile widened into a hyper-American grin, greater than the Great Outdoors. "Course, there will be plenty of good rides even if we're never able to make it out of the solar system! But listen . . . Even though I'm jealous as hell that you get to go out and be Buck Rogers—"

"Dad, it works!" Crichton could feel the singular rush of scientific thrill again. For a few moments, he had been a god! "I made the mission. But I hit the gravity wave of a black hole, Dad. I got sucked in and spat out in another galaxy." And the other gods saw his hubris and struck him down. It had been a rollercoaster ride with a downside that had never yet stopped, and his stomach was still a few light-years behind him. "Faster-than-light travel exists already—and there are plenty of extraterrestrials out there that use it!"

The Old Man's face creased into a frown. "I don't understand. What happened?"

"Dad," said Crichton, "I was shot out of a wormhole and right into something out of *Star Wars* directed by Alfred Hitchcock. There are a bunch of races out there. One's called the Peacekeepers. They keep the peace by stormtrooping around the galaxy, taking over planets. They had this great big living starship called a Leviathan, Dad. They'd collared it and turned it into a prison ship. But three of the prisoners—this beautiful blue woman named Zhaan, a huge warrior with fleshy dreadlocks called D'Argo, and a deposed midget monarch named Rygel—escaped and liberated it. Well, it's a long story, but seems my ship smashed into a Peacekeeper's fighter ship and killed the brother of a head honcho who's now vowed revenge on me. I tainted a female Peacekeeper called Aeryn Sun by association, so she's stuck on Moya—that's the escaped Leviathan, run by a huge crab-like creature called Pilot. The Peacekeepers are after us, and all we want is to find our way home! Our problems are way bigger than finding a way out of the solar system."

The Old Man sniffed. He pushed a bowl toward his son. "Jellybean, son?"

Disbelief and consternation filled Crichton. "Dad! Aren't you listening to me?"

"The popcorn-flavored ones are amazing."

"Dad, you've never listened to me my whole life. All I wanted was to grow up to be as strong and courageous as you. Now that there are light-years between us, I realize that's the way it's always been: me speaking, and you not hearing me. Listen to me this time, Dad."

The Old Man looked away, out toward the view. A seagull was diving down towards prey in the marsh. Clouds the color of shale were moving in from the east, over the Atlantic. "Whatever happened to that sweet girlfriend of yours, John? Your mom and I really liked her."

Crichton Senior was looking out of the window.

Seagulls swooped onto window ledges. They stared in. They all looked like even shorter versions of Rygel XVI, Dominar of the Outer Whosiwhatsits.

"Ashlay? Ashlay?" they squawked peevishly. One flapped up, and squirted a long white trail of droppings across the window. Two others fought over a green food cube.

"What's going on? Is this some kind of government conspiracy, Dad?" said Crichton. "Am I in *The X-Files*? Am I loaded with experimental drugs?"

He looked at his father.

Commander Crichton was morphing into Crais, the fanatical Peacekeeper pursuing him. Crais's black hair shone, drawn back into a severe ponytail. His dark eyes glittered with intense hatred. He wore a belted leather robe that flapped at his ankles as he paced, his hands clasped behind his back. He smelled of spicy scented oil and gave Crichton a creepy feeling. Crais was a being for whom vengeance was the highest pleasure. He wheeled around and looked at Crichton, his face darkening.

"You killed my brother," said Crais, pointing a

gloved finger at him as though it were a sharp weapon. "You shall die."

Crichton hopped up. His chair crashed back. "Look, I told you. It was an accident."

"I am going to cram all of these into your mouth!" said Crais. His hand reached for the bowl. The jelly-beans had turned into a roiling mass of black alien insects. "They will bore through your innards like riplasers! They will eat your eyes from the inside out!"

Crichton turned and ran. He opened the door of the room. It was a doorway into space and time. Rod Serling stood before him, arms clasped, cigarette smoke twirling around his head. "You've entered a dimension of sight and sound . . ." he said.

"No," said Crichton, "I've entered a dimension of insanity!" He turned around just in time to see the jel-lybean bugs growing into giant heads filled with angry eyes and razor teeth.

"Sic!" ordered Crais, black eyes flashing with psychotic intensity.

The heads bounced off the table and started rolling his way.

"There's a signpost just up ahead," said Rod Serling raising a ragged black eyebrow, speaking through his clenched teeth.

The edge of the door canted. Crichton, losing balance, grabbed the dark coat-tail of the big-eyebrowed man, but the host of his nightmare jabbed his lit cigarette into the back of his hand. Like Alice into Wonderland, Crichton fell. A dark wind blew up from the caverns below, and Crichton found himself drifting past shelves stacked with complete collections of Tom Swift and Hardy Boys books, hula hoops and Furby dolls, and action figures, heavy on soldiers with weapon belts.

"Abandon Hope All Ye Who Enter Here," said a beanbag animal wielding a nasty-looking red pencil. "Beware, John Crichton!" said Robbie the Robot. "It's illogical, Captain," said a pointy-eared man with a bowl haircut, raising a razor-sharp eyebrow. "Force the Use, John!" cried another figure in a robe and a hood. "There's no place like home," said the Wicked Witch of the West, swooshing past him. "There's no place like home." Instead of Margaret Hamilton on the broomstick, though, it was Crais the Peacekeeper in black drag. "Which you'll never see again!"

With a maniacal laugh the last figure swept away.

"Crichton!"

Somebody was slapping his face. He felt cold liquid running down his front. He could feel a comforting and concerned emotional presence suffusing him. His fall stopped, and he was floating, floating. . . .

Crichton opened his eyes.

The light from Moya's lamps was dazzling, and he closed his eyes again to shut it out. His head hurt. His stomach was sour and there was a taste of fear in his mouth.

"Crichton! Are you all right?"

The soft voice felt like heaven. He opened his eyes again, slowly this time. Zhaan was kneeling beside him, her silken blue robes a soothing pool of tranquillity. The throb in his head began to subside. Zhaan leaned over and gathered him in her arms, and it felt good. He reached up and touched his face, and his hand came back sticky and red. Blood.

With an influx of adrenaline his focus sharpened. He surveyed the expanse of the bridge: the arc of the steel-skin ribs framing the chamber, the walls studded with lamps, the gleam of the copper-colored floor, a DRD scurrying bug-like toward one of the dislodged cables hanging from a console. D'Argo stood behind the console, shaking his head as he tapped the controls insistently, and Aeryn stood looking at Crichton asprawl on the floor. Her arms were folded, her face clouded. When she saw that he was fully conscious, she nodded and moved to one of the scopes, a grim expression on her face.

Then he remembered. The impact and the fall and that tractor beam—

"Zhaan!"

"I am here, John," she said from his side. "You were unconscious and experiencing severe psychological disturbances."

Although usually he felt only aloofness and mystery from this alien woman, now he felt comfort and warmth and trust. He just wanted to fold himself up in her arms and weep and tell her about how he'd found his father and lost him again. "Extreme psychological disturbances? My life as I know it," he said. "I was having a terrible nightmare."

"Welcome back to a terrible reality," said Aeryn.

Crichton pushed himself up. Now that his head was beginning to clear, he could see that the bridge was in disarray. The repair DRDs were tracing a jagged path between mechanical bits and pieces jarred loose from the consoles, and a crack had opened between two of Moya's metallic ribs. The entire chamber was showered in yellow light from the vu-screens. Another group of DRDs whirred and clicked defensively and adoringly around Rygel, their eyestalks waving. Aeryn and D'Argo hovered over the scopes, working away but also clearly wanting to be near something solid if that kind of cataclysmic collision happened again. "The alien ship!" said Crichton, remembering the event that had pushed him into nightmareland.

"Got us dead to rights, and moving in," said Rygel, eyebrows agitated. He fingered one of the whiskers sprouting from his face. "Pilot seems to be taking a nap."

"I am prepared for docking and boarding," said D'Argo, who had his Qualta Rifle—half rifle, half deadly sword—ready on his shoulder. "We shall not be captured without a fight!"

Crichton wobbled over to his own control area and punched up some scanners. "I see no sign of any kind of activity that would indicate they're preparing weapons. Looks like absolutely nothing is happening over there." He whistled. "That's one big piece of hardware. How big is that ship?"

"230 zacrons in diameter, 150 zacrons in length," said Aeryn. "No Peacekeeper ever made a ship this large." She was bathed in cool light from her display, looking grim but controlled. The worse the situation was, the fiercer she got.

The alien ship was more massive than any he had seen, easily the size of a small moon—or the pocks and rubble of a small moon bound together with great sinews and arteries. It seemed to be a contorted mass of spatial geometries, filled out with hills and valleys and twisted fissures through which arced flashes of electricity. Next to something that immense, Moya must seem like a flea gazing at a dog.

"And all that mass," continued Aeryn, "is getting closer and closer."

"Where's Pilot? Can we possibly use some other method to separate?" said Crichton, looking down at the organic cables below him. "Damn, I see the problem." Lucky thing this part of the operations was his speciality. He refastened the loose connection and squeeze-sealed the tab. The impact must have shaken it loose.

Instantly, the holograph of the arthropod frizzled back into view. It was much fuzzier than before, though it had white blips and futzed on and off.

"Moya is frightened!" said Pilot instantly.

"Can she maneuver?" said Crichton.

"She is helpless. It feels as though the Peacekeeper collar is on again," said Pilot, raising his articulated arms as though to slough off invisible chains. "Only this time, over the entirety of the hull. There is no room for movement."

"Damn!" said Crichton. "What does that ship want from us?"

"Whatever it is, it needs to be close to get it. And," said Zhaan, "it's getting closer."

Crichton looked up. The sharp outlines of the vessel stood in vivid relief against the stars. Then, one by one, the stars were edged out as the monstrous ship filled more and more of Moya's vu-screen.

"Oh, great. Next it'll be nuzzling up against Moya,"

said Crichton. "What is this, some kind of starship mating ritual?"

"Fortunately, the vessel does not appear to be sentient. Its approach is not a sexual advance," reported Pilot.

"No, I didn't mean it literally," said Crichton. "Well, good, if it's not organic, then presumably it doesn't want us for a snack either."

The problem with a starship like Moya was that, as big and spectacularly organically and technically equipped as she was, she had no weapons. The faster-than-light StarBurst route was pretty much her only trump card, and now that she couldn't move, that was right out of the picture. This was one of the ironies that had always bothered Crichton. To get whisked out of the twenty-first century into a new galaxy was a lark, but part of the package was supposed to be whopping great zap guns and light sabres and the like to fight with. Moya was more or less buck-naked, in space opera terms.

Then the tractor beam turned a bright red. The craggy hull of the vessel was so close now that if it were a seagoing ship, you'd be able to see the barnacles.

"What's happening?" said Rygel. The DRDs surrounding him had paused in their adoration, and the running lights that ringed their lower rims were quiet, as if they too were waiting.

"We're being towed in for docking, I presume," said Zhaan. "Any ideas?"

"I am still ready for defense!" said D'Argo, gripping his weapon in the crook of his arm with savage intent.

"You see," said Rygel, his voice tinged with disdain,

"we've absolutely nothing to worry about. One Luxan warrior should hold off a ship of any size, wouldn't that be so?"

Aeryn threw him a glance, her eyes narrowed. "I hear that in times of war," she said, "Luxans save two energy bolts should they be trapped. One for suicide and one for puffed-up arrogant deposed rulers."

"Fortunately for me," said Rygel mildly, "they are so dim they utilize the former first."

The Luxan growled and glared at Rygel, looking as though he was thinking of violence but was stymied by sheer wit. Fortunately for Rygel, vengeance, witty or otherwise, was interrupted by an outcry.

"What are those things?" said Zhaan, startled. "Oh no! They're coming toward us!"

CHAPTER 3

Crichton had never seen anything like it.

Thick tendrils of some sort, great vegetable stalks ending in barbs and snags, moved outward. They wavered towards them in a flock of perhaps twenty, like floating seaweed. This kelpy stuff seemed to move with a purpose. Even as they swam towards Moya the stalks coiled and separated, flinging themselves out to surround and enfold the Leviathan. Crichton flinched as they wrapped over the screens. The bridge shook and the screens frizzled off and then back on again.

The lights died to a soft ambient green glow which hushed all into a mordant sour yellow.

The Pilot hologram wavered but held fast, as though it were keeping itself alight through dint of sheer willpower. "Moya has been held fast by some kind of scixplast extensors," he reported, his voice calm but concerned. "Biosystems indicate no hull damage. I'm tracing through the internals for signs of difficulties, and DRDs are being readied for any necessary repairs."

"So we're under attack, then," said Crichton.

"We don't know if it's that," said Zhaan. Somehow her terse and steady voice exuded a calming peace. She seemed to glow blue. And the deep floral scent of her still had a pacifying effect on Crichton. "There is something unusual about these attackers. For one thing, their ship is a giant plant."

"A plant?" said Crichton. "You can't be serious."

"I know plants," said Zhaan, "and I am serious. And remember, they've shown no signs of weapons and we haven't been harmed."

Crichton touched his hand to his head and held out evidence to the contrary, slick and slimy and upsetting. Still, its iron smell was familiar and as he looked at it, he realized that it had been brewed in the genetic labs of Mother Earth—and therefore, so far from home, it seemed worthy of reverence—almost holy. "That's called blood." He held up his hand with its smear of red for all to see. "Red blood. Human blood. My blood."

D'Argo leaned over, sniffed it, grinned and seemed to approve of the smell. He clamped a brotherly hand upon his companion-in-arms and looked toward the alien ship, wiggling like a Picasso squid in the sea of space.

"Let them attack," said D'Argo. "I am prepared." Eyes afire, he reached back and touched the gleaming golden weapon slung over his back in an almost ritualistic way. "I shall fight with tooth and tentacle, should it be necessary."

Aeryn turned her molten eyes toward the others. The sides of her white shirt were damp with sweat. "I stand ready as well. Pilot! Access Moya's data banks. We need all the information we can get on past encounters with such vessels—mythical or otherwise."

"A number of the starfaring races used to have legends about the Nokmadi," said Pilot after a moment of concentration, the dome atop his head tilted down in a decidedly monkish manner. "The legends say this is a very ancient race indeed. They named their ships Navigators because their quest was to map the universe. Whether they succeeded, the stories do not say. This is where my knowledge of the legends ends. But there is unknown data and foreign matter of the past, far, far beyond my ken. And there are also bits and pieces of information in the biocomputer that have been partitioned away over the years." He paused and glanced down at the complex consoles that made up his interface with Moya. "There is a very small amount of information about the Nokmadi there, but it is fragmentary, like a star map that shows only half the stars. Moya has the silhouette of a Nokmadi ship recorded, but it is an ancient silhouette, produced from a drawing, and the ship in it differs from this one somewhat." Pilot's hands reached out to punch buttons, and the outline of the ship came up on Crichton's screen. Zhaan, Aeryn and D'Argo gathered around the console to study the drawing. It was clearly drawn by someone whose skills were rudimentary: barely more than an outline. Like the ship in front of them, the vessel in the drawing was a large ovoid like a distorted moon, but in the drawing its sides were smooth and featureless.

"Any idea how big the ship in this drawing is supposed to be? And who made this drawing, and how long ago?"

Pilot shook his head slowly. "Incomplete data. I'm afraid Moya can tell us no more."

"Very well," Aeryn said. She turned to face Zhaan. "Why don't we access your databanks, Zhaan? Knowledge could be the only kind of power we've got now."

After some moments, Zhaan nodded and closed her eyes. The gently draping aquamarine robe that hung from her statuesque body shimmered. As always, John Crichton felt he was in the presence of something deep and enigmatic.

Zhaan rubbed her fingers lightly over her forehead, as though massaging memories to life. "Yes," she said. "There is something there. I can remember tales of the Nokmadi—" She sighed. A moment passed in stillness. Then her eyes opened again and she shook her head. "Ships, travelling, Navigators, ancient stories. But like Moya's memories, they're only fragments."

"And in these fragments, did they travel the universe capturing innocent Leviathans?" asked Aeryn. With a slim but muscular arm she wiped away the sweat on her brow.

Zhaan took her fingers from her temples and sank onto one of the seats. "I don't know," she said with a trace of sorrow in her voice. "It's as if the Nokmadi were so ancient that no memory is deep enough to reach them. I can retrieve a fragment here and a fragment there, but nothing to put together into understanding. I suppose it's as if I too have a star map with only half the stars."

Rygel fingered the purple collar of his pint-sized potentate's robe impatiently. "Any emperor would know," he declared, "that you get the scribes to copy the maps onto translucent pieces of paper, and then lay one over the other. In my day I had sixty-six autoscribes copying night and day, and those were just the accounts of my glory. Of my glorious ancestors, Rygels I through XV—"

"The miniature one has had a good idea!" interrupted D'Argo. "Parwenian gneezels are flying! The fiery deserts of Flameworld are freezing over! The—"

Aeryn rolled her eyes. "You say there was a good idea, D'Argo? The rest of us missed it."

This time Pilot interrupted, his four arms working simultaneously on the controls, his brow furrowed. "Yes," he said, "yes, that might work. If we combine databanks, we will certainly improve upon the partial knowledge of each. And with her particular physiology, Zhaan can establish a direct link to Moya's neural circuitry for a brief time, if I can locate the exact neural connection."

"Combine databanks?" said Crichton.

Zhaan strode over to Pilot's hologram. He nodded at her, the carapace that domed his head shining in the light. "As if we laid one star map over another."

Pilot's head dipped. "Zhaan's metabolism is slow enough that she can take in the data from Moya without overwhelming her own system. But it must be brief. Zhaan?"

Zhaan gave a quiet smile. "Certainly, Pilot. I welcome any opportunity to gain knowledge."

"Excellent! Then it will all be taken care of!" said

Rygel, who looked decidedly bedraggled and roughed up by all this bouncing around. His clothes were awry and his eyes looked as though they'd just spun around inside his brainpan, while the usually well-groomed threads of hair growing from his face were all fuzzed and mussed. "If you find something out, I give you leave to act on your own. Now I need to use the little king's room." He started away, trailed by DRDs.

"He is going to hide!" D'Argo barked, glaring after the little alien. "Rygel, stand fast and do the honorable thing! We prepare for battle. Select your weapon and stand by our sides. If our lights of life are to be extinguished, let it be only after battle. Come, repair your good name with honor and glory!"

Rygel lifted a hand in a dismissive manner, fingers doing a toodle-oo. "You know where I can be reached!"

"Yes, in a room full of helium farts!" said Aeryn. "Are you ready, Zhaan?"

Zhaan nodded. On Pilot's instructions, they detached the thickest of the living cables from the main console. Zhaan took her position on a bench just behind the console, and D'Argo volunteered to attach the cable to Zhaan. He took a fiercely serrated short knife and held it above Zhaan's neck. She craned her neck to look back at D'Argo and nodded slowly.

Crichton heard a sharp intake of breath from Zhaan. A cable was now trailing into the console from the back of her blue robe. She saw Crichton looking at her with shock and gave him a wan smile. "I regenerate very quickly," she said.

"We must begin," urged Pilot. "Data transfer commencing."

Zhaan closed her eyes and brought her head down to her chest. She became as silent as a stone settling to the bottom of a pond. The only noise was the sound of a DRD whirring past and a muttered curse from Aeryn as she tapped on her console panels.

Abruptly, Zhaan opened her eyes. It was like flowers blossoming, full and rich, abounding in deep color. But she wavered and seemed about to pitch forward.

With astonishing speed, D'Argo jumped forward and caught her. With a swift flick of his knife he yanked the cable free and dropped it to the floor. He cradled her in his arms for a moment, then gently lowered her onto the bench. "Aeryn, water!" he barked.

"I'm doing a vital job here!" said Aeryn.

"She needs water, now!" said D'Argo.

Crichton moved to the bridge trough pool. He filled a beige ceramic cup with good old H_2O, pleasant and cool, the same throughout the universe and thank God for that. He brought it over to D'Argo, who attended to Zhaan, letting some of the cool, sweet water slip into her mouth. Zhaan imbibed gratefully and smiled up at the warrior helping her.

"Thank you," she said. "How did you know I was parched?"

D'Argo smiled down at her warmly. "There is nothing like water to feed life. Water is precious and your life is precious." He shot an annoyed glance back at Aeryn. "Are you all right, then, Zhaan?"

She nodded gratefully. "How soon the healer needs healing."

"Are you ready to tell us what you saw?" said D'Argo.

"Yes, and why did you have that odd attack?" said Crichton.

"I don't know. It was as though . . ." She paused and a haunted expression crossed her face.

"What's wrong, Zhaan?" asked Crichton.

"It was as though someone was looking at me," continued Zhaan. "Studying me. Learning. An odd, overpowering presence."

"Moya," said Crichton.

Zhaan tilted her head to consider his suggestion. "No," she said after some moments. "I could feel Moya—she is a strong presence as well, but one that we feel to some degree around us all the time. This was different—as if I suddenly had been caught in the beam of a great spotlight pointed at all of us."

"That doesn't sound fun."

"No. But I'll be fine. Thank you for the water. And Moya's memories did help me learn more of the Nokmadi." She smiled faintly. "Or rather, now I remember more—although some of my memories are Moya's."

"The Nokmadi were explorers and warriors?" prompted D'Argo.

"No," said Zhaan. "They did not wage war. They did travel the universe. Mapping. Learning. They merely sought to understand."

"Things might have changed in a million cycles or so," said D'Argo. "It would help us to know the weak points of this race and their ships."

"Wait a moment. I'm remembering . . ." Zhaan shook her head. "Many peoples have legends of a vessel that appeared at a distance from their home planet. It floated into their territory one day, and floated away again."

"Maybe the ship itself was sentient? Maybe no one was aboard?" suggested D'Argo.

"No," said Zhaan. "Someone was aboard. They could feel her."

"Her?" said Crichton.

Zhaan opened her scintillant eyes and looked at them. The depths of the universe and of time itself glowed in those eyes. "Some kind of being, or perhaps beings. In a vessel that wandered throughout space. The legends say that the vessel never returned home."

"Lost navigators," said Aeryn. "How very frelling poetic."

Zhaan rose from the bench and strode around the chamber, her hands clasped behind her back, her silken robes shimmering under the light. She stopped to gaze up at the vu-screen, which showed the great pits and valleys of the other ship at a range so close it seemed as if the two ships might bump together.

"That ship is so pitted, it looks like the surface of an uninhabited moon. Like a moon, it could have been moving through space for aeons."

Aeryn moved beside her, craning her long neck to study the vu-screen. "So you think that this . . . this ship . . . it's that lost ship. Only it's found us?"

"I discount no possibility. However, it does seem extraordinary."

"I am sick as hezmana of myths. Pilot, have you had any success yet on the communication bands?" asked the ever-practical D'Argo.

"None whatsoever, I'm afraid," returned Pilot. "However, there has been activity with the tendrils. They have sought out and found the cargo hold. I have also managed to realign my anterior screens. We can now see what's happening along Moya's side."

The screens flickered and showed a different view. Crichton could see the thick tendrils wrapped around Moya—and beyond the jagged hull of the ship. Something was happening.

"Looks like they're pulling us even closer, for actual docking," said Aeryn. "They've scoped out the cargo hold and know what to do."

"Like opening a tin can," said Crichton.

"Crichton, Aeryn, join me," said D'Argo. "We must greet the intruders."

"And me?" said Zhaan.

"For this endeavor we need warriors," said D'Argo. "We will contact you from the other vessel—if we can."

The warrior's coat-tails and head-tentacles whirled as he swept away. Grabbing up her own gun, Aeryn gave Crichton a significant glance, threw him a pulse pistol and then followed.

"Show time!" said Crichton.

His name was Rygel XVI and he was a right and royal sovereign. With dignity and composure he looked out upon his subjects, who whirred and squeaked with awe and servitude. From his lofty height, looking out over his personal chamber, Rygel held out his hand and made the royal gestures of acceptance of this adoration and praise.

"To you, good sirrah, I bestow my beneficence!"

Rygel twiddled his fingers. His expressive eyes lowered upon the small, metallic, bug-like subjects, who twittered and responded with a jerky motion. Rygel had

absolutely no idea what the twittering meant, but he
rather fancied it being something along the lines of,
"Hail, holiest of masters, and hallowed be thy stool!"

Savouring the odors of this royal moment, the Great
One turned to another subject, who seemed to be doing
some kind of herky-jerky backwards-and-forwards
dance of praise itself.

"To you, good subject, I bestow my beneficence."
Happy now in his element, sensing familiar smells with
his delicate nostrils as the gases started to percolate and
whisper up, feeling pleasant tingles, the Once and Future King felt that all was right. Rygel XVI, Dominar,
was on his throne.

"I well remember the time that two women came to
me," said Rygel to his subjects, raising his voice slightly
so that they could hear every exalted word from their
lowly positions. "Each claimed ownership of a baby.
They came for me to judge who was the rightful mother.
Now, in this era of extreme genetic confusion, it could
well be that both were the mothers and there were no
fathers. But, my loyal friends, in my wisdom I cut to
the true matter at hand. 'I have decided,' I told them,
'that I shall eat the baby and thus determine its rightful
parent.'" The diminutive Dominar raised both eyebrows and looked expectantly down at his subjects.

"And it was very tasty in a fresh Baza wine sauce,
barbecued over naga coals."

They wiggled their eyestalks and buzzed. One began
to turn around in circles, and another zoomed back and
forth until it ran into a wall.

Rygel laughed uproariously, farting with sovereign
authority.

"Nincompoops!" cried Rygel. "Of course I didn't eat the baby! Both mothers set up such a fuss that I had it cloned, and happiness was had by all!"

The DRDs winked and buzzed.

Rygel XVI sighed and gazed down at his subject. Although he was grateful they attended to him, they lacked certain something. What was it? Intelligence? Personality? Character? Certainly all those things, but then those were never qualities he'd looked for in subjects before. Ah well you had to take what you got, and be grateful!

What was it that that odd earthling had called him the other day? The Dunce and Future King? Hmm. That sounded right and royal. Rygel rather liked this new fellow. John Crichton had told him that he'd come from a world in which succession of rulers was, until recently, decided mostly by blood, so the earthling well knew the power and majesty this process visited upon the peoples who practiced it.

In fact, Crichton had told him of a dinky and foggy island that had once been a mighty empire and that still honored and appreciated its royal line. Alas, the place was now so diminished in stature that it was best known for witty conversation, good universities, and proper beer. Rygel identified with this island and thought its people might appreciate him. In fact, hearing that the current royalty was rather out of favor with its subjects rather perked up Rygel's hopes.

"Perhaps," he had told Crichton, "if we find your Earth first, I can apply for the job, and they can get the kind of monarch they deserve!"

Crichton had allowed that yes, he'd do his best to see that proper inquiries were made.

Still, it was tough for a former Dominar, imprisoned for many cycles, tormented and terrified and abused, to tend to his needs, even in freedom. Certainly it had taken long enough to persuade Pilot and Moya to lend him some DRDs as "assistants." Even then, if there was some kind of internal emergency, they'd buzz off to be about their duties like defender cells sensing an infection. They were just little mobile robots, the Diagnostic Repair Drones, round bug-like things on treads and wheels that patrolled the highways and byways of this intelligent ship's innards. Crichton said that they were the first thing he'd seen when he'd entered Moya; they were the beings who'd given him the microbe injection that served as a universal translator. They were the workfolk of the place, Moya versions of nanotech custodians, techs and mechanics. When Rygel saw that the rest of the crew weren't inclined to elevate him to the status that was his due, he immediately saw the potential of these creatures, smaller in size even than him.

"Now then," said Rygel XVI. "It would seem that Moya has got herself in a bit of a spot. Captured by a strange ship—my word! A careless bunch. If the other members of this silly crew would only listen to me!"

The DRDs buzzed and chirped in agreement.

"Yes," Rygel said. "When you're adored by millions of subjects, it seems to me much easier to go home and have myself restored to my rightful power. Then I can find out the location of the homes of the rest of the crew, but only after much sport, merriment and leisure. But do you think the crew listened to me? No! The fools. Yes, it is true, they pointed out that I was a deposed ruler and that not only might I be executed upon sight by the new rulers, but that they, as my associates, would meet a similar fate. Even though I told them that there were thousands and thousands of subjects who missed my benign rule terribly, they would not believe me! Can you see why I am so dejected? Can you see why I have this attitude?"

One of the DRDs scurried off and bumped into a wall. It twittered forlornly.

"Idiot! Fool! Lord, what I have to settle for!" The Dominar rolled his fingers over his lips, contemplating the puniness of his throne. Oh, how the mighty had fallen! But the truly mighty remain strong! The truly high-born are never less than royal. A higher breed, with higher brows and higher brains and higher intent and purpose. Somehow he must convince the others that he should be in charge, and his work with these DRDs was the only thing he could do right now.

Yes, he would shape them up!

"The others can deal with that little matter of being captured by an alien ship," said Rygel XVI. "They need practice in coping with minor difficulties on their own. Besides, I need to keep my magnificent self as safe as possible in such matters, in order to preserve what hope for order this galaxy has!"

The DRDs chittered and wobbled and bumped into walls with mechanical joy.

"Right. Now, let's see if we can't teach you a few things!" said Rygel.

He pushed the lever to flush, and then hobbled off

his throne, savoring the music of the gaseous sympho-
nies rising from his gurgling issue.

The docking bay of Moya was huge.

It had to be, thought Crichton, in order to accom-
modate the mammoth cargo that this Leviathan must
have carried in her day. He never failed to get a frisson
of awe when he looked at the opening that had accepted
him that fateful day of his arrival, when he was fleeing
the snarling storm of the Peacekeepers. Moya had accepted him like a mother receiving a child into her arms,
and she had sustained his life and his hope.

Now the sound of something big and mighty was
echoing through her massive halls like the rumblings of
cymbals prefacing a Wagnerian opera.

"The doors!" cried Aeryn.

"Prepare for invasion!" said D'Argo, assuming his
warrior stance. This time, instead of merely ritualisti-
cally touching the grip of his Qualta Rifle, he reached
behind and pulled it out at a speed that seemed to rival
the StarBurst itself. Tentacles waving slightly, the warrior stood alert, ready for anything.

"Let them do their worst!" spat Aeryn. She took a
stance right alongside D'Argo, her jaw set, her arms
outstretched to hold her pulse pistol at the ready.
Aeryn's Peacekeeper training was first-rate, and she
fought best in a group, as she had been trained—even
a motley group like this one. Crichton had complicated
feelings about her, but they were simplified in survival
situations like this. Fighting is a good sublimation for
other emotions.

"We should be behind a bulkhead," he said, switching off the safety of his own pulse pistol. "They could come out firing."

"We will retreat if necessary," said D'Argo. "It is bad form to show anything but bravery to a stranger. Courage is courage in all languages."

"Call it courage or call it curiosity," said Aeryn. With a shake of her head she flipped raven-black hair behind her shoulders. "I just want to have a look at what's there."

"We're not going to get sucked out into the vacuum, are we?" said Crichton.

D'Argo shook his head. "Moya has seals. She will compensate for any apertures, particularly since Pilot knows we're down here."

They stood poised, ready, and as they watched, the great cargo door began to ease open.

CHAPTER 4

The Peacekeeper ship, the *DarkWind*, had set loose the hellhounds. But instead of enveloping Moya in a radiant cloud of devastation, the untried weapon met the energies of StarBurst—and opened an envelope into the unknown.

Moya shimmered and disappeared into StarBurst, and the *DarkWind*, blown back by the lethal power of the combined forces, erupted into space in a flurry of quanta energy. As retros and stabilizers fought for balance and equilibrium, the cutter tumbled through a new space and a new time.

Its captain, Sha Sutt, struggled with the g-forces, fighting to maintain consciousness. She was rattled from the top of her handsome and determined face to the bottom of her prosthetic right foot. Anything that was not locked in place on the bridge tumbled and banged, scattered or thunked: the rectangular metallic case of a mobile tracking apparatus, a black light-sconce that had been jarred loose, the techs' palmtop dataholds. Everything seemed lighter, airier, as though the crew's minds had stopped short of their heads and their weight hadn't quite caught up with them. A young forcefield monitor, complexion pale as a moon, threw up in his maintenance bag. A sour smell permeated the atmosphere even as lights flashed on and off and an alarm sounded deep in the heart of the *DarkWind*.

"Stress levels on hull unacceptable," barked a grizzled pilot, grimacing through the map of wrinkles that was his face. "Captain, unless there's a transfer of energy from directional impetus to form equilibrium—we're going to implode."

"Do it!" snapped Captain Sutt.

Damn it! she thought, struggling not to be sick herself. Crais would not have ordered the pilot to sacrifice pursuit for survival—he would have driven the ship until she cracked up. But then again, Crais was light-years away. Her own judgement needed to be brought into play here.

The pilot's hands danced across the controls. He touched bulbs and pulled switches, and the graphs on the monitors slowly began to fill with energy—the power that would keep the crew of ten on the small Peacekeeper cutter alive. As he did so, a sub-pilot calibrated the power to stabilize the artificial gravity. It seemed to Sutt as though the universe was suddenly piecing itself back together again. The strange and hellish trip they had just experienced, seemingly through eternity and infinity, both of them lit by rainbows of an almost hallucinogenic intensity, coalesced into dull quotidian reality. Here she was, Sha Sutt, strapped in her captain's chair, surveying the bridge of a fourth-unit cutter, an old piece of junk that had seen far better days. The surfaces were dull and the upholstery on the chairs was thin. It smelled of Sebacean sweat glands and yesterday's dinner—and of that idiot's vomit, of course. But these were biological smells, and the wear and tear of a Peacekeeper's bridge, the odd tassels and rockshells and knickknacks from other planets (forbidden on the clean and neat First Class ships controlled by the tight-rectums further up the chain of command) made her feel as though some semblance of normality had been achieved. Even the gravity was settling back to normal, and she felt the return of weight dropping through her body, until she felt newly heavy, as if she had just climbed out of water. It made her head ache.

She shook off her wooziness and unclipped the harness that was biting into her chest. The straps fell to the sides of the chair, and she was able to breathe again. She looked up at the vu-screen. The Leviathan was gone—and so was the asteroid field.

"Where are we?" she demanded.

The navigator rumbled to himself for a moment, shaking his hair as though to remove the vestiges of the null-space they'd just been through, and then consulted the parabolas and digitals on the screens before him. "Indeterminate at the moment. If you'll just give me a second, Captain. Ah. Yes. Defining. Referencing. Out of range of all Peacekeeper ships, including the *LightMessenger*. But still in the galaxy, Captain."

"That's a relief," said Sha Sutt. "Keep on it, Hendrin.

I know you can refine our location. Sensors? Have we got a bearing on the Leviathan?"

"Objective not within scope of parameters. Will enlarge," said the queasy-looking woman near the sensor-bank, leaning over the sproutings of controls. Although she had the Peacekeeper veneer of calm and control, her eyes betrayed a gleam of fear. Peacekeepers were used to fear, though. They had to be in control, after all, not merely of their domain in the universe, but, above all, of their inner universe. They could not rule the outer without iron control over the inner. Equilibrium was everything—according to the rule book, anyway. Captain Sha Sutt well knew that this was not the case. One of the top Peacekeepers, after all, was Crais—and Crais was a volcano. Sha Sutt herself, despite the fact that she affected a composed and glacial countenance, knew all too well that this was a facade.

"Continue sensor scouting. We have our orders," she said with as much calmness as she could muster. The oblong vu-screen at the front of the bridge showed a scattering of unfamiliar stars. "We must locate the Leviathan. If we can recapture it and its crew, then we must do that. If we cannot recapture the Leviathan and its crew, our priority then is to capture the Earthman known as John Crichton and bring him back to Crais . . . And if we cannot capture him, then we must destroy him."

The crew was silent. They knew the importance of orders. Orders kept chaos out. Orders were structure. Orders, particularly orders from a commander as high as Crais, were the stuff of a Peacekeeper soldier's existence. Whether the crew knew how wild and unusual these orders from Crais were, they gave no indication. Even the fact that they knew that they were beyond the boundaries of Peacekeeper authority did not seem to deter them. Orders, for Peacekeepers, were orders—even unto death.

Again, Captain Sha Sutt saw the asteroid, hovering before them.

Again, she saw first the spangled thrashings of light, glimmering like a shattered spectrum from the pitted rim of the space-rock. The convex oval of the Leviathan heaved into vision—but even then its outlines were shimmering and shivering, about to take leave of solid space/time. Gut fear touched her, but she kept her composure as the magnificent sight glittered—and the words of her commander sounded in her ear.

"Too late for conventional weapons. Use the hell-hound—and send Crichton to hell." The dark mellifluous sound of his words filled her with emotion. The strength, the command of the man—it made her weak even to hear that voice.

"The hellhound! But Crais—sir! We're not cleared to engage the hellhound. We were en route to System Five for preliminary testing when you called us to join in the attempt to destroy the Leviathan."

"I know about the testing—and about the hellhound. Only a weapon this powerful can destroy the Leviathan before she evades us once more. Weapons Command will think it fired accidentally. Engage it now!"

"But, sir! That could be suicide . . ."

"Hurry, Captain! Do you want to be a lapdog of the bureaucrats, or do you want to kill the enemy?"

She knew what Crais would do—even at the risk of

destroying his own ship with an untried and dangerous weapon.

"Move into position! Fire the hellhound!" she commanded.

The DarkWind *blasted past the asteroid. The Leviathan was already disappearing, its form folding up into raw space. A blast into the boiling energy that enveloped it now might well backfire catastrophically. She watched as the blinding gleam of energy that was the hellhound lit the darkness and streaked toward the Leviathan.*

"Excellent—" said Crais.

But by then the comm window was closed, and a trapdoor of the universe had opened.

"Wherever we are, that Leviathan sure isn't here," the navigator said, a touch of resigned pessimism in his voice. "And the hellhound is completely unresponsive. Something about the explosion ripped our entire weapons systems wide open. It's far beyond anything we can fix before returning to home base."

A fearful lieutenant named Stribben, eyes wide, could not help but quaver: "Something's wrong. I can feel it."

Sutt glared at the perpetrator of the gaffe. Some less patient Peacekeeper might have given this fellow Stribben a space-walk. This was no time, however, for extreme discipline. "We do not know what happened. From my internal impressions, however, time is a definite factor. Chronometer reading?"

"Why—you're right, Captain. A full day and two frac-units have passed since we attacked the Leviathan," said a startled co-pilot named Dinn. His troubled dark eyes looked up at her. "We've moved in time as well as in space. Fortunately, the scanners are picking up the energy-trail of the Leviathan. We seem to be just where it emerged from StarBurst. Only more than a day behind it."

Sutt mentally scanned options as her eyes flicked along the read-out board. "Not only do we have enough energy, we seem to be entirely revitalized—except for our weapons systems. When the hellhound interacted with the energy from StarBurst, it must have unleashed a force no one could have predicted in the tests. I wonder how—" But now was no time for careful analysis. There were other matters of vital importance to deal with. Their directive, for one thing. Their mission.

"Sensors! If the Leviathan was here, we must be able to follow it. Gamma radiation!"

The sensor tech looked down at the readout. "Yes, Captain. We can follow its path."

"Excellent!" said the captain. She stood up carefully, unflexing herself. She was an uncommonly tall and slender Sebacean, with a disciplined physique and well-formed muscles. Her dark leather uniform fitted her like an oiled glove, and her eyes glittered with her intelligence and cunning. It was good, she always thought, that those eyes were dark, for dark eyes seldom betrayed weakness. And in part of her, Sha Sutt well knew, there was weakness.

"Plot a course to follow the trail. Calculate the speed of Leviathan and then be sure to exceed it. But there is no immediate hurry. If we are a day and a fraction behind it, then they have no way of knowing we are here, following. Leviathans do not StarBurst often, I think.

Particularly when they are under the impression that they are alone."

"Course plotted," said the navigator. There was a troubled look on his wizened face, reflected in the expression of the others on the bridge. He added cautiously, "Where were we for over a day?"

Sha Sutt did not care to pursue that question now—with the crew, or in her own mind. They had a ship to destroy.

"That is for the physicists to determine—our job is to track down the Leviathan. I am going back to my cabin for a moment. I shall return directly. Lieutenant Verno, take command. Stay on the trail of the Leviathan. Notify me instantly if there's any additional sign of the ship. And get the bridge swabbed down, Lieutenant."

Her movements dignified, she rose from the command seat, gave the shell-shocked crew a final glance, and strode from the bridge and down the corridor, her expression impassive. Only in the lift compartment, with the doors shushed closed behind her, did she allow herself to fall against the wall and put her hands over her face.

Crais, my commander in all things!

You have sent me in pursuit of my most mortal enemy.

As they waited to enter the mysterious giant ship, Crichton didn't know what to expect. Helmeted aliens? Creatures with many heads? He'd seen all that before. He'd been through a lot already—plus the weirdnesses and peculiarities of his crewmates.

Anything could be beyond that door—

Only it wasn't. The door had pulled open to reveal a hollow cylinder, large enough for a man or a Luxan to enter, and paved with a pebbled walkway. In that cylinder there stood—precisely nobody.

"Nothing!" said Aeryn, frowning, her dark eyebrows lowering. A consternated look crossed those severe but striking features, and her mouth twisted in concern. She lowered her pulse pistol but kept both hands on the grip.

"I wouldn't say 'nothing,' " said D'Argo ruminatively. He relaxed his stance ever so slightly, his hands still holding the Qualta Rifle at the ready. "It's clear what this is."

Crichton pondered a moment, studying the gap before them.

"It's some sort of connecting corridor," he ventured.

The interior of the cylinder showed odd glittering interstices on the ceiling. A strange wind wafted in, warmer than the cool temperatures of Moya, and bearing with it a hint of spices.

"Invaders: nil," said Aeryn.

"I read: invitation," said Crichton.

"I proclaim: caution!" said D'Argo.

"What, and just stay here and rot?" said Crichton. He was not only surprised at D'Argo's response, but also shocked at his own gung-ho eagerness to seek out the unknown. What was he doing? Hadn't he seen enough movies to know that the door of the sinister mansion always creaks open on its own, and there are always the undead waiting on the other side?

But would he have come out into space in the first

place if he weren't intrigued by the unknown on the other side of those doors?

"I believe that you have the explorer mindset, John," said Aeryn. "I preserve the peace. D'Argo survives. Maybe we make an interesting threesome, eh?"

"The Three Musketeers," said Crichton, almost to himself. "One for all and all for one!"

D'Argo raised an eyebrow and looked both Crichton and Aeryn up and down. "Threesome?" he rumbled. "All for one and one for all? Only if I'm truly desperate!"

With a gingerly step, Crichton peered into the corridor. The air was definitely warmer, with a brief stream of cooling breeze; the sensation was like stepping in front of a porch fan on a warm summer day. The corridor curved around to the right. Crichton looked up; the glittering of the ceiling made it look as if it had been sprinkled with stars. He took another step forward, past the cargo door. He felt more than a little cautious, but as always, action was much better than inaction. Inaction led to such things as death and boredom—and of the two, boredom was really the scariest thing out here. When there was too much boredom, he had other strong feelings. Like desperate loneliness and existential fear.

Standing half in the alien corridor, Crichton hit his comm. "Are you reading this, Zhaan? We're got what looks like a corridor here—can you get a view of the exterior?"

Zhaan's voice arose from the comm. "The exterior seems to match the interior, John. A bridge to Entity X.

It appears to connect to the alien vessel just at the mid-section."

Crichton turned to the others. Aeryn had lowered her pulse pistol to her side.

"So what do you say?" said Crichton. "Should we shoot for direct personal contact?"

"We are still getting zero on communication bands," reported Zhaan. Crichton could visualize her, steady at her station, working her controls with the grace of a ballerina. "I would guess this is as much communication as we're going to get."

"The bridge over the River Void," said Crichton. "It's a funny way of saying hello, but I guess we won't get anywhere by refusing to come out and play." He took a final look at the other two. Their faces were unreadable.

"Just call me Christopher Columbus," he said. "I'm just hoping I don't fall off the edge of the world."

He took a few cautious steps further into the tunnel, craning his neck to try and see around the curve.

He heard footsteps behind him and turned to see both Aeryn and D'Argo keeping pace.

"So who is this Columbus creature?" said D'Argo.

"Let's just say he sailed the ocean blue." Crichton grinned, turned back and started for the unknown.

The tunnel took only a few minutes to traverse. It appeared the tractor beams of the alien ship had managed to dock the two vessels quite close. True, it was a little eerie walking along a bridge over a billion-light-year drop, on their way to a massive silent vessel, but then Crichton had pretty much come to expect that kind of thing on the other side of nowhere. They reached what seemed to be the end of the corridor and stepped through some kind of airlock. It opened into a spacious passageway; as they entered, a door cycled itself closed behind them and gasses hissed. The briefest fragrance of cinnamon sparked with bitter mushrooms and cardamom tea drifted and then faded.

They found themselves in metal corridors that were much more to Crichton's tech taste than Moya's organic halls, where he sometimes felt like he was moving through Godzilla's digestive system. They were conventional squarish passageways with smooth gray walls, bathed in a subdued ambient light. There were no side corridors, which made deciding which direction to go pretty easy.

They travelled with Crichton in front, his pulse pistol at the ready once more. Aeryn walked at his shoulder, one pace behind, every sense alert, her weapon held in front of her. D'Argo kept watch behind them as they walked. Every minute or so they stopped to listen, but the ship was silent. The atmosphere was breathable, even sweet, and once again Crichton thought he caught the faint evocative scent of spices.

"I calculate this passageway runs along the periphery of the ship," said D'Argo. "We are tracing its circumference."

"Which leaves the question of what's in the middle of the ship," said Crichton.

"What's this?" said Aeryn. She stopped and, unwilling to take her hands off her pistol, tapped the toe of her boot on the metallic floor. Etched into the surface was a radiant star no bigger than a handprint. When

Aeryn lifted her boot, the star faded from view.

"Do that again," said Crichton.

She touched her foot to the ground and the fine lines of the star appeared on the floor once more, growing in detail and complexity until it sparkled with a faint glimmer. Aeryn stepped back and the star faded to nothingness.

Crichton took a few short deliberate steps around the corridor, staring down at his feet. Nothing but the gray sheen of the corridor. He moved his left foot forward again, and underneath it, very slowly, there blossomed another star.

"I've found one," said D'Argo, pressing his toe into the floor and looking at it with amazement.

Aeryn had moved forward and was now standing on yet another, glittering faintly under her foot.

"Stars," she said. Somehow they had all begun to whisper. "Nokmadi."

They exchanged glances.

"Navigators," said Crichton.

"The people," said D'Argo, "who have the maps."

They proceeded cautiously down the passageway, and from time to time another star blossomed faintly under their step. Then the corridor angled to the left and abruptly opened into a larger room. They paused at the doorway, their grip on the weapons tighter.

The chamber looked alike some sort of dining hall. After the eerie alienness of the ship and the passageway, Crichton felt as if he had suddenly been StarBurst light-years away, back to Earth. But what would have been familiar and comforting there was eerie in the vast depths of space.

The walls were panelled in a dark mahogany. A long table set upon an ornately patterned red carpet stretched down the room. Polished wooden chairs stood around the table. Candles in brass candelabras wavered with flames. Gleaming blue-and-white-patterned plates were set at each place along the cream-colored tablecloth, and gleaming silver utensils were set alongside the plates. On each plate was a mound of food: slabs of meat with a layer of gravy, tucked up against stuffing, mashed potatoes and glazed carrots. Steam rose from the food, and the smell gave Crichton the feeling that he had just opened the door to his grandmother's house back in Kansas.

Crichton found himself salivating. "Hmmm. Maybe it was just as well Rygel didn't come along."

"A dining hall, and a meal all ready." Aeryn touched the edge of a plate with an exploratory finger. "Yes, it's still hot."

D'Argo traced his way around the walls, examining the candle sconces and the panelling.

"Hello!" called Crichton. "Anybody here?"

"The modes of human inquiry constantly surprise me," commented D'Argo.

"We seem to have happened upon a mystery," observed Aeryn.

"So, food prepared," said D'Argo. "For us? Nine settings? That would be three per person—quite a feast. Or perhaps the crew of this vessel were interrupted by our arrival before they had a chance to get to dinner."

"And they've disappeared." Crichton was nodding.

Aeryn looked at him with a perplexed expression. "You look as though this is all familiar to you."

"It is familiar," said Crichton, "in an odd kind of way. There's a counterpart to it in the history of my planet. Something that happened on nineteenth-century Earth. I loved to read about it when I was a child. It was known as the mystery of the *Mary Celeste*."

Zhaan sat calmly and waited.

She sat upon the bridge, bathed in her blue self, looking up at the screens and yet not quite seeing. She felt more centred now, more ready to peer into the vast emptiness of her true self, with the distractions of space and time set aside. Her brief union with Moya had given her a glimpse of the depths of memory and understanding still to be gleaned. While she was waiting for word from the others, she could search those depths.

The first trick to true concentration, true attunement to the doorways of beyond, was to imagine herself back in the sun and warm soil of home, back in the whirlpool of sensation and growth. These poor all-meat sorts she was travelling with had no idea of the joys and breadth of experience enjoyed by the floral world. Photogasms were the least of the pleasures and sensations. When she meditated, Zhaan would envision herself in her home garden, transfused with chlorophyll and sunlight, rooting into the cool underlayer of the deep dark earth and probing for sweet moisture. The perfume of the aaaakkik flowers, ah! the odor of the winkwort! She could feel her kindred surrounding her, even now, the precious plants she had grown up among and the sweet tangle of growth in her little plot at home.

She closed her eyes to the confusions of material reality and reached out . . .

There was something out there beyond Moya. Something calculating and assessing. Something . . . Something beyond the edge of today and yesterday and yet far, far from tomorrow.

Shifting energies . . .

Yearning and fear . . .

Hunger and hope . . .

"Ahoy!"

There was a sharp slap on her cheek. She opened an eye and found herself confronted by Rygel wobbling on his ThroneSled. The plains of transcendent understanding twisted and evaporated away.

"Damnation and tribulation!" she cried, scowling at the loss of the understanding she had felt coming over her.

"Whoa!" said Rygel, pulling back on his controls and backing up. "My goodness, I thought you were the princess of peace."

"I believe it is Aeryn who's supposed to keep the peace," said Zhaan. "My race, like all races, has turbulent episodes in its past. Survival, unfortunately, seems to demand such things. Of course lately, now that I have met so many impolite creatures, I'm afraid I occasionally have aggressive feelings myself."

"You accuse me of lack of etiquette?" exclaimed Rygel. "I am a walking encyclopedia of etiquette!"

"Which volume contains the rules for slapping meditating people?" enquired Zhaan politely.

"Actually there are some directives in the Mystic Manners section . . ." mused Rygel. "No! You confuse me. I had to slap you awake. You were going into some sort of seizure."

"Seizure?" She looked down at herself: she looked normal, felt clear-headed, strong, centred.

"Yes. Normally you're quite still when you meditate, Zhaan, but you were twitching and your eyes were rolling back and you were saying something about 'the Orb of All.' "

"The 'Orb of All?' " replied Zhaan. "What is this 'Orb of All?' "

Rygel held his arms up in exasperation and looked to the cluster of DRDs who'd followed him to the bridge. "That's what I want to know." He sighed melodramatically. "Well, at least you're not going to die. And at least I didn't have to administer artificial respiratory resuscitation." Rygel worked his mouth around with dramatic contempt. "Far too much like osculation. Liable to get blue all over me!"

"It might do you some good." She leaned over and touched the high ridges of his brows, which were expressively tufted with fine sprouts of hair. Rygel's eyes went wide and he tried to get away, but Zhaan had him. With just the right touch of her fingertip she stroked the ornery mound of trouble, indignity and pompousness, and kept on probing into the little fellow, hoping to touch some glow of warmth and sweetness. The amount she found was just enough, she reflected, to make him appealing—although sometimes it was a close call.

"Oooooh . . . ahhh . . . no . . . no . . . oh, that's nice!" said Rygel, making contented noises. His rubbery face worked around with reluctant pleasure.

"I didn't know your race osculated, Rygel," said Zhaan softly, purring like a tiger considering a pounce.

"That must be a dreadful sight. I hope you close the doors and clean up afterwards."

Peevishness flared in the deposed ruler's big eyes and he jerked his head away from her hand. "I am the ruler of billions who save the soil I pass over as a relic of my glorious—"

"Speaking of loyal subjects, Rygel, what have you done to the DRDs for them to seem so taken with you? Usually they seem quite happy to scurry around and monitor Moya's interior condition. Have you been osculating with them?"

Rygel chortled. "Kissing them? Oh, heavens no!" He pulled out a contraption from his pocket, always a veritable bag of tricks. "I've just befriended them, that's all, just been trying to communicate with them. Sometimes people don't give little beings the reverence that's due them." He looked at her pointedly. "While the others are off playing brave explorers, I have been getting better acquainted with our small friends. You need all the friends you can get, especially if you might be losing three of them."

Zhaan drew her head back in indignation. "Don't say such a thing, Rygel. I believe John, Aeryn and D'Argo can handle themselves, and you have to give them credit for daring to go where others might not."

"Fiddlestickoids! Stay with what's right here, I say. And that's exactly what I'm doing. Which is to say, learning the means of electrical vibrational ethernet pulse-feedback communication!"

"My goodness," said Zhaan. "Do you mean comm units? So that's how you're communicating with them?

But the important point is: what are the DRDs saying to you?"

"I'm not terribly sure, really. Although they seem to be quite responsive. Look here—" He pulled out a device that could be pasted over the ear like skin, connected to a matrix of wires. Zhaan could see them sparkling like nano-stars. "I found this in one of the workshops and started puttering with it. The DRDs responded immediately. They started to follow me and make encouraging noises."

"Click, click . . . beep . . . click?" Zhaan bent her head in gentle enquiry. "That's encouraging?"

"Yes. I believe that they have discerned me for the royalty I am. There might be some kind of biomagneto-genetic overlay tech here that is similar to what was used by technicians in one of the ancient civilizations on my world. A civilization that might have had early contact with Leviathans. And our rule is: never throw away a good piece of technology."

"An early civilization?"

"Which one, of course, I haven't a clue," continued Rygel. He looked down with fondness at the DRDs. "But these creatures detect my sovereignty, surely. We just haven't got our codes straight yet." He harumphed thoughtfully and regarded the beetle-like things. "These fellows can do much more than repair things. I'm not yet sure what they're capable of." Rygel stuck his finger up. "But I shall find out. The first thing I shall teach them is to feed me!"

"I should think you do that well enough on your own. And Rygel, have you actually asked Pilot to check with Moya on this?"

"Peripherally," said Rygel, sniffing. "She allows our work to proceed. Now, if you'll excuse me—"

Abruptly the room shook. A thunderous boom echoed through the ship. Rygel stepped back and tripped over one of the DRDs, then fell onto his rump, his little feet kicking. The DRDs scurried around, bumping into each other and into the walls. Zhaan retained her balance only by grabbing hold of the nearest control grid. "Pilot," she cried, "what is happening?"

The Pilot holograph flickered into view.

"Moya!" said Pilot. "Moya is in great pain!"

CHAPTER 5

The *Mary Celeste*?" asked D'Argo, his voice rumbling deep within his massive chest. "Is this some Earth legend?"

They stood in the chamber, next to the dining table, its burden of food still steaming and fragrant. What Crichton found particularly unnerving about it all was that everything looked so Earth-like. The blue-and-white china, the candelabras with their curving brass branches, the pattern on the silver handles of the knives: it was all so familiar it was almost comforting—and alarming. Chandeliers hung from the ceiling, resplendent with teardrop crystals. The goblets were crystal as well, sparkling in the lambency from above. The silver shone bright, and the food—he could see the food was his favorite.

"Some sort of composite flesh-like substance," said D'Argo, poking at a slab of food with his knife.

"Meatloaf," said Crichton.

"And they had this meatloaf in the legend of the *Mary Celeste*?"

"Not that I know of," said Crichton, smiling despite his growing feelings of apprehension. He could feel the nape of his neck tingling with a retro déja-vu frisson. "And it's not a legend—it really happened." As he talked, he began to walk around the room, scrutinizing every detail: the panelling, the table, the settings, the ceiling with its glittering chandeliers.

"When I was a kid," said Crichton, leaning over to look under the table, "I was obsessed with the sea." There was nothing under the table except the legs and seats of the chairs. He fingered the hem of the table-cloth. "I loved those stories of sailing into the unknown, and the most unknown mystery of them all was the fate of the *Mary Celeste*. She was an American brigantine of the nineteenth century—"

"A sentient ship, then," said D'Argo.

"No, no, we just call ships 'she'—well, for the heck of it, I guess. Anyway, she left port on the seventh of November, 1872. She was carrying a cargo of denatured alcohol. Did I say she was a middle-sized freighter with sailpower? The arrangement of the sails is complicated—"

"You were very interested in all the details of the *Mary Celeste*," summarized Aeryn. Her finger was still on the trigger and her expression was grimmer than usual. "I think you've made that point."

Crichton was running his hands over the curved back of one of the chairs. He tapped it. It felt real, sounded real.

"It's a mystery in Earth history. Weeks after it left port, the *Mary Celeste* was discovered just as we've found this ship: completely deserted, with a table set, its crew and passengers mysteriously gone. There were many inquiries. No one has ever been able to figure out what happened. I spent hours working out different scenarios when I was a kid. Amazing how it all comes back to me as if it were yesterday. The past just swallows you up like that sometimes."

D'Argo pulled out one of the chairs and began to examine the upholstered seat. It had a design of a spray of flowers on a green background. He ran a thick finger over the surface, then prodded it.

"It may be that none of the crew on that ship ever returned," he said, "but somehow I doubt that we will be so lucky."

Aeryn was still standing by the door, keeping watch on the passageway with her pulse pistol held in front of her. "So you were fascinated with the *Mary Celeste*," she prompted.

"Totally," said Crichton. He picked up a knife and hefted it: it was heavy, like silver, and gleaming. "I had a model of it, a perfect replica of the real thing. Well, maybe not perfect—the topsails were inaccurate. But then my aptitude for astrophysics went off the chart and suddenly I was a scientist. And since there weren't too many mysteries left on the seas, it was time for the stars."

D'Argo leaned over to smell the food. "We've been here quite a while," he said, "but the food is still steaming. Don't things cool down on this ship?"

Crichton picked up one of the empty side plates. It

was white with a blue weeping willow tree in the centre. He turned it over. On the underside was an inscription in small faint blue letters. He raised his eyebrows.

"Hey, D'Argo," he said. "Do Luxan plates have lettering on the bottom? Is that a common thing in this part of the universe?"

D'Argo took the plate from him, tilting it to the light to get a better view. "Luxans don't have plates like this," he said. He turned it over. "There's a drawing of a growth on the front."

"That's a weeping willow."

"A sentient growth. In an unhappy mood."

"No, it's—never mind. Do you recognize those letters?"

They scrutinized the lettering on the plate. It scarcely looked like lettering at all, more like the jumble of marks on the smallest row of the optician's chart. His grandmother's plates had had some kind of maker's mark on the back—now what had it said? Who would have thought, the last time he had been helping wash dishes in his grandmother's kitchen, that the next time he would be studying the backs of plates would be in the starry back elbow of beyond?

"Did your model of the *Mary Celeste* resemble this dining room at all?" asked Aeryn.

Crichton set the plate down. "It was just a tiny model; you couldn't see the inside. I have to say that this is the way I imagined it. But of course, no one knows what the real dining room of the *Mary Celeste* looked like."

"No photographs?"

"No, photography had hardly been invented." At this Aeryn smiled with wry amusement. "Of course, people drew pictures, but they made up all the details, just as I did." Crichton looked around the room with pleasure, despite his worries. He must have read half a dozen books about the *Mary Celeste*, back when he had first realized the world held such wonderful enigmas. He'd never thought he'd be in on something so similar himself. "You've got to admit it's a heck of a mystery," he said.

Aeryn gritted her teeth. "There are no mysteries. There are only questions that have not yet been answered."

"And this place is full of them," said D'Argo. He had traced his way most of the way around the room, examining the panelling from floor to ceiling. Crichton joined him, feeling the panel near the door. "The old mansions used to have—" he began. "Hey, here's something." His fingers had found a vertical seam. Working carefully, he was able to slip his fingernails in it. To his extreme surprise, the side of the wall gave way under only a little pressure. Crichton pulled on the panel. A door-sized piece of the wall moved back.

"What the heck?" he said.

The panel swung away from the wall, revealing a control array of the biomechanoid variety that composed Moya. Here were cantilevered levels of varicolored squibs and fleshy things that looked like mushrooms and ragged fungi. Embedded in the mesh were nodes and toggle switches, while on one screen profoundly alien letters and schematics blinked and snapped with sparks all the shades of the spectrum. There was the odor of burnt oil here, in marked contrast to the savory scents from the food on the table.

"Controls?" Crichton wondered.

"Yes, but to what?" rejoined Aeryn.

"It looks a little like Moya's controls, doesn't it?" Crichton observed. "Can we operate these?"

D'Argo moved forward to study the panel more closely. "There are all manner of crossovers between the biological and the technical. I must say, this is a particularly odd one. It looks to have a full sensor array. Here, let's all hold our hands spread over the top and let it have a good reading."

They all held out their hands. The biomechanoid contraption wavered and blinked sharply, then started to expand and contract, expand and contract, as though it were breathing.

Suddenly eyes opened. Two large brown eyes with brown pupils and bloodshot whites.

"More sensory apparatus all the time, it would seem," said Aeryn. "It is developing as we watch it. Or as it watches us."

The eyes regarded each of them, one by one. When they fell upon Crichton, for a split second he felt as though they were peering way deep down into his soul, sifting and sieving and weighing the fragments of self and reality.

Then, below the staring eyes, a mouth opened up: thin white lips parting to reveal long fangs. It exuded a rancid smell of charnel. A puff of smoke and wisp of fire breathed up and a tongue began slowly lolling out. This time they all stepped well back, fingering their weapons.

Covered with barbed polyps, the tongue was red and dripping with fluid. It slowly undulated out. And out.

And out. Two prehensile barbs reached toward them, probing. Then the tongue withdrew, slurped and slapped and made the motions of chewing.

Crichton, backed up against the wall, grimaced. "What is it?" he said. "I swear I had a nightmare like this once."

"I may have nightmares like this for the rest of my life," said Aeryn, her face a grimace of disgust. "D'Argo, do you know what this is? What does this disgusting thing want with us?"

D'Argo was standing at some distance from the face, regarding its staring eyes warily. "I have no experience of such a thing."

The eyes closed.

Crichton stepped forward once more and addressed the peculiar alien face. "Hey!" he said. "What's going on? Are you in command here? You've got our ship and we need it back!"

He took another cautious step forward and slipped in some of the mucus that had dripped from the flowing tongue. He felt his hands coming down on the polyps, into the skin—and slipping through.

He tried to pull back, but something gripped him forcefully from the other side. The lights went dim. Crichton found himself up against the panel—and then face to face with those large alien eyes again.

"Crichton!" cried Aeryn. Crichton could feel her grabbing him—but the force on the other side was grabbing him harder.

And it began to pull.

"Help!" he cried. "Something's got me—it's pulling—"

He saw the mouth open again, morphing larger and larger, wider and wider, pulling him free of Aeryn's grip, then in and through and into gastric darkness.

Pilot's voice was strained and had a touch of panic.

". . . great pain . . . great threat! Moya is being engulfed!"

Zhaan's heart leaped to her throat. She looked at the screens with horror.

"Good Lord, this alien ship is an uncivilized thing!" said Rygel. He raised a hand and addressed the air in the direction of the alien ship. "Stop it! Stop it, I say!" he commanded, his voice quavering slightly.

The tractor beam was slowly phasing off, roiling around the large alien ship in wavelets of dying energy. Now, from the side of the vessel, holes had irised open and tentacle-like appendages had thrust out, wrapping around Moya like a giant squid seizing a submarine.

Moya started to shake.

"Moya is applying full-parameter integrity defenses, but synapses are shorting out!" Pilot's voice, usually calm, betrayed his distress. "I feel the pain myself . . . it is horrible!"

"Pilot, is there a hull breach?" said Zhaan anxiously. Pilot was working the controls frantically, his yellow eyes wide with worry. Zhaan thumbed the comm unit. "John, Aeryn, D'Argo! Come in! Are you there? John! Do you read?" The comm unit gave forth only silence.

"I knew it!" said Rygel. "They've been squished to death by Things on the alien ship! And now we're about to have a hull breach! Our air will escape! We'll die!"

He swivelled to the DRDs. "Vassals! Go forth! Do something!"

The DRDs turned, their eyestalks agitated. They circled around for a brief moment, then accelerated and swarmed away.

Zhaan felt the pain in Moya in a surge of empathy.

"Oh," said Pilot, in a suddenly quiet voice. "Oh my. Yessssss . . ."

"What!" said Zhaan. "What's going on?"

Rygel covered his head with his hands. "We're gone. This is it. It's your fault, Zhaan. You've failed us! Oh, come for me, noble ancestors. I shall take my throne in the afterlife. I—"

"Moya is much better," said Pilot, back to his normal voice.

"Better?" said Zhaan, more than a bit taken aback. "There isn't a hull breach, then? Moya's not being squeezed any more?"

"No," returned Pilot, "although the alien vessel remains connected through the cargo bay. There are now also four connections to other sections of Moya, but they cause Moya no pain. In fact, some sort of neurochemical electrostimulus is making Moya feel better. She hasn't felt this good in cycles. Nor have I, being intimately connected with her."

Rygel peeked through his fingers. "Well, well. You see, Zhaan. It was your hysteria that panicked us all."

Zhaan shook her head sadly. "Rygel, must you be so . . . so . . . Rygel?"

"Oh dear," said Rygel. "You're starting to sound more like Aeryn again."

"Rygel, you would try even a stone's patience." She

turned back to the control. "Pilot. So then, tell me that we're all right!"

"Yes," replied Pilot, actually sounding rather bright and chipper. "There are a series of new connections between the alien ship and Moya, but they are painless to Moya, and there are no breaches to vacuum. There is a homogeneous transfer of genetic materials for adhesion purposes. But there is no what I would call destruction."

Zhaan nodded thoughtfully. "Can you contact whatever intelligence is doing this?"

"Moya detects no intelligences in the person of the vessel. It seems totally autonomic," replied Pilot.

"But we're still prisoners! Just like with the Peacekeepers!" whispered Zhaan. She rose to her feet and moved from console to console, checking the screens. All systems were holding steady, but she could not throw off a feeling of dread.

"Well, all in all I prefer this to Peacekeepers, actually," said Rygel, zooming up to hover above the consoles. "True, that last experience was troubling, but anything rather than being back under the Peacekeepers' thumbs."

Zhaan shook her head. "For a supposedly canny ruler, Rygel, you can be magnificently thick-headed. The whole idea is to escape the Peacekeepers. We've managed to stay about one heartbeat away from them so far. So that leaves us about half a heartbeat away from them now. We're losing our lead. And what if they find us when we're in the grip of this alien vessel?"

"Hmmm. Well, we shook them off pretty successfully last time, and they have no idea we're here," Rygel responded. "I personally am fearless, I can't speak for others. Now if you'll excuse me, I will go and collect my subjects. Actually, come to think of it, I shall call them 'acolytes.' Yes, acolytes of the Church of the Royal Sceptre."

"See if you can do something about contacting the others in the alien ship. If we could know what was going on there," Zhaan continued, "maybe we could do something here."

"Yes. Perhaps with my electronics genius my subjects—acolytes, rather—can work something up," replied Rygel. He settled himself more comfortably on his ThroneSled and floated serenely off.

Taking a deep breath, Zhaan turned back to the controls. "Pilot. Is Moya maintaining equilibrium?"

"Absolutely."

"Good. Tell her to continue to attempt communication with this ship that has captured us." Zhaan peered down at her control console. She squinted at the readings. Indicators seemed to be flopping about willy-nilly, just as confused as any of the crew, or indeed the ship itself.

"I will, and then—" Pilot paused for a significant amount of time. "I . . . Oh dear . . . Spectronomic and gravitational changes are occurring. Radiation levels are increasing. Something is happening out there!"

Zhaan turned and watched, mouth agape, as the entity that had captured them erupted before her eyes.

The Queen of All Souls sat in her chambers, head resting in coiled tentacles, binocular eyestalks staring out into the night.

Things moved out there. Black things, coiling and darting. The stench was acrid, but she could not smell it. The wash of the night was sour and salty, but she could not taste it. The breezes were cold and clammy, but she could not feel them.

Once she had felt, the Queen of All Souls. Once she had great passion. Lovers! Ah yes, and feasts! Wine and the choicest food and exotic sensations. Oh, but she longed for those days again . . .

She sighed, and the sound of the sigh was like an angel's wing flapping in a storm.

A door opened behind her. Energy-candles fluttered in their sconces. An OverLord drifted in, his own tentacles curling and uncurling dreamily. His white hair drifted behind him like a frozen comet's tail and his black robes flowed like gaseous streams from a dark star.

"Your majesty," said the OverLord, bowing. Outwardly he was calm, but the Queen of All Souls sensed trouble beneath his surface. OverLord Foxxnak Rookin, Minister of the FauxPlain, Tertiary Tier House Baron, was a strikingly tall creature, skeletal and slightly bent, like a winter tree gnarled by the winds. His eyes burned like ignited anthracite: fervid silver and magenta. Roo-kin was perhaps the most powerful of the Queen's courtiers. He not only kept a bent finger on the pulse of news of the World, his powers of divination were extraordinary, his methods the result of a life-long dedication to the DataVols of knowledge, both scientific, mystic, and all the dark shadows in between.

"Roo-kin, why do you disturb me?" the Queen asked.

"Your majesty—Queen of All Souls and Mistress of

the Revelation Cabal. O Empress of Night!" Roo-Kin's eyes began to sparkle like dew in the moon as the stalks moved about, fairly trembling with excitement. "The MagicTechs have examined the stars with intense scrutiny."

"They do so enjoy their auguries. And so, what news of the future did they find?"

"He comes, your majesty!"

"Comes?" said the Queen of All Souls. "Who comes?" These damned courtiers. They were all melodrama and muffled meanings, full of decorative ways of saying things that lacked a great deal of substance. She well knew how to warp and weave words herself. This, after all, was part of the job of being queen. However, amongst her own people, she preferred coming straight to the point.

"They last saw him in the area where the double sap-pouches meet the pancreatic—"

"Spare me the details! Who's coming?" The Queen's voice was shrill and commanding, as befitted one who knew the secrets of the Books of Future Knowledge: the Book of Abeshill, the Book of Conoster and the Three Books of Pollup predictions. Threaded through these books was the prediction of an event that would change everything. An Arrival.

With a gasp of awe, the OverLord Minister Foxxnak Roo-kin let out the words that they had all waited so long for.

"The Promised One, your majesty," said the Minister. "The Promised One is coming! He is being welcomed by the Dayfolk! And with his help they seek to destroy us."

CHAPTER 6

A eryn and D'Argo watched with horror as the last part of Crichton's foot slipped into the mouth of the wall.

Aeryn felt stunned. She could do absolutely nothing. The obscene tongue licked out, did a run around the lips, and then the lips smacked.

The big warrior roared with frustration. D'Argo pushed a hand forward to jam it into the maw, but almost instantaneously the mouth became a control panel again.

D'Argo yowled with pain as his hand rammed into the solid metal of the panel. He stepped back, snarling, and picked up his rifle, anger flaring in his eyes.

"No!" said Aeryn. "You might hurt Crichton!"

"It ate him! We can at least try to save him!"

"No," insisted Aeryn. "If it meant to kill Crichton, he's already dead and we can do nothing. But if he's not dead, you could kill him if you interfere before we know what's going on."

D'Argo stepped back, shaking his head.

Aeryn looked at him. The warrior looked as though he were on the point of tears. "D'Argo. We must compose ourselves!"

The warrior bellowed. He stepped to the table, reached out an arm and swept it across the lower end. Dishes and goblets and mounds of food flew off and smashed against the wall.

If the crew comes back now, they'll really be upset, thought Aeryn, looking at the mess on the floor and feeling sick to her stomach.

Then her Peacekeeper instincts kicked in. If she lost control, gave way to fear or disgust, then how was she going to keep this berserker here from making things even worse?

"Right!" she said, straightening herself and shaking her hair back with a determined look. "We must evaluate the situation."

"Evaluate the situation?" echoed D'Argo. "Our battle companion has been consumed by an enemy! We must act, and act decisively!"

Aeryn studied the room, the candles still flickering, and the control panel on the far wall as solid as if it had always been there.

"No," she countered. "Nothing is really as it seems in here, is it? We can't automatically jump to the conclusion that Crichton is dead. We must find out more about this ship."

"Find out more?" D'Argo roared. "I know what I need to know! He's in the belly of the beast and I can't imagine he's coming back! I'm going to shoot that thing into pieces so small that it will regret—"

Aeryn took her place in front of the control panel, her eyes flaming. "You'll do no such thing, D'Argo. Blasting the control panel won't bring Crichton back. If we want to find Crichton, or find out what happened to him, we need answers, not revenge."

D'Argo grunted, but the words had softened the warrior's eyes. He nodded. "But let that devil-tongue touch me and I shall rip it out by the roots!"

Aeryn holstered her pulse pistol and put her hands on her hips, thinking. "Clearly this ship has unusual powers. We're not going to get out of this by shooting—we're going to get out of it by thinking. So let's think—and quickly."

D'Argo folded his arms and nodded, still keeping an apprehensive eye on the control panel.

Aeryn began to pace. "This room. No sign of any crew. The food always hot." She glanced over at a plate, its pile of food still steaming. "There's something uncanny here."

D'Argo strode around the table, looking at the food balefully.

Aeryn seized one of the candelabras and examined the candles. "And look at these. A form of wax, and yet the wax has not melted down at all since we've been here."

D'Argo nodded. "Illusions."

Aeryn stared around the room, at the panelling, the sconces, the long table and the chandeliers. "I think whoever controls this ship has been reading Crichton's mind," she said finally.

"What?"

"It's all straight out of Crichton's story about the mysterious Earth ship! The meal prepared, the crew gone—and the furniture and the food! Crichton seemed to recognize it! It was just as he imagined it! Can that be a coincidence?"

D'Argo stroked one of his tentacles, considering. Then he turned to face the control panel. "But what about the mouth? Is that some kind of Earth mystery too?"

Aeryn thought back. "Didn't Crichton say he'd had a nightmare like that? What if he weren't just saying that—what if he really had? What if they plucked it straight from his memory?"

D'Argo thought for a moment, and shuddered. "A race that can read your memory." He put his hands on the back of one of the chairs and stared down at the table. "OK," he said. "It could be true. Suppose it is. I suggest—"

That was when one of the plates of food began to talk to them.

Down and down.

Down and down.

It felt to Crichton, half-conscious, that he had been going downward so long that he was turning upward. Falling felt like that to astronauts. That's what you were pretty much doing when you were hovering out in orbit . . . falling. Only you were falling for so long that there was no bottom to the fall.

Although, come to think of it, he didn't really feel as though he were weightless and unattached. It felt as though he were flowing down instead of falling down. As though he were going down some kind of chute in a dark game of chutes and ladders.

Falling . . .

The mouth . . .

The obscene mouth and tongue pulling him in . . .

Fear for his life, like some guinea pig being eaten by a python . . .

Now, though, there wasn't much fear. No, none of that at all. It was just flowing, falling . . .

Something.

Crichton struggled for awareness.

One of the great enemies for astronauts, or pilots of any kind for that matter, was unconsciousness. If you are unaware of your surroundings in any way, you are in danger, for you are not flying your vessel properly. When at the controls, at all times you have to be alert and awake, or the next thing you might know, you could be unconscious for ever.

Struggle.

Wake up, dammit.

Wake up, John.

There was some sort of light above, muddled and grim and streaked with a sinister band of dark red, like an artery slashed open.

But it was light, and light was awareness, and awareness was exactly what he sensed he needed.

He reached out for the light, like Adam reaching for God's finger in the famous Michelangelo painting.

He reached and touched.

And he landed.

Crichton opened his eyes. Around him was a shad-

owy room, rounded like the sides of a spaceship. Somewhere water dripped. There was a smell of gaseous rot
in the air. Some sort of lichen growing up bulkheads
and supports.

It felt like the guts of a dead tanker. Although it was
large, it somehow felt claustrophobic.

"Hello?" he said. "Hello?"

Silence, and then a faint rustling.

"Hello." This time his call was quieter, more cautious.

"He . . . llo," came a voice like a tomb grating open.

Three ghostly forms appeared.

On the reaches over the Chaque Vance River, at the site
of ancient ruins, the Queen of All Souls had built a
manse to her personal sensibilities: a weird structure of
eccentric gables, balconies, cupolas, and skywalks together with three glass towers through which the blue
moonlight shone.

Now, bathed in secret energies and draped in the star-
riest of gowns, the Queen lounged and stared out at the
filigreed rainbow of dawn.

"Cugel!" she called to a dwarf. The little creature sat
amongst a pile of thaumaturgical instruments, activans
and artifacts. Beside him lay a pile of books. He was
psionically juggling a number of librams, curiosa, tal-
ismen and amulets to amuse the Queen, using the powers of mind-magic alone.

"Yes, Your Majesty!" Distracted, Cugel lost his connection to the physical elements, which tumbled onto
the floor, scattering every which way.

Cugel pulled himself together again, peering up at the

Queen with small gleaming eyes, his nose twitching with polite vexation, his large ears flapping.

"Sorry, Your Majesty."

The Queen laughed faintly. "You do amuse me so much when you do not mean to amuse me."

"As long as I achieve amusement, my lady."

"A worthy achievement, to inspire mirth in someone so insubstantial." Her voice was a sigh of mist.

Cugel lifted up a fist, caught the mist and made a moth out of it. The moth flapped back to the Queen and disappeared, melding into her body.

"Energy is not insubstantial, Your Majesty. It is the raw stuff of the kinetic universe," said Cugel.

"It makes me insubstantial," replied the Queen, "and without substance, and the decay that comes with it, I am immortal. I cannot fathom why anyone would choose differently." She stretched out her insubstantial form, enjoying the last of the darkness.

"It is indeed unfathomable, Your Majesty."

A light smile flickered over the Queen's face. "Thank you, Cugel. But I have been thinking—these events. You heard the results of the auguries, did you not?"

"Aye, my lady."

"Then you should know that we have indications that the Dayfolk have captured a ship of the stars."

"Yes, Your Majesty."

"Cugel, what do such small Nightfolk as yourself say about the Promised One? Recount the legend to me as you understand it."

"Of course, there are many variations on the Prophecy of the Promised One," began Cugel, his small eyes bright. "The version of my clan has always been thought very reliable. I have it in a book, just here."

"Read it to me, then."

Utilizing his special forces of psycho-kinesis, the energy-creature lifted one of the volumes up into the air. It hung, then spun, then opened up to a particular point. Cugel's transparent finger took on stronger force and with it he paged further through the thin vellum. With the book suspended before him, he took up buzz-lute and began to strum it as he read aloud.

"For lo! All is off-kilter and the light knows not the dark, and the dark refuses the light. But there shall be One who shall bring both to the World.

"And who is this being? He is no being of ours, and yet he is us. He is no being of space, and yet space is his home. He is not a creature of happiness, and yet happiness is in his heart.

"And from a great distance he shall come, and he who attends to the words and needs of the Promised One shall find balance and harmony.

"And home shall at last be found.

"And lo, he shall have disciples who know him not—and they shall love him and yet hate him, and they shall speak harsh words though they are sweet of heart. And he shall show us a new way, and we will understand the deepest meaning of our voyage."

Cugel put down his lute. The Queen closed her eyes, and after a moment she spoke.

"The Dayfolk. They have been looking out for the Promised One as eagerly as we have."

"That is why they have captured him, my lady."

She smiled. "They do our work for us. Will they be able to figure out what he can be used for?"

Cugel shrugged in a coruscation of spectra. "I know not, Great Queen."

"This is not good."

"No, my Queen."

The Queen sighed, an evanescent whisper of breath as insubstantial as herself. "We survive," she said, "and as long as we survive, we may yet conquer time and space." She paused for a moment. "Sing on, O Bard of Night. Sing on, and I will consider the matter fully."

The buzz-lute rose into the air and stillness became sound and the music of prophecy drifted through the draping sleep-ivy drowsing upon the trellis above, holding flowers like cradled babies.

CHAPTER 7

The immense vessel bloomed in the vu-screen like some new-born planet.

Zhaan watched, overwhelmed with wonder and dread. What had once been discernibly an alien ship was now something much more. The tendrils that held Moya fast had sprouted tendrils of their own, and those tendrils had grown tendrils yet again. It was like an unworldly garden. In her wide knowledge of the universe, Zhaan had heard of ships larger than moons, ships that grew out of anyone's control, but the reality dwarfed everything.

The stars had simply disappeared, as if the thing erupting into space took hold of all the universe and shook it. As she watched, a snake-like root detached itself from the greater mass and came grasping toward Moya, disappearing from sight of the vu-screen. It was as if the alien ship were some dormant plant that had been awoken by contact with another living thing.

Zhaan looked away and called out, "Pilot!"

Silence.

"Pilot?"

A tremor of alarm went through her. Had something happened to Pilot? Was Moya all right? A new fear came to her. Not of dying: she had stared down death many times—and many times had almost gladly embraced its sweet relief.

No, this was worse. She was afraid that the others were gone, that she was alone to face this monstrous entity on her own.

"Pilot!" she shouted, standing up.

"Sorry, Zhaan. My deepest apologies." The familiar voice and image swept onto the bridge, the forlorn face of Pilot. "I am somewhat taken aback."

"I should think so! I am as well. And Moya?"

"Moya is still in a state of health, even bliss. The electro-chemicals flowing through her now are most relaxing."

"Well, thank goodness for small favors. At least our ship is happy." She pointed towards the growing vessel and the new tendrils snaking towards Moya. "What's going on?"

"Sensors are down."

"No speculation?"

"I do not speculate. Insufficient data. Would you care to speculate for us?"

"I've never seen a ship like it. A vast plant with a slow but powerful metabolism."

"And still growing?"

Zhaan nodded her head. "And still growing."

"Whatever it is, it has its grips on us," said Pilot. "Suggestions?"

"I'd guess we have something it wants. It could destroy us, absorb us—there seems to be absolutely nothing we can do." She sat back down wearily, averting her eyes from the sight. Even when under prison guard of the Peacekeepers, she had felt the possibility of escape and redemption. Now, though, so utterly dwarfed, she felt like an insect regarding the sole of a descending boot.

A thought came to her. "Unless . . ."

"Yes, Zhaan?" Pilot prompted.

"Continue to attempt to re-engage communication with Crichton, D'Argo and Aeryn," she replied.

There was perhaps something that she could do, Zhaan thought. And there was also something that His Miniature Majesty could do as well.

"Please request Rygel to get back up here. And tell him to bring Moya's DRDs with him, if you please! No dawdling permitted. Immediately!"

"Xarchshlkjikjjh . . . globble . . . Eat me!" said the plate of food, as if tuning in to Aeryn's language slowly and not entirely accurately.

"What?" Aeryn asked. She pulled a chair out of the way and moved close to the edge of the table, scrutinizing the plate.

"Eat me!" repeated the food.

Steam curled up from the food, and the smell was quite savory. Nonetheless, neither Aeryn nor D'Argo were in the habit of eating things that talked. As the sounds emerged from the pile of food, it quivered.

D'Argo was looking down at the plate in front of him as well. His food was also coaxing him, and presumably it was trying Luxan: "Grfujarkh! Eat me!"

Aeryn hit the back of her head with the heel of her hand to get her colony of translator microbes back into gear.

"What the frell? Are you talking to me?" she said to her food.

"Eat me," pleaded the food, seeming less and less appetizing all the time, despite the pleasant smells that wafted up from it. The voice seemed to be emanating from the carrots, or maybe the gravy.

Aeryn took a step back and clenched her jaw. "OK. This is frelling weird. This is one I can't explain. Crichton never mentioned talking Earth food as part of the legend."

D'Argo's brows were knitted in concentration. He pulled a chair up and sat down. "No, it's nothing to do with Crichton. It's not an Earth legend. It's a Luxan legend."

"It is?" Now Aeryn's brows were sky-high.

To her amazement, D'Argo scooted his chair up to the table and surveyed the food calmly. "The Dinner of the Enlightening," he explained. "It is one of the foundational Luxan myths. Three warriors, seeking the Gem of Constancy, came across a magical table laid with the most delicious of foods. It was a table in an island in the middle of the ocean, as I remember."

Aeryn gave a dubious scowl. "Was one of these magical foods 'meatloaf?' "

D'Argo shook his head. "No. But clearly Crichton's memories of the lost Earth sailing ship have determined

this set-up to some extent. In the Dinner of the Enlightening, the key factor is that the food asks to be eaten.
In fact, as I remember, only the noblest of warriors have
the ability to hear the food speak."

Aeryn gave a short laugh. "I'm comforted that the
food thinks I'm noble. But then do the noblest of warriors get food poisoning?"

To her great alarm, D'Argo took a linen napkin from
beside a plate, unfurled it and tucked it into his belt.
"The food does not hurt them. It's called the Dinner of
the Enlightening because when the warriors eat it,
they're able to understand what's happening to them,
where dangers lie and how to overcome them."

"Eat me," coaxed D'Argo's carrots.

"Nice story," grunted Aeryn. "Fantasy always has a
happy ending, doesn't it? That's what makes it fantasy."
She watched D'Argo as he reached to pick up a fork.
"Oh, no. You're not going to! D'Argo, you can't seri-
ously eat that."

D'Argo picked up his knife. "I can, and I suggest that
you may want to achieve enlightenment too."

Aeryn moved away from the table and walked around
the room with an impatient stride. "First you're trying
to shoot up the place, and then you're about to eat the
food! D'Argo, this is the ship that swallowed Crichton!
We should not be tucking into dinner! Have you lost
your tarbles?"

D'Argo cut into a slice of loaf and loaded some potatoes on top of it. "It is a powerful myth in my culture.
To gain further knowledge, I must eat the food. I will
do as my ancestral warriors did."

Aeryn paced back and forth. "Fine. Fine," she said

in a clipped tone that suggested it was not fine at all. "Imitate an old myth. Leave me to rescue Crichton and save Moya on my own. Behave in a completely irrational way just because some food told you to."

D'Argo was chewing. "Mmmm," he said. "Loafmeat, he called it? I haven't had it before, but it's not bad. Come and have some."

"No, thank you."

His expression changed again. He looked down at the food. Aeryn could see that it was quivering again, and she could hear a faint coaxing coming from it.

"Yes," said D'Argo. "Yes, of course." D'Argo turned to Aeryn. "It wants to know why you won't try yours. It wishes to speak to both of us together. It understands our reluctance, but in order to communicate, you must partake."

Well, the big guy wasn't exactly choking and turning green. Aeryn paused, hesitant.

"It's saying something about Crichton. But it wants you to be listening before it tells the whole story."

"It can't explain unless I eat some food?"

D'Argo paused and listened. "The beings here are not of a substance that can interact with our substance. We must ingest something of their world to understand them."

Aeryn snorted. "They couldn't just leave a sign? They had to construct a whole chamber and eat Crichton? I don't trust them!"

D'Argo was listening to the small alien voice and nodding.

"Eat me!" clamored the gravy on the other plates.

Aeryn scowled. Then, putting down her gun, she

went to the table. With an efficient no-nonsense grab and swallow, she ate one of the carrots.

There was a tingling in her throat, and a commingling, it seemed at the back of her neck. Microbes getting together for a party?

The rest of the food quivered again. "Excellent. You have taken the first step. Thank you—Aeryn."

Her first question was: "What's happened to Crichton?"

"Thank you," said the food.

"John Crichton!" she cried. "Why did you eat him?"

"Ah ha!" said the pile of food. "You enjoyed our little joke, then. We didn't exactly eat him. We just borrowed him. His own dreams supplied us with quite an interesting way to do it." The voice had an undertone like a bee's buzz.

"Then where is he?" cried D'Argo.

"He is safe in another part of the ship."

"We demand that he be returned!" said Aeryn, pushing her chair back abruptly and rising to her feet. "This is an insult and an outrage!"

"I'm sorry you feel that way," said the food mildly. "But now that you've finally partaken of our offering and can understand everything we need to say, we can move to the next level of understanding—and perhaps rejoin Crichton, once he has fully conferred with our elders."

"Elders?" said D'Argo. "Who are they? Who are all of you?"

"We are—the Nokmadi. Yes, I believe that is the name we were called long ago," said the buzzing voice.

"The Nokmadi!" said D'Argo. "Zhaan was correct.

The legends were true. We have stumbled upon a fabled lost race." A look of wonder crossed his hairy face.

"A race that has trapped our ship and imprisoned our friend!" Aeryn turned away from the table and directed her demand to the ceiling. "We demand that you release us. Allow us to get back to our ship and depart."

"We cannot stay here!" echoed D'Argo. "We are warriors fleeing a terrible enemy."

"The Peacekeepers," said the food. "Yes. A curious race . . . but no matter. You have plenty of time. Time, after all, is merely a form of space, and there's plenty of that in the universe."

"Look, it's very difficult speaking to either a plate of food or thin air," said Aeryn. "Why don't you come out of hiding? You will not be harmed if you promise the same."

An odd tinkling; fairies prancing on dew-dropped leaves.

"Harm? No, that's not an issue."

A man appeared, sitting in the chair at the end of the table.

"Not an issue at all," said the beautiful alien, brushing back his romantic jet-black hair and turning a scintillating, sly smile at Aeryn.

CHAPTER 8

In her cabin aboard the Peacekeeper cutter *DarkWind*, Captain Sha Sutt dreamed of a past that even now set her heart pounding.

She stood on the balcony of the HoverTel as it settled down near the Inverse Falls. The water flowed upward, defying gravity, cartwheeling back into spray. The mist was warm on her cheek. She could smell the Algean sea, strong and vigorous and fresh, light-years from the skycamps in which she had been raised.

She was a junior adjutant at a summit about the struggle to contain bands of malcontents in outlying Peacekeeper territory. Something had happened to Crais's personal adjutant, and at the last moment she herself had been assigned to him.

He strode between rooms at the summit headquarters so fast she could barely keep up. He entered chambers without knocking, and she could see from their faces and their deference that the officials within were frightened of him. He stood up in the middle of meetings and issued commands like "Destroy them!" and "Have him killed," pounding his fist on the table. He always got his way. He embodied power.

She wanted that power for herself, and she wanted him for himself.

She did his work faithfully.

And then on the final day he summoned her into his private chambers.

He was dressed entirely in black, his sleek dark hair pulled back in a ponytail, his beard neatly trimmed. He played with a ring on his finger as he spoke; his voice was low, calm, as if he were amused at something.

On a table were two long-stemmed glasses and a bottle with a long slender neck. "This is Ardenturan port," he said, thumbing the top so that the pressure released with a long hiss. "It's a strong drink, too strong for some." He poured a thimbleful of the amber liquid into one of the glasses, and a sharp fragrance filled the chamber.

"It reacts to the chemicals in your bloodstream," he said, raising the glass to his nose and inhaling the scent of the liquid. "It combines very badly with the chemicals of fear. You might even say it diagnoses fear. And if you're afraid when you drink it, it kills you."

He smiled and took a sip.

"That would be a good joke if it were true," she observed.

"Wouldn't it?" he replied. He took another sip and set the glass down on the gleaming wooden table.

"Sha Sutt, I have observed you now for some time."

He drew a chair up to the table, sat down, and moved closer to face her. She could feel the heat rising off him. He looked at her with intensity.

"You have an important future ahead of you. It may be that I will play a small part in that future. I will ask only one thing of you."

He was so close she could have reached up and touched his face. "Anything, Captain," she said.

"All I ask is loyalty." He looked into her eyes with a dark and burning gaze. "Tell me," he said with intensity, "that loyalty is not too much to ask."

She was flattered, even heady, that he would care so much about the loyalty of a lower-level functionary such as her. The flattery made her bold.

"You have my loyalty," she said, "even if it should kill me."

He sat back in his chair, relaxed, with a small smile on his face once more. "I don't think it will," he said, "or at least not this time. Some Ardenturan port? It's no joke about it being lethal if you're afraid—it killed my former adjutant just last week."

And because she had that one moment of heady boldness, she drank it down to the last drop.

Sha Sutt groaned. She writhed in her flatmat. The tissue threads of the filament-warmer knotted about her in her cabin. Although she had stayed cool throughout the entire ordeal of the battle amongst the asteroids and the harrowing dive into the Leviathan's StarBurst, although she had not perspired across the light-years nor in her command decisions aboard the bridge on the other side of the jump through space and time, now sweat stood on her brow and dripped into her massage-pillow.

For a moment she awoke, shivering. For a moment, just a moment, she thought that Crais was with her, reassuring her. However, reality intruded and she remembered that the affair had been over before it had really begun. Crais had gone elsewhere and returned with some other young officer in his thrall, and he politely but firmly detached from Sutt. She had warned herself not to hope for too much, but still it was painful. Nonetheless, she was promoted to captain of a ship and found that her family back in the Pods had received mysterious gifts. She could not complain. She could only grieve, for when Crais looked at her now, he was distant, as if he had other things on his mind entirely. And in her heart, Sha Sutt said to herself: he shall not ignore me.

The wrench through space and time had taken its toll. Sha Sutt still felt dizzy, and the tug of sleep once more pulled her down upon the mat of the tiny cubicle she called "The Captain's Cabin." Sha Sutt dreamed. She dreamed of another past. She dreamed not of a lover, but a rival—an enemy.

"So, Sha. Peacekeeper starship captain now! What a great honor for someone so young."

The words in the officers' bar were cutting. But then, the words of Sub-Lieutenant Aeryn Sun often were. The two women were of the same age and skills—they had known each other since they had met on a special training course on the desert planet B'Nalli. That had been a torturous time—two other Peacekeeper soldiers had died in that camp during a particularly gruelling set of practice maneuvers. And Sutt firmly believed, although she had never been able to prove it, that she herself had come to the brink of death—because of Aeryn Sun.

"Yes, Sun. I am a starship captain," snapped Sha Sutt. "I earned my wings. I'm a qualified officer and I'm proud to serve the cause!"

There were murmurs in the shadows. Sha Sutt thought she heard a whispered slur: "Qualified! Qualified to serve under Crais, perhaps." She whirled around. But there many people here now in the Calm-time, and she could not tell who had spoken.

Aeryn Sun sighed. She took a gulp of her drink and shook her head sadly with a wry smile. "Always on each other's case, aren't we, Sha? Let's just celebrate, pure and simple. Let me buy you a drink."

Captain Sha Sutt's eyes flared. "And let my guard down? The last time that happened, I ended up in the hospital—hanging on to life by a thread."

Aeryn Sun frowned. "Oh, come on, Sutt. We've been through this before. What happened back on B'Nalli had nothing to do with me. And you know damn well that if I'd known you'd been blasted half dead I wouldn't have run back to that emplacement. I never saw you."

"I saw you. I swear you looked at me, damn you!" said Sutt through gritted teeth. "You were trying to get the best time in the squadron. You knew I would slow you down. And so you left me. You didn't even check to see if I was dead or alive."

"It was dark and the ground fog—" Aeryn Sun shook her head. "What's the use? We've been over this a

dozen times. I would never leave one of my own troop behind. You choose not to believe me. But even if you don't take my word for it, the inquest into the matter found nothing to prosecute."

"The inquest protects its own and you know it, Sun. It's survival of the fittest." She moved toward Aeryn, towering over her. She pulled up a finger as though it were a weapon and pointed it. "And I survived. But let me tell you—not only did I survive, I learned who I could trust. And it's certainly not you."

"Sutt, can we never move beyond this?" said Aeryn. "Let's have a drink; it's on me." Her tone of voice was still friendly, but her eyes betrayed how tightly wound she was, how exasperated she was becoming.

"Buy me off, is that what you're hoping to do? Not quite befitting a glorious soldier of the Peacekeepers, is it? And I'll say right now, Sun, it's not just me who's wondering about your conduct. I've been hearing some very questionable things about your loyalties."

Absurd. Aeryn Sun looked as though she were about to toss her drink in the captain's eyes. She was volatile, was Sun—always was, always would be. The damnable thing was that when they had first met, they had immediately seen each other as kindred spirits. They enjoyed the same read-crystals and would talk not just about the men they had fancied in their short lives, but also their goals with the Peacekeepers. They'd been tough but wide-eyed, and together they saw the mission of the Peacekeepers in the universe as something almost sacred. Who else would bring order and stability to a chaotic universe? Who else would bring law and philosophy and intelligence to unruly civilizations who *could develop into destructive terror? Who else but the Peacekeepers? And how could the Peacekeepers accomplish this without steadfast determination on the part of its warriors, its young soldiers bred for just such tasks?*

But it had not all been seriousness back then in the training camps of Yunez. No, Sha Sutt had taught Aeryn Sun many games. Games of cha-cards and mooka-dice. Brain games and strategy games. In turn, Aeryn had begun to teach Sha a secret language of the L'Bu, something they alone could understand when out with the rough and rowdy fellow soldiers. Also, Sun had taught Sutt how to drink woozy Cak with a big stein of zooka ale to wash it down. And they had taught each other an inkling of what very few studious and serious Peacekeepers seemed to know how to do: to let down their guard and learn to enjoy life.

"I'll say it again. Absurd. I would not abandon any fellow Peacekeeper or friend."

"Former friend, Sun," said Sutt. "And you've made me hate the very word!" With that she had spun on her heel and walked out without a backward glance.

That had been three cycles ago. When Sha Sutt had heard how Aeryn Sun been contaminated, she knew it must have been no accident. She had abandoned the glory of the cause and fraternized with the enemy, and Sutt was not surprised. There was no loyalty in the woman: nothing like the loyalty and honor that lived in Sha Sutt.

Now she had a chance to show her loyalty.

Now she could prove herself to Crais. Even now, he seemed to fade into view in her dream and she saw him

standing on a balcony on that paradise world, smiling
again, saying, "Do this for me. Follow them and kill
them—for me."

A beep-beep-beep stabbed into the dream. The misty
form of Crais evaporated and again Sha Sutt was in her
tiny cabin, sweating.

Automatically, she pressed the comm-stud.

"Yes. Sutt here."

"Captain, please come to the bridge," said a voice,
the excitement in it barely controlled. "Immediately."

The ghosts that appeared to Crichton in the depths of
the alien starship looked as if they were composed of
glittering points of light sketched into the frame of a
person: sparkling, and yet transparent, insubstantial.
They were clothed in long ghostly robes, and they gazed
at Crichton with unmistakable relief and happiness. At
first they had spoken nothing but gibberish, though they
had offered him a platter full of ripe and glistening
fruit—Earth-fruit, it seemed: cherries, grapes, peaches
with the blush still on them. The smell was delectable.
They gestured to him so much that he had finally
shrugged and sampled a grape—and immediately
found, to his surprise, that he could understand their
speech.

"You have come!" said one.

"Blessed event!" said another.

"The Promised One!" rejoined the third.

Crichton stared at them. In fact, he stared straight
through them. Yes, they were ghosts! At first he had
thought maybe they were holograms. But no . . . there
was something ineffably different here. This was no

play of light, no laser-digitalized magic, but something stronger and more intense. The ghosts dazzled as they moved, and their colors were clouded by a pure and shimmering white.

Their shape conformed to the visual evolutionary model Crichton found out here: two arms, two legs, head, elongated body, binocular vision. Actually, though, as he looked he could see that the "arms" were in reality tentacles, with even smaller tentacles for fingers. Their figures were long and willowy, and they moved as if they were floating.

The room they were standing in was much less sterile and metallic than the corridors that had led into the ship; instead it seemed almost organic, a sickly green color, its walls soft with growths. A pale light filtered down from above. Except for the ghosts, the room was empty. Crichton had the uneasy feeling that he had been swallowed by some kind of alien Venus fly-trap.

"Who are you? I mean, what are you? Where am I? God, my head hurts!" said Crichton. "Tell me what the heck is going on!"

"Pardon the manner of our introduction. But you found the reality chamber, as we hoped, and we were able to read a signature of your thoughts. I am Pahl, and my colleagues are Leff and Igai."

Crichton frowned. "The reality chamber? The place with the table set for dinner? I couldn't detect much reality in that room!"

"Ah, you mean external reality," said Pahl. He pressed his front tentacles together like an Asian monk about to give a bow. "The chamber reads internal reality. It reads your memories. You were thinking of a story about a mysterious ship on your home planet, and the room interpreted it into 'reality' for you. Unfortunately, you were also thinking of a certain nightmare you had once, about a gaping mouth, and the chamber also read that and swallowed you. Often we find these little slips rather amusing, but we did not mean to subject you to any harm."

"It picked up on my thoughts? And made them into external reality?" Crichton thought of some nightmares he was glad he hadn't been remembering at the time—and some dreams that might not be so bad, transfigured into reality. "But why?"

"Thoughts are just electrical impulses," said the ghost. "We learned to translate them into reality long ago." He gestured down at his own sparkling insubstantial form. "In fact, you might say that we on this ship are just thoughts of ourselves. But in your case, we had to be sure of who you are. And what better way to speak to you than with your own images?"

"Huh." Crichton was having trouble taking it all in. "My head hurts . . . Well, that's nothing new, anyway." He shook off the throb and tried to focus on them. There was some question it was important to ask. "OK, so you can translate my thoughts into candles and meatloaf. But why do you need to know who I am? Couldn't you just ask me?"

The third alien stepped forward, this one a slighter version of the alien form, its pale and shimmering robe trailing onto the soft green floor. It spoke in what sounded to Crichton like a woman's voice. "We needed to know who you are in a deeper sense. We needed to know things about you that even you may not fully know."

"Whoa," Crichton replied. "Mind if I sit down?" He shook his head and sank down to the floor. The ground felt slightly fuzzy, like a dense carpet of moss. He scooted over to the wall and sat against it cross-legged. The ghosts took seats opposite him—on nothing. He blinked his eyes a couple of times to make sure he was seeing what he was seeing. They were sitting as if on low chairs, their tentacles in their laps. But there was nothing beneath them. They really were sitting on air.

"Let's start from first principles," said Crichton. "You're—ghosts? Spirits of dead people? Or some other kind of transparent beings?"

The ghosts looked at each other, and Pahl spoke. "We have consulted your concepts, scientific and otherwise, as we scanned your brain. In the Earth sense, perhaps you would not call us ghosts, because we are not the spirits of dead people."

Whew, thought Crichton. That's good. Everything was bizarre enough without finding himself talking to dead people.

"However, in an effective sense, in the sense of our appearance and our generation, we are the apparitions of people whose bodies no longer exist. In that sense, then, yes, John Crichton, we are ghosts."

"OK. You're people without bodies, just the illusion of bodies. Looks like all our earthly concepts of materiality are wrong." Crichton smacked himself on his head with the heel of his palm. "Nope. Still awake and now my head hurts even more."

Pahl shook his head slowly. "No. Our bodies as a

whole no longer exist, but an essential physical core lives on, kept safe elsewhere in this ship: tiny nodules of flesh, but enough. Those cores think us into being— generate us, you might even say 'remember' us. We are our own memories. But we are memories that will live for ever."

Crichton opened his mouth, but found he hardly knew what to say. "Live forever—it sounds great, but it's impossible."

Pahl lifted his hands in a gesture that must surely have denoted encouragement. "A great deal is possible. We have made it possible. We are composed of energy generated from our minds, thoughts and memories. Perhaps the term you would use for what we are is— souls?"

Crichton sighed. "OK. Ghosts, souls—you're some kind of generated energy-beings and you can generate stuff even out of my own mind. The technology sounds fascinating, and I'd love to have a look at it under better circumstances. But right now you're holding us prisoner and you've got our ship trapped. So enough of the illusions already. We're being pursued by people who want to kill us, and if you don't kill us first, they will definitely be happy to oblige."

The ghosts looked at each other, and then bent their heads together, blending their forms into a kind of whirling ectoplasm.

The leader pulled away and turned to Crichton.

"You are safe from your pursuers."

"Oh, you think so? These are Peacekeepers. These are the meanest sons of bitches in the galaxy! And they want to string us all up."

The ghost alien simply stared at Crichton for a moment.

"We are capable of dealing with any threat," the alien stated, finally.

Crichton climbed to his feet. "So you say. Fine. If the Peacekeepers arrive, you may think differently. But we've got more immediate problems. I demand that you release our starship at once. You've picked my brain. Now let me go!"

The ghosts regarded him impassively, and Crichton felt himself growing angry.

"Hey! Do you hear what I'm saying? Let our ship go! We mean absolutely no harm to you and your ghost buddies, and me especially—I'm just a lost astronaut trying to find a way home!"

The leader rose and stepped back a moment, gazing intently at Crichton.

"Yes," he said. "Yes, indeed. You are the Promised One!"

"The Promised One," said the Queen of All Souls. "Yes. I sense him now, Roo-kin." She lay stretched out on her daybed in the inner chamber of the palace, deep within the hip. She had generated herself a long robe tinged with a midnight blue, one that she remembered from long ago, and she watched the blue shimmer as it lay spread out on the daybed around her. She lifted her gaze to Roo-kin once more. "The Promised One is closer, is he not? He has entered the World."

The OverLord bowed, the cuffs of his robe fluttering in a phantom wind. "Yes, Your Majesty."

"This is not good, Roo-Kin," said the Queen. "Would

that I held full power over the World! Then that vessel would have been allowed to pass by. But no. The Day-folk! They are fools!"

"Yes, Your Majesty." The OverLord had a worried, tense expression on his face, as if too much stating of the obvious might bring even more unpalatable truths into being.

The Queen rose, drifted to a window and looked out into the World. Currents of night drifted and shifted, smelling of slumber and soil.

"Tell me the Dayfolk version of the Prophecy of the Promised One," said the Queen. "You have been studying it, have you not, for just such an event as this?"

" 'Oh, in the tides of night, from the beams of day . . . ' "

"Not the full version, please. Condense."

"Very well, Your Majesty. It is said that there will come a Promised One to the Dayfolk, the Dreamers Who Would Go Home. And this Promised One would wear a Mortal Coil. Thus armored, he would be able to descend into the Hole in the World, and wrest from their Moorings the Jewels of Dreaming, and return to the Dreamers their forms enfleshed and alive, and at last the Dreamers could go home."

"The fools," the Queen spat. "They were not made to go home. They deny their destiny. I shall not deny my destiny."

"We shall then put a stop to the Promised One?" ventured Roo-kin.

The Queen stared off into the slumbering darkness.

"No," she said quietly. "We will be able to turn him

to our purposes. He has in him a love of night too. He would not be out among the stars without a love of night. I will take care of the Promised One." She smiled. "Myself."

CHAPTER 9

"All right," said Captain Sha Sutt, her boots pounding resolutely on the floor as she strode towards the command chair. "What do you have for me?"

Her leg felt particularly heavy as she clumped it along onto the bridge. Its servo motors seemed to whine and grate inside her. Damned alien thing. She was grateful to be able to sit and let this new information cascade over her. Depression and mordant memory were gone now, evaporated under the input of new information—information that could factor into a victory. And victory, for a gamesman like Sha Sutt, was everything.

The sensorman punched up the vu-screen. "It's some sort of archaic ship, Captain. We're running analysis right now, but we thought you'd want to get the visuals immediately."

The visual impacted, registered—but her iron will kept Sutt from betraying her inner surprise. The ship was monstrous, filling up the entire screen even at what the read-out said was quite a distance away. Sutt leaned forward and widened the display. The strange ship was an ovoid the size of a small moon. If it were hollow, you could fit a complete colony inside it. Sutt had heard of vessels this size, but never of this structure and style. But then, they were light-years outside Peacekeeper-known space. What could be expected?

"Impressive. But what's the importance? We're pursuing a Leviathan—though I must say this makes a Leviathan look like a guppy. Can we get in closer?"

"I suggest not. I'll get better visuals," said an adjunct officer. Once more gloved fingers tapped over controls and once more the vu-screen shifted, this time with a close-up. The visual registered with Sutt—and this time she allowed herself a smile. Near the surface of the gigantic star vessel, held transfixed by some kind of kelp-like projectiles, like a fish caught in the tendrils of a sea anemone, was the Leviathan that called itself Moya.

"You see why I suggested we keep our distance," said the adjunct.

"I do indeed. A wise suggestion," said Captain Sutt. "Are we safe from those tendrils at this distance?"

"As usual, I have scrambled force fields for radio-astro-camouflage purposes," said the sub-lieutenant. "We are maintaining distance and being judicious with sensor reads. So far there is no indication that we've been detected in any way."

"Well, clearly the Leviathan was detected," said Sutt. "And captured as well. What can sensors tell us about the interior of the alien vessel?"

"The readings are confused. Strangely, we're having a hard time picking up life signs. With the ship's grip on the Leviathan, you'd think there would be someone at the controls. But we're only picking up three biological forms—and some kind of background energy. Other than that, nobody. Or nobody alive."

Sutt frowned. "What—our quarry is dead?"

"I did not say that. A cursory scan of the Leviathan itself reveals two life forms."

"Hmm. So two are there on board the Leviathan—and the others are on the unknown vessel—or dead. I like those odds. Continue monitor scanning." She turned to the navigator. "What have you got so far from the computer banks?"

"We've scanned and done comparisons and I'm showing positives, Captain. I think we'll have something in just a moment."

Sutt nodded. "Excellent. Good work." She tapped the hard shell of her leg. A staccato dance of fingers. A habit. Inside, Sutt was thrilled. This was far better than she could possibly have hoped. Not only had her quarry been halted in its escape, but there, before her, was an unknown. And the Peacekeepers tended to profit from unknowns. All signs pointed to the conclusion that this thing was the product of a new race. When the Peacekeepers encountered a new race, their valiant forces were able to bring order and meaning to a species that had known only the chaos of freedom—and, most important, the Peacekeepers always profited from the new technology the aliens brought.

Sutt was given very little time to muse further before the screens started flashing with new output. The navigator leaned forward. "Captain, I believe we have something here. We've not only been cross-referencing history but myths and legends from all cultures that our people have brought peace to. What is coming up, sir, is bits and pieces about a truly ancient race who once plied the galactic starways."

"Myths? Legends? We're in greater need of solid information right now."

"There are strong indications that these myths are more like history, Captain," said the navigator. "And they are myth only in that there has been no verified evidence to support them. Until now."

"Keep me in suspense no longer," said Sha Sutt.

"The race, Captain, was known as the Nokmadi. They were explorers, it has been said. And carriers of knowledge that has seeded many legends amongst the planets. Most interesting of all these legends are the stories of holy gems."

"Holy gems? Say more." Sutt could feel her heart rate speed up.

"Objects with tremendous capabilities, Captain. Some say they are not jewels as such, but vessels of power—what some people would call power gems, a melding of natural properties and technology far beyond our capabilities. The Forthari have legends of such gems going back a thousand cycles: they say they were possessed by an ancient race who used them to see through the chaos of the universe. There is a similar legend among the Koppalu: they say that such gems were used to wake the dead. Their scientists investigated the legend for many cycles, but they were unable to make progress. However, neither the gems nor the ancient race said to possess them have ever been encountered by a Peacekeeper force, and some have said that we can dismiss the reports as the childlike beliefs of lesser races."

It was true that such beliefs were officially discouraged. What the navigator could not report was what the insiders in Peacekeeper missions knew—what Captain Sha Sutt knew. There were indeed power gems in the universe. Some had been located. Nothing with any of the puissance or potency described in legend, of course—but artifacts nonetheless, crystalline silicon forms of quanta-batteries that not only gave off light and heat, but small doses of other kinds of quanta-energy. Mysterious quanta-energy that Peacekeeper scientists had not been able to qualify or really even use to any effect. What they had been able to determine, these scientists, was that the crystals were not natural. They had been formed by an intelligent race. The call had been put out to captains of all Peacekeeper ships: keep a lookout for anything remotely resembling these crystal-gems, for they could be a great source of power for our noble cause.

A thrill of excitement coursed through Sha Sutt. Could this not only be an ancient Nokmadi ship—but could it also contain the power gems? Fully powered? Why, if that were so, not only might she be able to seize the Leviathan and its crew, but she would be able to bear a prize of great value back with her as well. No: prizes! Nokmadi power-gems—and the location of an ancient Nokmadi vessel, filled with knowledge and treasures beyond estimation.

"Ah," she said coolly, "I see." Her eyes swept the

bridge, looking at her crew. "We are a small bunch. Ten Peace-keepers. But we are a Hunter ship, are we not? We were born for such a mission as this. This is the way in which we shall not merely serve our cause and our masters, but become masters ourselves, eh?"

Even as she smiled slightly—something she very rarely did—she could see that her smile and what she said made its point to every mind on the bridge. Their eyes mirrored her enthusiasm. If they had been fearful before of this new sight in this new and dark sector of the universe, now they knew that the adventure ahead of them was not merely dangerous duty, but potentially rewarding on a very large scale indeed.

"Sensor officer," said Sutt, "what other kinds of energies are you reading?"

"Many, Captain," said the sensor officer, gazing down at his displays. "Most abundant is a low-level background energy, a type unknown to our tracers. However, what seems most significant is the kind of energies I am not reading."

There was a moment of silence as the officer squinted at the controls and tapped in orders.

"What I am not registering is any evidence of propulsion. No active motors, rockets, quanta-engines—no faster-than-light drives whatsoever."

"So what you're saying," said Sha Sutt, tapping upon her artificial leg in a musing fashion, "is that the alien ship has merely been drifting—out here in the middle of nowhere."

"And nowhere is correct, Captain," the navigator chipped in. "We're more than half a light-year away from any kind of star or solar system."

"Then it's been this way for a very, very long time."

"A hundred thousand cycles at the least," said the sensor officer. "The kind of energies utilized for FTL have a long half-life, and unless the über-physics here are truly beyond our ken, no engines have been used for at least that long."

Tap tap tap of short fingernails on hard metal-and-plastic prosthetic leg. "Go on, sensor officer. Continue analysis."

"Analysis continuing, Captain. But as I said—"

Sutt smiled again. Oh, but the Lords of the Peacekeepers gave their captains wonderful little bags of treats and goodies.

"Lieutenant, take over for a moment. I must visit the evac."

"Yes, Captain."

Captain Sutt rose from her chair. With one last glance at the image in the vu-screen, she turned and clumped back toward the utilities room. She could have made it so that it was not so obvious she had a false leg—but prosthetics were not uncommon amongst Peacekeepers. In fact, the loss of a limb in service to the cause was an emblem of great honor.

Still, Sutt did not wish any of her crew to know exactly what other uses she had for her false leg.

In the small, antiseptic-smelling evac chamber, Sutt unsnapped her trousers on both sides and let the material slide down to the floor. She lifted her false leg up to the commode's edge. Thought impulses from her brain directed servo-motors reasonably accurately. Nonetheless, she helped things along with the guidance of a strong hand. Balance then steady, Sutt commenced to work on the faux-flesh of her thigh. The tapping was coded. Freckles served to locate pressure points. The faux skin peeled back neatly. The tertiary storage drawer was exposed, and Sutt tapped the necessary pressure-point. The drawer slid open, exposing a mass of slots, all occupied by neural-data cells. She thumbed on a guide, examined the glowing green result and then selected one of the cells. A tiny disc of slender but sturdy silicate slid out, and Sutt took it. When she had pulled her trousers back on and secured them properly, she waved her hand over the evac unit. It made an almost undetectable flushing sound, and she returned to the bridge.

"Here. Read this data and compare radiation quotients," Sutt told the sensor officer. "Determine if there are any matchups."

The sensor officer stared at the tab of silicate. His training meant that he knew better than to ask any questions. He laid the silicate tab carefully in a small depression on the sensor panel and clicked it into place. "Assessing, Captain."

As Sutt returned to her chair, she fancied she could feel the power—no, all the powers—thrumming in her right leg. *You gave this chance to me in your way, Aeryn Sun. Perhaps I should thank you, because in doing so you have brought about your own demise.*

The sensor officer looked up from his console. "Captain, there are matches."

"Excellent. As I thought." She stood and leaned on her chair, addressing the crew. "Hunters of the *DarkWind*. We now have more objectives than Commander Crais gave us." She smiled fully now, letting all of her satisfaction show. "And I promise every one of you that should we succeed in those objectives, you all will be rewarded fully!"

She looked at the Leviathan and the ancient ship that flowered around it, but saw only her own destiny.

"Rygel," said Zhaan, "we need to talk."

"Talk? Yes, talk is my speciality!" Rygel XVI brightened and hoisted a commanding finger in the air. "Why, do you realize that I had diplomats during my reign, yes, thousands of diplomats and emissaries and aides de camp with the best rhetorical skills in the business! And these people could talk the stars from the sky and the great gazoom bird from its plakuu nest. But who was the best talker? Me! Me, me, me! Why, yes, let's talk!"

The diminutive despot sat now amongst his minions. The DRDs murmured and buzzed about him, eyestalks waving adoringly, little lights bleeping with electronic love. The crowds of them nearly filled the bridge, and they had whirred out of the way with seeming reluctance when Zhaan had moved to take a seat between Rygel and some of his acolytes. Ensconced on his ThroneSled, fingering his whiskers with satisfaction, Rygel looked happy, thought Zhaan, which was very strange, considering that a gigantic alien planetoid-thing had just stuck tendrils into the side of Moya and their chance of survival had diminished considerably.

"Rygel, we need to talk, not prattle! We could die at any moment!"

"As ever, my dear, I panic only when actual pain and disaster nip at my tail. Believe me, what I do now is appropriate. The royal intuition instructs me on this course. In the last few cycles I often wondered if I would see another dawn. In fact, I didn't see a dawn for many cycles. But you see what I mean. When tomorrow may not bloom, you seize the moment and squeeze all the pleasure in it. Correct, my acolytes?"

The DRDs squeaked, grouped around him on the floor.

"We must begin to take action," Zhaan continued in a firm voice. "We can't reach the boarding party, we can't speak to what's captured us—"

"Time to loll about and create pleasures for ourselves, I say. Speaking of which, I have been experimenting with the food cubes and have discovered that lightly sautéing them in copper gives a pleasant aftertaste . . ." Rygel sniffed and licked his lips. "I'm feeling a bit peckish. I wonder if I can interest you in cooking a meal for us?"

Zhaan grabbed the ridge of his eyebrow and held fast.

"Rygel, this is an emergency," she said emphatically.

"Let go of me. That's the emergency," insisted Rygel. He tried to squirm away, but Zhaan held fast. "Let me go . . . ouch . . . oh my, oh dear! Zhaan, Zhaan, you're going to rip the Imperial brow right from its roots! Oh . . . oh . . . oh! Subjects! Help me! Help!"

The DRDs buzzed and chittered, as usual.

"Forget help for you," said Zhaan, administering a tad more pressure. "I need help *from* you."

"I'm only a little fellow . . . ooowwwwwww . . . I am so limited," whined Rygel. "Oh, oh! . . . in my present circumstances . . ."

"In your present circumstances, you are a cunning little piece of Binurian protoplasm, that's what you are," said Zhaan in a calm voice. "It's vital that we communicate with our friends, and perhaps even more vital that we contact the creatures who are holding Moya prisoner."

"I'll do . . . ow . . . I'll do whatever I can . . ." Rygel said in a strangled voice.

Zhaan looked straight into his bulging yellow eyes. He tried to turn his head, but her hand was steady on his protruding brow. "Rygel, you've accomplished quite a bit in learning to work with the DRDs." Her voice was now soothing. "This communication system—remarkable. And the intelligence displayed. I am magnificently impressed. I think we can use this for the good of all—as befits a royal personage such as yourself." She released his brow.

"I would feel flattered if I weren't in such agony!" sniffed Rygel, rubbing the side of his head.

Zhaan bent down and patted one of the DRDs thoughtfully. "I want you to talk with Pilot and Moya. A communications genius such as yourself may be able to figure out exactly what sort of communications systems this alien ship uses."

Rygel blinked. "Radio, surely? Isn't that the usual?"

"Obviously Pilot has tried all bands—and we get nothing. What else can we try? Can you find something in those voluminous and unpredictable pockets of yours? Or reprogram the DRD communicator? Get to it, Rygel. We need answers."

Rygel folded his arms and heaved an immense sigh. "A king is often called upon to help the lowly. And pray tell, what will you be doing while I'm tinkering with the innards of Moya's comm units?"

For the first time, Zhaan was the one to sigh. "There is very little I can do, it seems. I will enter into a certain Delvian trance. This will enable me to go deep into my memory and the ancestral memories of my people that are passed down within me. Perhaps I will find more about the Nokmadi there."

"Meditating!" cried Rygel, nodding his head forcefully. "Sitting quite still! That is a strength of mine as well, although I find the process goes better with a food cube or six to nibble on . . ."

Zhaan rose abruptly from her seat. "You know the communications networks, Rygel. Confer with Pilot and the DRDs. The second you work anything out, rouse me. I shall be at the opposite end of the bridge." She strode away without a backward glance.

Rygel reached into his pocket, rooted around for a minute, and withdrew another small mechanical gadget. This one was a scrambled piece of wire with a short yellow tube hanging off it. Rygel turned it around in his hand, feeling the shape of the wire and peering down the tube. The tube was full of pocket lint. "Don't think so," he said to himself, and reached in his pocket again.

Zhaan moved to the far side of the bridge, where the trough of water brought to mind the tranquillity of her garden, back on her home planet, so many light-years away. She felt a momentary rush of sadness that she had not seen her garden for so long—and that she might never see it again. She had a brief image of the way the sunlight slanted through the dark green fronds of the chappa tree. Sighing, she sank into her meditation position, trying to focus her mind and to ignore Rygel's mutterings.

She spread her aquamarine robes over her lap so that they draped onto the floor without any folds. It was time for the rite of Urgashanou, the one rite that could reach the ancestral memories deeply buried like seeds in loam. The rite was a sacred thing, usually reserved for the very top echelon of priests. She had read the books, but like all but a tiny handful of the priesthood, she had never attempted the rite. Traditionally, those who undertook it devoted many years of study to the process.

This was because there was one problem with the rite.

It either vaulted you to a level of understanding at which all the memories of the Delvian ancestors were available to you.

Or it killed you.

She took a deep breath and began.

CHAPTER 10

"Who are you?" D'Argo demanded, moving to stand in front of the alien figure sitting at the end of the table. "What are you? Where is our friend? Why are you holding our ship? We demand answers!"

This ghost was humanoid, and he had all the exemplary features valued in Sebaceans. The sleekness, the strong brow and fine eyebrows. The long nose, the pinched lips—the deep, deep eyes. He looked, in fact, a bit like Crais, only slimmer and with a better musculature.

Musculature? How could a transparent being, wondered Aeryn, have a musculature? She could see right through him!

The being wore a tunic, a cape and a simple pair of breeches. He looked not at all like a spacefarer, but rather some kind of gentleman farmer.

He smelled, thought Aeryn, of the first day she had

ever set foot on her native planet, after being in space for so many, many cycles. He smelled of the sunlight she felt on her face, and the fresh air and the wind. He smelled of happiness and freedom, and fulfilment. He smelled like warmth and safety.

Her defenses went up immediately.

The transparent being simply looked at them, his gaze mild.

"Welcome to the World," he said. His voice was soft and low.

Aeryn found herself lowering her eyes. She looked up again. The figure seemed almost real, but his outlines were just a touch insubstantial, the colors of his clothes, hair and complexion just a bit pale. She noticed that his eyes were green.

"I'm glad we can finally speak with you," she said finally. "I hope you will help us."

"And so it is with us, I think," said the ghost.

"Who are you? What are you?"

"My name is Yanor. My people are the Nokmadi."

D'Argo nodded with satisfaction, pulled out a chair, and sat down, his Qualta Rifle across his lap. "Zhaan was right about your identity. And what about our comrade, Crichton, the one swallowed by the wall-thing—or the nightmare-thing. Is he alive?"

Yanor spread his translucent arms wide and a smile lit his features. "I am happy to say that Crichton is not only alive, but he is being enlightened. And he's at a higher stage so far than you."

D'Argo looked over at Aeryn: he looked as if a weight had been taken off his shoulders. Aeryn felt a rush of emotion: great relief, even joy. So their new adventure was not fatal—so far.

D'Argo leaned toward the ghost and said with great intensity, "And why have you captured our ship?"

The figure nodded in sorrow, as if he knew the questioning would come to this. He pushed back his chair from the table and rose. "We have captured your ship because we need your help—and we are desperate," he said. "I hope you will help us, and in return we may have great powers to help you."

Aeryn noticed that the mounds of food on the dishes had stopped steaming. She touched the edge of a plate: it was cold. Indeed, the plate, the tablecloth and the whole room looked as if they had lost something: as if they had lower resolution, or not quite as high a degree of reality. She had the not entirely pleasant feeling that things could start to become transparent at any moment. The candles flickered, and the light was perceptibly dimmer.

"Do you have maps we can consult?" asked D'Argo.

"When will you return Crichton to us?" said Aeryn.

The ghost moved to the wall. "We have nearly as many maps as there are galaxies," he said. "And we will set off for the place where Crichton is, and as soon as we get there, you may see him. Now, so you know what is at stake, I would like to show you the World."

"Your ship is called the World?" said Aeryn.

"No," said the ghost. "Our ship is the World." Now he almost had a twinkle in his gemlike eyes. He turned to the panelled wall and beckoned them.

Cautiously, Aeryn advanced. She kept her pistol in

her hand, and D'Argo maintained a grip on his Qualta Rifle.

Yanor touched a panel on the rear wall and the whole thing slid aside as soundlessly as a curtain parting over a screen.

A blast of sweet wind blew over them, and the smell of grass and honeysuckle was in that wind. A pair of small suns hung in the sky, among a froth of cumulus clouds. Light of blue and green lustre fell down upon brooks and fields choked with flowers. Beyond them were craggy mountains, splendid and mighty. Aeryn could almost taste the freshness of the air.

"Come, come," said Yanor, striding forward into the grass. He seemed much more solid against the vivid colors of the landscape. "It is a lovely world, is it not? Worth fighting for?" He smiled. "Let me show you our home, and then we will talk, and you will know how much is at stake."

"Promised One?" said Crichton. He had struggled to his feet again, and he was standing in the low light of the mossy chamber shaking his head, which felt no better than it had the last time he'd shaken it. "Look, friend. I'm an astronaut. I'm a scientist. No way am I a Promised One. Even my mother didn't think I was a Promised One."

"We beg to differ," said Pahl mildly.

"Well, there's sure been a mistake somewhere. The fact that I'm even out in this part of the universe is a mistake. Sorry, but I'm not a metaphorical guy. What do you want with us? I want straight answers, scientific answers."

Pahl pressed his hands together again and assumed a stance of great solemnity. "It has been prophesied," he said with reverence, "that a Being would arrive who would be the Promised One. The one to descend into the depths, to journey to the Orb of All, and to let us go Home again! We have sensors that have been looking out for the Promised One, and when they analyzed your ship, they knew the Promised One was aboard. Everything you have said merely confirms that you are indeed the Promised One."

"What? 'I have seen the Promised Land?' 'Let my people go?' Who am I supposed to be, Moses? I can promise you I've never even seen a bulrush."

The ghost sighed, a sound like the rustling of leaves over a grave. "Perhaps it is better to show you." He flowed back to his two companions. Again, the dip of heads. Again, the ectoplasmic conference. The ghost turned. He held up his digits, which rippled like a sea urchin's tentacles. "Come, Crichton. Come with us, come to our World."

With a shiver Crichton followed as the transparent aliens turned and floated across the spongy floor. At the far side was a wall criss-crossed with metallic fibres. They did not stop at the wall, but simply floated through the metal, the folds of their outlines sparkling and shivering with light as they disappeared.

Crichton stared at the wall with disbelief. It seemed as solid as it had when the ghosts had disappeared through it, and pushing on it with his hand confirmed that it was rock-solid. He pounded his fist against it in frustration. "Hey, you guys!" he called. "I'm solid! I can't just walk through things."

Nothing.

Silence.

Crichton stared at the gray wall. A clammy cold was creeping into his bones, and a sense of something dangerous lurked in the shadows. He could feel goosebumps forming on his skin.

"Hey, guys! I'm still here. I'm—"

The wall began to open. An irising effect started at the very middle of the wall, and the whole area began to open up, like an inverted metal bloom. The gray peeled away; as soon as the round hole grew to about a metre wide, a shaft of light poured through, illuminating the dank room. It was golden and mild, a sweet sunlight, and as it speared through the dimness, Crichton found his heart lightening.

Slowly the hole opened further. Crichton stepped back and watched. Slowly the panorama unfolded in front of him. It was like something in a painting, framed by the gray metallic grids of the wall. A landscape painting: more than that, a magical landscape painting.

In the foreground of this painting-come-to-life was a meadow of lush grass peppered with color: fuchsia and chartreuse, opal and azure. There were exotic plants, the nearest earthly match for which would be vines and flowers, and rows of strange trees with azure fruits and verdant leaves. After the clamminess of the room, the smell of fresh air was intoxicating. Crichton felt suddenly charged and happy.

Beyond the meadow a gleaming river wound through the countryside, and beyond the river rose mountains. The sight was breathtaking. Crichton's soul took a deep breath of it all.

"Lovely. It's . . . lovely," he said.

The ghosts materialized below a tree in the foreground.

"We are glad you approve, John Crichton. It is the Now Home. You will be the Bringer of the Yesterday Home and the Tomorrow Home."

"I like to be useful."

Crichton eagerly stepped forward into the grass, and as he walked he sent little sprays of floating things like dandelion seedlings drifting into the air. The effect was as though his boots were releasing fairy dust from the turf. He walked over to the ghosts.

"What about my friends?"

"They are here now as well."

"I need to see them."

"When the time comes. First, you must help us."

Crichton sighed. This all would be fascinating under other circumstances: the idyllic landscape of fields and mountains, the winding stream, the scent of the flowers on the warm breeze. But now all he wanted was answers.

"OK. You've got my attention. How am I supposed to help you?"

"We need you to do a very simple thing," said Pahl. "We need you to go into a certain chamber and gather some items for us." The ghost leader looked around at his companions, whose expressions were of the utmost solemnity. "We have been waiting for you to come and do this for so long."

Crichton looked from one face to the other. "You're making it sound so easy. What's the catch?"

The womanly ghost, Igai, stepped forward. "Our ship

has lost all engine capacity. And so after you get these items for us, we will need to take your ship."

A jolt of alarm shot through Crichton. The peril of the situation seemed so at odds with this peaceful landscape, the warm sweetly scented wind, the luxuriant carpet of blossoms.

"I cannot give you our ship," he said.

The lead ghost looked at him as if with great sadness for one who understood so little. "The passage of centuries has damaged our engines beyond repair," he said. "Our faster-than-light drive is useless. We have been drifting in space, helpless, for untold millennia, until you brought us your ship. In return for our passage, we can take you home, or give you eternal life. Do either of these interest you?"

CHAPTER 11

Zhaan meditated.

Meditation was usually like a fresh pool of luxurious warm water for her. Not as blissful, perhaps, as the photogasms she experienced when exposed to certain kinds of light, but far more soothing and peaceful.

She sat on the side of the bridge under the arch of one of Moya's great copper-colored ribs, quietly settled. To someone who was standing beside her, it might have seemed as though Zhaan was sitting in a pool of silence. But not to Zhaan. Being over eight hundred cycles old and having a body derived from a flora-genetic background had its rewards. For one thing, when she tuned into her plant awareness, she never failed to note all the details around her that simply slipped by when she was in her more outwardly aware mode.

Now, for instance.

As she meditated, she kept her hand closed around a

radi, a small Delvian crystal and one of the few things from her homeworld that she still possessed. It was a sparkling clear crystal shot through with Delvian sunlight: and if one looked closely enough, the very eye of the crystal held a spot of intense blue. Zhaan liked to think the blue was Zhaan herself in the sunlight of her garden on Delvia. The crystal had been incubated in the fertile earth of her homeworld and hardened in a cycles-long bath of dried buh leaves, so that the crystal had the rich elusive scent of Delvia itself.

As she sat, the warmth of the radi in her hand, she was aware of subtle noises that were not only calming but profound. The dominant ones now were the hum and whoosh of Moya's inner systems beating out their synchronous beats. Pilot had been correct—Moya was content. Whatever kind of sedatives those invading probes had jabbed into Moya, they were marvellously effective. With all the barbarous things that the Peacekeepers had done to this Leviathan, this living ship, this beautiful being, there had been much pain echoing through her. Her own work with Moya had eased that somewhat. Alas, there had still been pain in the ship—until now.

In control, Zhaan let herself drift past the harmonious and synchronized chuffs and flutters of Moya's energies right into the perfume, the delicate jasmine-and-talc scent of the buh leaves.

As her meditation deepened, she sank into her own past and the past of the thousands of cycles of Delvian ancestors, thriving and growing in the fruitful soil of the planet. Straight on went her perceptions, winding around the scents of the fillgran plants and pushing on through the olfactory into the gustatory. Mint and age, java-mort and kaki-leaves. Past these joys into soul, past and past again, deeper than cutaneous sensory arrays, through photon awareness to a more primal memory.

Zhaan gathered up like a storm of lilies. She harmonized and focused, she blended and burst. Up and out, up and out, forward, backward, null-tomorrow, nano-yesterday, microts upon microts . . . Here is Zhaan . . . not-Zhaan . . .

She could see thousands of cycles into the past, back to the infancy of Delvia, when its inhabitants had barely begun to pierce the veils of esoteric understanding, and when their primitive technology made it perilous to venture beyond their own solar system.

She was in such depths of antiquity that Zhaan felt her grasp on memory weakening. She squeezed the crystal harder, as if she could gather the strength of the planet from it.

Down, into the past . . . She saw the crude Delvian rocket that had first been sent out to greet visitors from the stars. She saw a huge alien ship like a featureless moon newly afloat above Delvia, and a ramp extending from that ship to the Delvian emissaries, just as it had been extended to Moya. She could feel enormous yearning from those aboard the alien ship—a yearning for true sunlight and the rich Delvian soil. A yearning to go home. And a bitter, devouring aloneness.

She felt dizzy with the power of the memories, and fragile, as if she might slip off the edge of consciousness. She tried to steel her mind to remember.

The touch of cerulean night . . . the caress of antiquity . . .

The yearning of alien minds on a sparkling soulscape of light and dark . . .

A spiral staircase leading down to never never and up into . . .

She felt a strong tug on her consciousness, as though she were being pulled to some place south of oblivion. The yearning, the aloneness—were those in the past, or in the present?

She started to de-escalate the rite, to step down from the heights of memory and understanding, and once again she felt the tug, pulling her off in another direction. Should she close down her enquiry into the secrets of the Nokmadi, or throw herself open to them? She might never again have the opportunity to penetrate the secrets of this vessel, this new world, this jagged rift in space.

She took a deep breath.

Here I am, she thought. Take me.

And the dark and the light took her and wrenched her and carried her down.

D'Argo looked at the drifting clouds of fairy-dust thrown into the air as they walked through the thick grass. He was grinning.

Aeryn watched the big creature as he stopped and took a huge, fulfilling breath of the fresh air. He looked invigorated, as though he were wearing Peacekeeper stim-boots and had just pressed for a hype-jab.

"This is good," he said. "This is . . . beautiful. I

almost didn't know how much I missed being on solid land."

Aeryn shook her head, determined to fight the feelings that were enveloping her too. "You planet-huggers. Damn if I can see what you get out of tufts of vegetation and rock hanging off a pile of dirt."

Yanor said, "This is no planet, nor is it simply a ship. It is more than either: it is our World. Sometimes we call it the Now Home. Welcome."

Aeryn looked out at the impossibly serene landscape and then back at the strong, slim figure of Yanor. "Great. The Now Home. We've got one of those riddle-wrapped enigma puzzles, huh?" she said. "More mystery. Just my cup of wak-tea."

Yanor turned and looked at her with those penetrating green eyes. He definitely appeared more substantial now, more solid—and yet there was still the smoky moil inside him, moving clouds of translucence.

"We must travel now," he said simply. "You will see the World and understand why we need your help. And then, I hope, you will give it."

"And Crichton?" pressed Aeryn.

Yanor folded his hands. "Crichton and his companions are some way ahead. They dare not stop and wait for us. Time is of the essence. If we set out now, however, we may be able to catch up with them."

Aeryn looked at D'Argo, who had a wary expression on his face. D'Argo grimaced. "If we set out now, that will be because you have agreed to tell us what we need to know," he said forcefully.

"I understand," said Yanor. "The meeting-place is up ahead, and there the answers will become clear." He began to walk through the thick grass of the meadow. D'Argo and Aeryn looked at each other for a moment; then Aeryn set her jaw and started after him.

D'Argo turned and took a last look behind them. The panel they had stepped out of was nowhere to be seen; around them was nothing but meadow and forest, lush and fragrant. Almost too lush and fragrant. The twin suns had made their way almost imperceptibly farther up from the horizon, and the sky was still a piercing blue.

D'Argo touched his Qualta Rifle and followed Aeryn.

Yanor led them through the meadow and down a gentle slope towards the stream. They could hear the water babbling and see the stones along the shore. A well-worn path opened up before them, paralleling the path of the stream, and Yanor joined it. At each step his feet seem to rise above the path for a moment and then sink down again.

They walked for a few minutes in silence. Aeryn allowed herself the luxury of relaxing just a bit. But it was easy to let something like relief sweep through your bones and blood when you had such warmth and fragrance to walk through.

Despite what she'd said about planet-huggers, Aeryn always had to admit that certain aspects of planet's surfaces she always found intriguing, even comforting. Although this was not, strictly speaking, a planet's surface—it must be a space within the sphere, Aeryn calculated—it had all the elements of one, from mountains to streams, and it seemed a very attractive one as well.

The path traced its way along the river for some time,

and they drew closer to the forest ahead. The trees were dense with small red berries. Shrubs with drooping branches grew to waist-height, and when they brushed past them the leaves gave off a faint odor of something wild, something that made her pulse race. The colors and the fragrances had a heady intensity.

Eventually they emerged into a clearing in the woods, the ground leafy and dappled with sunlight. For the first time Aeryn could hear the singing of birds, although whichever way she turned in the dense forest, she could see none in the trees.

Yanor came to a halt, and D'Argo drew along side Aeryn. And slowly, before their eyes, a meeting-place shimmered into existence.

CHAPTER 12

P ilot!"

"Yes, Rygel?"

"Pilot, would you please present a request to Moya for me?"

"Of course, Rygel."

"Would you tell her to do something about these ridiculous DRDs?"

Rygel XVI, the great and glorious, eternal object of adoration, highest and most venerable power of innumerable realms, etc., etc., lay upon the cold floor.

Near him hovered his ThroneSled, looking more than a little wobbly and uncertain.

His acolytes were clustered around him, clambering over him. They had his robes engaged in their gears, and when he tried to pull away from them, they were heavier and more resistant than they looked. Their exploring eyestalks tickled, their little wheels gouged.

They seemed totally out of control and, what was worse, they simply would not let Rygel up.

"Moya does not give orders to the DRDs, Rygel."

"Look, I don't care if it's the Grand Vizier of Rumley Nimkin Major who gives the orders—they're going crazy, and I want them to stop!"

One of the DRDs started to bump him in the side. Others started to push at him with a little back-and-forth scouring motion.

"I am not familiar with Rumley Nimkin Major, Rygel. It appears the DRDs are attending to you."

A DRD started nuzzling his foot.

"Stop that!" cried Rygel. "That's . . ."

He kicked at the DRD, but it clung to him and its nuzzling motion was making him feel ticklish.

"Yoooooooohooooooheeeeeeeehaaaaa!" cried Rygel. "No, no, please! Pilot! Moya! Stop it . . . please . . . oh my . . . oh dear . . . Stop this thing!" He tried to twist away from the DRDs, but they had him surrounded, and kicking and flailing didn't discourage them in the slightest. Their shiny yellow carapaces shone in the light as they swarmed around him. "Stop it now!" cried Rygel, almost out of breath.

"Rygel?" said Pilot. "Are you all right?"

"Please . . . no . . . noooooooo!" Another DRD had fastened itself to Rygel's other foot and was proceeding to work on it, applying some sort of maddeningly ticklish electrical current to it. Even as he writhed, a whole slew of DRDs whirred and chittered through the door to aid their fellows in this important operation.

Pilot cleared his voice. "Rygel? They have determined that there is maintenance necessary to your neurostructure, and so they are performing stimulus-node massage to encourage energy flow," he reported.

"My neurostructure is fine! Why won't they stop when I tell them? Oooooh . . . Ah . . . Ooooooh! Eeeeee!"

"They will only take orders from the mental communications networks you have established," said Pilot, looking down at the console that constituted his interface with Moya. "Your voice no longer has authority clearance."

"My voice . . . ahhhhhhhhhh . . . they won't obey my voice?" cried Rygel. "It's . . . ooooooh . . . a voice that has commanded billions! If I can't use my voice, I can't use the furze!"

Pilot looked quizzical. "I do not understand that term, Rygel."

"The furze, the furze . . . that's the device that stimulates the rudimentary glandpod at the base of the herpian suplex in the sphirochetia lobe of my brain! Ooooooooooh . . . stop . . . oh . . . That's why I can talk to them . . ." Rygel shook with painful laughter.

There was dead silence from Pilot, then with low and sincere tones, he commanded the former ruler, "Use the furze, Rygel!"

Even as Rygel tried to jerk himself away from the workers, he caught a glimpse of a new batch clattering and clicking away through the doorway. Oh, Zurrka-mounds! They were going to tickle him to death!

He closed his eyes and tried to concentrate, to ignore those expert extensors massaging and sending spurts of low energy to sensitive parts of his nerve endings. It was all rather like Grope Day at the Festival of Tentacles on the planet Marfar. As a ruler, a proud emperor, the latest and finest and most magnificent in a line of astonishingly magnificent rulers, he should be able to rise above even a crowd of DRDs reenacting Grope Day. Once, billions had fallen silent with awe at the slightest motion of his little toe. He must recapture that magnificence now.

He directed the impulses of his brain towards the furze, into it, and beyond it.

He was there. The tactile attentions of the DRDs faded to the background. He could feel the buzz of interlocking communications as those flows of connection mixed with the mechanical frequency inducers and—

Acolytes, behold my command, cried the Right Royal Rygel. *Cease your ministrations*!

The DRDs stopped moving. The extensors were retracted. The tortuous tickling halted. In relief and triumph, he blasted forth his decree: *Always you shall heed my thought-voice so*!

Rygel opened his eyes. The creatures were a good metre away, waiting quietly, dozens of them, their eyestalks bent towards the floor. They were silent, the running lights around their lower edges still. Their silence was somehow reverent. They looked as though, if they only had legs, they would bow down to him.

"Good, stay there!"

The DRDs did not move, twitch, or blink.

Rygel righted himself and patted himself all over, to make sure there were no scratches, punctures or unseemly disturbances to the royal robes. As he became calmer, he realized that he felt fresh, stimulated, full of vigour and energy. It was as though his circulation had improved.

Cautiously, the DRDs began to move again, circling him with joyful whirring noises, coming closer, pointing their eyestalks at him, and then backing off shyly.

"Ah ha," he said to the little scrabbling machines. "What do you know? You did an excellent job of maintenance on the Royal We!"

The DRDs were now turning in circles, wriggling and waving their extensors. It was all rather like Asteroid Day on DanceWorld. Rygel was about to order the servile creatures about, make them do a shamba dance or something equally graceful, when the memory of Pilot's voice played in this mind: "Use the furze, Rygel."

He reached up, touched the mechanism he had attached to his ear earlier, and thought his command.

Vassals! Turn and dance the other way!

Immediately the DRDs, like some kind of demented chorus line, spun about and began dancing in the opposite direction.

Left!

They jumped left.

Right!

They jumped right.

Order by order, Rygel instructed them to zig and then zag, to dance by threes, fours, and sevens, to shake their rears and to blink their lights in syncopation. They obeyed in unison.

"Quite the sight! Quite the sight indeed!" said Rygel. He felt an inner glow of great self-satisfaction as he surveyed the dancing fools he had created.

"Stop!"

The DRDs stopped.

"Very good. Now—stay here. There's someone I

need to speak with." Rygel scrambled onto his ThroneSled. My my my! Did he have some news for Zhaan: his powers were even more magnificent than she might have anticipated. The ThroneSled zipped around the consoles and Rygel hummed happily to himself. Oh my, wasn't he the clever one? There she was, that blue Zhaan, staring into her blue roots and stems, totally ineffectual, and he, Rygel XVI, with his vast ability and intelligence forging the way toward problem resolution, had made a breakthrough in communication.

Rygel angled the sled around the trough pool. "Zhaan? Zhaan!" he called. "You'll be happy to know that I, Rygel XVI, have—" As he reached the far end of the bridge, Rygel could immediately see that there was a problem.

Zhaan had fallen from her meditation place and now lay sprawled on the floor. A blue-green fluid leaked from her mouth and ears. Her eyes were wide open, staring into nothingness, and a clear crystal had fallen from her hand.

"OK, let's get this straight," said Crichton. He was sitting with Pahl and his companions in the shade of a large tree, around a stone table that had shimmered into view. Despite the fact that it had appeared out of thin air, the table seemed substantial enough, its rough stone surface cool to the touch. Pahl and the other two ghosts, Leff and Igai, were sitting on stone seats gathered around it rather than on air, which Crichton found reassuring. The tree sheltering them seemed to emit a faint fragrance of morning and springtime, and the landscape was as bright and peaceful as ever.

The ghosts looked at Crichton, their glittering translucent hands folded on the table.

"You want me to help you do something," said Crichton, "and in return you'll take me home?" A sense of excitement was building in him now. "You know where my homeworld is?"

Leff spoke. "We do know. I can guide you there myself. I am the keeper of maps among the Nokmadi."

Crichton's pulse quickened. So they had indeed found the Nokmadi! He really might be close to going home.

"Where are the maps? How can you know if my homeworld is on them?"

At this all the ghosts smiled. Leff spoke again. "The maps are all over this ship. You have already found some—and met some. And your homeworld will be on them if you come from this galaxy or one of the six hundred other central galaxies."

Crichton blinked. "Central galaxies?"

Leff smiled again. His face was almost human, and Crichton could see the amusement in his eyes. "The galaxies nearest the centre of the universe. We have been mapping a very long time. From your physiology and your neurological construction, I would guess that you're from either the planet Xomsi or the planet Farworld. Of course, those are our names for the planets, not those of your race. Tell me, does your planet have a binary sun?"

"No."

"Then it must be Farworld. Do you recognize this?" He passed his hand above the centre of the stone table, and as his hand moved through the air it left a trail of stars and planets floating above the table. In the middle was a fiercely glowing golden sun no bigger than Crichton's thumb.

In orbit around the sun were planets of varying sizes and colors. Crichton felt his heart pounding in his throat. There was Mars, tinged with red, and Jupiter with its cluster of moons, and Earth, blue and green, clad in a mantle of cloud! "That's it," he said. "That's my home!"

The ghosts exchanged glances. "Who would have thought," said Pahl, as if to himself, "the Promised One would come from Farworld!"

Leff swept his hand over the table once more, and the solar system folded back into air. "Farworld," he said. "Then you are in this very galaxy. Not far from home at all."

Crichton clenched his hand into a fist. "OK. You have the maps. What do you want in exchange?"

A cloud passed over one of the suns overhead, and Pahl glanced up with a worried expression. "Our desires are neither more nor less than yours. We have been voyaging for millennia of cycles. We have seen stars born and extinguished. We have been away so long that we would have lost all memory of where we came from except that we have this World, which is a perfect replica in every respect except one. It is not real."

Crichton took in the soft fragrance of the blossoms, the sweetness of the air, the panorama of flowering meadows and jutting mountains extending back to the horizon. "None of this is real?" he said.

Pahl shook his head. "Only as much as memories are real. We have had the universe, John Crichton, but the vast emptiness of space has wearied us. Now we want only one thing: to go home."

"And I can help you do that?"

Pahl looked at him, troubled. "Now that you are here, Promised One," he said, "you do not know? Your ancient memory has not awakened?"

"Jog the ancient memory a bit, OK?" said Crichton.

Pahl nodded. "We must travel to the Hole in the World, where the gems of power are kept. The gems of power keep us in this energy-state—as ghosts, in your terms. They have made us immortal, but they are also our jailers. We need you to free us from the gems of power, to take on our fleshly bodies once more: bodies that can die, but that can also go home."

"And this Hole in the World—is it nearby?"

Both suns overhead were now wreathed in cloud. The air had a chill to it, and mist had begun to gather above the river.

"It is far enough." Pahl stood. "We must start." Crichton got to his feet, and the other ghosts rose as well. When they moved away from the table, it began to fade away until nothing but a dazzle hung in the air, and then that too disappeared.

Somewhere there was a cawing. A screech echoed through the valley. Suddenly the mist that rose from the river seemed not so mystical and beautiful, but mysterious and deadly. A cold shiver went up Crichton's back.

The ghostly aliens drifted into the forest, moving like part of the ground fog that had suddenly sprung up and curled around the trees, like mist about gravestones. Crichton hurried after them. The odors of mold and mushrooms and rotting leaves was thick here, and the electricity of something more ominous prickled at the back of Crichton's neck.

"Have you told me the whole story," he said, "or is there something more I should know?"

"You know the essentials," said Pahl, drifting deeper into the forest. Ahead there was a cliff face rising up from the forest, an abrupt frozen cascade of rock riddled with crevices. The ghosts headed towards it.

Abruptly there was a loud report from the sky. A slash of lightning raged through the gathering clouds, and thunder grumbled. There was a distinct touch of ozone in the air, like a surly promise.

"Does it rain here?" said Crichton. He looked at the ghosts. "Are we in danger from the storm?"

Pahl turned to him with a troubled look. "The lightning cannot kill us, but it is a threat to our stability. Any discharge of electricity will disable us for the space of a day. Come, we must hurry. We know a place where we can wait."

They came to the face of the cliff and Pahl located the opening of a cave. Even from the entrance Crichton could smell dampness and clamminess. The inside was impossibly dark, like the entrance to a tomb.

The ghosts passed inside, one by one.

"I hope you're not expecting me to do anything crazy like spend the night in here," Crichton said, stopping at the mouth of the cave.

Pahl turned to him once more. "Night in the World has far worse terrors than these," he said.

He turned back and plunged into the darkness.

Despite his better judgement, Crichton followed.

CHAPTER 13

Zhaan!" cried Rygel. "Zhaan, I command you to stop this silly charade. I want you to get up immediately, clean yourself and apologize for playing such a nasty joke!"

Despite all his bellowing, Zhaan did not move. She lay still on the floor, blue-green blood oozing from mouth, nose and ears.

Damn her! thought Rygel. More problems! What has she done now? He lowered his ThroneSled and waddled off, bent over Zhaan and poked her.

"Zhaan?"

Still nothing. Her eyes stared straight ahead, with a glazed look to them.

Arggh! Pulse, did she have a pulse? Was she supposed to have a pulse? Did plant-people have pulses like normal galactic folk?

Rygel peered down at his fallen comrade. She did

look beautiful, beautiful and bald and blue, especially now in repose, with the classic lines of her face—those high cheekbones, that perfect chin and that magnificent head. Rygel preferred the feminine lines and bulges of his own race, but he had to admit that Zhaan's face was really rather stunning.

He put a hand on her long blue neck, trying to detect a pulse. Her skin was even bluer than usual, it seemed, and her neck was chilly. Rygel held his sensitive fingers first at one pressure-point, then at another, hoping . . .

At the top of Zhaan's throat, just below that noble chin—

Rygel pressed in. Yes. There it was: a flutter, a throb! Zhaan had a pulse!

There was a clatter and scutter. Rygel looked behind him. A group of DRDs had clustered in the entrance-way, looking on attentively.

"Well, don't just stand there! Help me!" said Rygel.

They scurried over and grouped around the Zhaan.

"Now, Zhaan," instructed Rygel. "I demand that not only you not die, but that you return to consciousness. I need to speak to you about vital matters!"

Zhaan remained still. Rygel grabbed a cloth from a table and dabbed the blood off Zhaan's face. "Zhaan? I know you're in there somewhere. This is no time for you to have a crisis. I think you're being selfish here, very selfish indeed."

Apart from the faint flutter of her pulse, Zhaan seemed utterly lifeless.

"Very well. If you insist on being obstinate, we will have to address the problem here without your help. I'm going to make one more attempt: this is your last chance."

Rygel zoomed over to the nearest trough, filled a pitcher with cool water, and poured it over her face. The water formed a pool around her still form. The DRDs backed away.

Then Rygel made the ultimate sacrifice. He kneeled down by her side and got the hems of his royal robes wet.

"Zhaan!" he screamed into her ear. The sound made the DRDs scurry about excitedly, but Zhaan lay unmoving.

Rygel addressed the DRDs. "Help me pick her up."

The DRDs hurried over. Rygel positioned his ThroneSled by her side and together they pushed her onto the Sled, and over to the bridge.

"Pilot, Zhaan's unconscious. Something's very wrong, but she's alive."

"She must have had some astral catastrophe," said Pilot with a worried tone.

"Whatever the reason, there's nothing I can do here and now. I thought you might have some sort of biological adaptation place where she can be monitored. You know, stick her with that, pump her with this; keep her body ticking."

"Moya has compartments that may fit the bill."

"Excellent. But I want to keep her as close as possible. There's something I'm working on that may help here—may help all of us—but I need access to her powers and abilities. And I certainly want to know if and when she becomes conscious again."

Pilot assumed a reflective expression. "The biogenetic chambers might be modified for these purposes. They are on this tier."

"Sounds like it hits the mark. Direct us, please."

"Gladly. Take the hallway around to the right—I will open a pod and we shall see what we can do."

"Excellent. Come, slaves!"

Rygel guided the ThroneSled bearing Zhaan into the hallway, toddling along beside it, trailed by a host of DRDs. As he came around the curve, he saw that Pilot had indeed been able to open a pod in the wall. Moya's copper-colored inner cladding had slipped back to reveal a chamber several metres high, its inner surface soft and organic. It exuded warm air, as if giving forth an exhalation.

"Acolytes, prepare to heave ho!" The ThroneSled settled on the floor and the DRDs gathered around it, their eyestalks waving. Physical exertion was normally below a magnificent ruler's dignity, but Rygel could make an exception in times of emergency. He took hold of one of Zhaan's forearms and tugged. "Acolytes, heave ho now!" he commanded in his most imperious voice.

The moment they entered the cave, Crichton knew something was wrong. The ghosts went ahead of him, their forms emitting a dim and eerie phosphorescence in the gloom. Then Crichton heard Pahl choke, "No!"

Before Crichton could move, jagged bolts of light shot out of the darkness. In the flares of light he could see wraiths, the dark outlines of creatures who seemed to absorb the light like black holes. If the ghosts were constellations, these new and terrifying creatures were the black spaces in the sky—and they had weapons.

"Ambush!" cried Pahl. "We must turn back!"

But before they could do a thing, ragged bursts of fiery snarls belched out from the maws of those weapons. The fire consumed the ghosts. Crichton watched in shock as their ghostly mouths opened in ghostly pain—and then they were obliterated into a raging furnace.

He turned to flee, but there were wraiths blocking his retreat. Desperately he drew his pulse pistol. The smoky darkness began to clear, and the light from the entrance to the cave showed only the dark spectral figures of the wraiths, who waited, silent and menacing.

"What do you want?" cried Crichton, his pistol held in front of him.

He watched in horror as the gun maws lowered and took aim.

But a voice rose above the crackling of the power in those weapons. A woman's voice: "No. Do not kill him. He is the one we need."

A form stepped forward into the dim light. It was a woman's form, tall, dressed in a cowl and a mantle. She wore high leather boots and at her belt was a curving silver dagger.

She stared down at him for a moment, her face in darkness. "Greetings, John Crichton," said the smooth and silky voice. It carried magic and mystery with it: a voice of music.

The woman flipped back her cowl. Staring at him was the face of Zhaan.

Aeryn and D'Argo had had a full parley with Yanor in the clearing beneath the trees. It was a place of council, Yanor had said, one of many that the Nokmadi had established—or, in his words, remembered. He had spoken of their desire to map the universe, and how they had travelled the galaxies for millennia, until finally, weary and homesick, they wanted only to go home.

"We have been waiting and hoping for the Promised One," Yanor had said, leaning towards them across the stone table. His black hair glittered as if sprinkled with stars, and Aeryn found herself distracted by it. "He is your companion—John Crichton. He alone can enter the chamber where the Orb of All guards the power gems that keep us in our ghostly, immortal form. We have programmed our sensors to look out for such a one, but in hundreds of cycles of searching we have found no one with the neurological patterns that a Promised One must have. Other of our people are taking him to the Orb of All even now."

D'Argo made a noise of impatience. "What is this Orb of All?"

Yanor stared at them earnestly. "A device set in place when this ship, this World, was first constructed. It was originally meant as a safeguard against the destruction of the power gems. It reads the mental patterns of all who penetrate the chamber. And it destroys interlopers."

Aeryn slammed her hand against the table. "Then it will destroy Crichton?"

Yanor shook his head. "It will not destroy him, because he is the Promised One. It was necessary that he hurry on ahead, before anyone could stop him. But since you are concerned for him, we will follow. Our transport will be arriving at any moment." He rose to his feet.

D'Argo and Aeryn rose to theirs. "Who would try to

stop him?" asked D'Argo with a worried tone.

"What if you're wrong, and he's not the Promised One?" said Aeryn in an angry tone.

"The Nightfolk wish to stop him," said Yanor. "And we are not wrong." He was looking up at the sky, and their gaze followed his.

There, blotting out the blue of the heavens, were the vast, ragged wings of a dragon.

Once the dragon had landed, Yanor strode forward and unknotted a kind of harness it wore, letting down a rope ladder just in front of the dragon's folded leathery wings. The wings were a pale color, shot through with gold, and the rest of the dragon was covered in gold and red scales. It had a long head, now resting on its front claws, and steam came from its nostrils. A long scaly neck led down to its substantial body, the top of its back being even higher than D'Argo could reach, and the body ended in a long scaly tail that did several loop-de-loops as it diminished in size.

"I've heard of these," said Aeryn. "We have myths of them. A mythical beast for a mythical race?"

Yanor slapped the dragon's side fondly. "We call it Mortcalm. Of course, it's mechanical: we couldn't keep a whole colony of real dragons in space. But it reminds us of home."

D'Argo walked around the dragon, studying the folded wings, the curling tail. "Remarkable. I've heard of a number of races that have such a species in their mythology, but I've never actually seen one. And you have real ones on your home planet?"

A look of sadness crossed Yanor's face. "Had. Who

knows whether they still survive on Nokmad? And as for the myths many races have about dragons . . ." A small smile crossed his face. "Perhaps they saw one of ours when we came by?"

D'Argo contemplated this possibility.

"Come," said Yanor. "We must board. Time is passing, and the Hole in the World awaits us."

The shadow that fell across them was dark as the stuff that clung to distant stars in a sky full of forever.

The countryside spread out before them, lush and picturesque, like a living map of tiny trees and miniature streams threading their way through fields. The dragon's flight was smooth. In its back was a compartment with six seats, one behind the other. With safety webbing pulled across their chests, Aeryn and D'Argo were free to look down at the passing wonders of the World below them.

The light from the two suns was bright until suddenly a shadow passed over the dragon, a dark rectangle above them; a trapdoor in the sky had opened.

Aeryn could not make out what it was at first; it was so dark, blotting out all illumination.

"By the Sky Gods!" cried D'Argo.

"Stay calm!" said Yanor. "We shall evade capture." His hands were busy at the controls, yanking throttles, pulling levers, keying in coordinates. The right wing of the dragon dipped. With a roar, the flying beast drew its leathery wings to its sides and dropped like a stone. The g-force threw them back against their seats. Aeryn looked down and saw craggy mountain peaks rushing toward them. At the last possible moment, the dragon's wings opened, caught the wind and pulled up.

Maneuvering to follow was what looked like some kind of metal raft. From the underside it did indeed resemble a dark trapdoor hovering above them. Now that they could see it from above, they saw that the upper surface was filled with knots and promontories and turrets. Even as they watched, a scarlet beam of energy zapped down from a nozzle of a gun emplacement, sizzling the air fifty metres away, exactly where they had been moments before.

"What is it?" Aeryn screamed above the wind.

"I will shoot it down!" cried D'Argo.

"It is a ship of our enemies, the Nightfolk," said Yanor. "It is better armed—but it is not as fast or as maneuverable as Mortcalm."

Yanor yanked on the controls and Mortcalm's huge wings stroked the sky again, pulling them faster through the air. They dodged and hopped around the mountains while the raft pursued them, firing energy bolts.

"We can take refuge soon," said Yanor, "and then we will have several options."

"I hope death is not one of them," said D'Argo.

The ship of the Nightfolk followed them relentlessly. As they flew on, swooping and diving, Aeryn could tell that the sky was darkening. The flashes of fire from the attacking skyraft seemed brighter and of different hues now: magenta and orange, hot red edged with deep blue. A bolt of fire touched the side of the dragon. The beast pulled away, flying more slowly now, its wings beating with what seemed almost like painful exertion.

Yanor remained intent on piloting Mortcalm. He

swooped and swerved, banked and looped, but the dark sky-raft remained behind them.

The sky was filled with a silvery gloom, as if the impending nightfall had robbed even the horizon of its customary sunset glow.

And then suddenly the dragon began to dive. Aeryn could feel the g-forces pinning her to her seat as their speed quickened. She expected the dragon to pull up again at any moment, but the winged creature kept plunging down and down.

Aeryn craned her neck to one side for a better view. The dragon seemed to be aiming at the side of a mountain, but she could see no flat landing space to give them refuge.

The side of the cliff hurtled towards them; in the space of a second Aeryn took in the shape of the stones, small bushes clinging to the rockface, a cascade of dirt where it looked like there had been a slide.

"The mountain!" she shrieked.

Still Mortcalm plunged, wings tucked against its side. Just as it seemed that their descent could only be stopped violently, the dragon's wings unfolded again, and the wind slowed their descent—but not enough. Mortcalm was still heading straight for the mountain. Its side loomed, great granite crags and all, a whole line of trees and roots, and disaster—the dragon flew straight into it, and they were swallowed by darkness.

CHAPTER 14

"Zhaan?" cried Crichton.

The beautiful woman looked at him, tilting her head in an inquiring fashion. But as Crichton looked at her more closely, he could see that though the woman looked like Zhaan, there were differences. First, she was not blue, but a pale and creamy color. Second, she had a beautiful mass of flowing brown hair. She seemed somehow both substantial and insubstantial—like Zhaan but not like Zhaan. Where Zhaan was ethereal, this woman had an intense physicality. Where Zhaan was cool and serene, this woman was warm and enticing. Where he had admiration and respect for Zhaan, this woman seemed to invite more. There was the delicate scent of perfume about her that crept through Crichton's nose and down his backbone in a delicious shiver. Her eyes surveyed him with an alluring excitement, a thrilling connection of all that was electric about sexual attraction.

At first glance she'd seemed just as material as Zhaan, but as Crichton watched he could see her materiality fade, the colors and substances that made up her form moving around like dense smoke.

"Zhaan?" repeated the beautiful woman.

Crichton almost stuttered in his confusion. "You— you look like someone I know," he said. "But you're not Zhaan, are you?"

She threw back her head and laughed a silvery laugh. "I'm as much as you want me to be," she said, moving closer to him. The rest of the cave was dark, and the wraiths had faded into the blackness, leaving him alone with the mysterious woman.

"I demand that you tell me what's going on," he said. "Are you another person who thinks I'm some sort of Promised One?"

The woman took one of his hands between her own two cool hands. "Are you some sort of Promised One?" she asked.

Crichton withdrew his hand politely but decisively. "My name is John Crichton. I am an astronaut from the planet Earth, stranded far away by accident. I mean no harm to you or your ship, and all I want to do is go home."

The woman gave a slow smile. "Yes," she said. "You yearn for the cold emptiness of space, and you yearn for home. Those twin yearnings give you great power, O Promised One."

Crichton sighed in exasperation. "I am not promised to anybody," he said, "and my companions and I only want you to let our ship go so we can leave in peace."

The woman smiled and her dark eyes seemed to glow with an almost hypnotic fervor. "Oh, no, John Crichton," she replied. She smoothed a hand across his shoulder and then pressed a cold, delicious kiss onto his lips. "You are in exactly the right place for what you seek." They were in a huge cavern, lit by torches that glowed with a cool, even light. Aeryn studied the cavern. The entrance through which the dragon had glided was as invisible from the inside as it had been from the outside: it was as if they had penetrated a screen of illusion, but from a distance it all looked real and solid. Rocky walls were to either side of them, and far above a ceiling dripped with stalactites. But they were standing on a shiny metal floor. This was what Mortcalm had landed on and now was curling up upon. A little puff of smoke rose above its nostrils. Aeryn was surprised to see its great head sink down upon the metal, eyes closed with something like a half-smile upon its face.

Yanor was also smiling. His hair was unruffled, as if the wind had no power to touch him, and his dark tunic was as smooth and pristine as it had been when they had first met.

"Quite the ride!" he said. "But I think we are safe now."

"Who were those terrorists?" cried D'Argo. "I swear I shall meet them in battle again! And they shall taste my fury!"

Yanor moved to Mortcalm and stood with a hand smoothing the dragon's great scaly neck. "If only it were that simple," he said. "In fact, you cannot kill them—just as you could not kill me, if you tried—without going to the Hole in the World, where our forms are generated. It is there we were headed, and they sought to prevent us from getting there, as they did. So far."

As Yanor was speaking, Aeryn looked around the cavern. Her eyes were adjusting to the dim light, and she gradually became aware of two more dragons, a little smaller than Mortcalm, tucked away in the corners, resting with their heads on their forelegs. Beyond them were countless machines, blinking with lights, angled with catwalks and odd alien architecture, colored in harsh jade, bright magenta, streaks of cerulean. The place smelled of burned insulation, oil and electricity.

"This way," said Yanor, and he turned to lead them.

"Where are we?" demanded D'Argo.

"We are in the mountain stronghold," said Yanor, moving ahead of them towards the far end of the cavern. "This is where many of the Dayfolk—our kind—live at night."

"I thought you were called Nokmadi, not Dayfolk," said Aeryn.

The ghost stopped and turned his green eyes on her. "We are all Nokmadi, but only some of us are Dayfolk. The rest are in the service of the Queen of All Souls, the Empress of Night. The Nightfolk oppose our desire to return home, and for that reason they seek to destroy us—as you have seen."

The ghost turned and flowed away.

Aeryn and D'Argo exchanged a glance and then followed.

As they walked along in the dimly lit cavern, Aeryn noticed that other ghosts were perched in the scaffolding. They seemed intent on technological duties with the machinery. One looked down at her, and she could see that its face was not quite human, its clothing flowing robes instead of the tunic, trousers and boots that Yanor wore.

"The other ghosts," she said to Yanor, "do not look like you."

"But they do look vaguely like your kind, do they not?" said Yanor, leading the way around a bank of machinery. "We take the form of memories, and we have gleaned enough from you to look comfortably like your species."

She processed this thought. That meant that Yanor, too, was not really what he looked like.

"And yet you," she continued, "you're dressed like one of my kind; you look so much more Sebacean than the others. Why?"

He stopped and smiled, looking at her squarely in the eye. "This is the way I choose to appear to you." He looked over to D'Argo. "I considered appearing as a Luxan, but in searching your mind for possible reactions, I found you would respond more favorably to this Sebacean form. Perhaps it reminds you of someone you once knew? Do you like it?"

Aeryn frowned. "What does it matter? Let's get on with this!"

Yanor nodded. He turned again and led the way until they came to a large cage-like apparatus with wheels, decorated with motifs of dragons that looked as if they were made out of wrought iron. Yanor pulled open the door, which groaned on its hinges. He stepped in and beckoned to them. D'Argo and Aeryn followed him inside. The door screeched closed. Immediately, the cage contraption was lifted. Shuttles and wheels spun and clicked and they were drawn up, then hurtled along horizontally into a narrow tunnel. The carriage rattled and shuddered as it passed along through a darkness punctuated by specks of light.

Finally the contraption clanked to a stop. Yanor opened the door of the carriage and they got out.

They stood on a tier—one of three—along the side of a vast room. These tiers and terraces were hung with tapestries of intertwined ivy and flowers and other plants, surmounted by a brilliant and glowing woven sun.

On the spacious ground level, a fountain spurted several jets of water, the centermost of which was the largest. Streams of water jetted in pinwheels and loops. Surrounding this fountain, statues of rock and metal floated about a metre above the floor. The statues turned to watch Aeryn and D'Argo as they followed Yanor along the upper tier.

On every tier, as well as on the ground floor, other ghosts moved. As they passed by, the ghosts looked at them with great interest; several seemed as if they would come up and speak to Yanor, but held back.

"What is this place?" asked D'Argo. "What is going on?"

"This is the city of the Dayfolk. We can take refuge here while we plan the rest of our journey."

Yanor guided them onward along the terrace, and then finally inside a room about twelve paces square. Smoky paintings of ochre and bronze decorated the wall. There were oddly assembled geometric figures in one corner, and to the right was a small fire, around which padded furniture was situated.

"Please. Sit. Make yourselves comfortable. I shall have some material vials brought. Something to slake your thirst. Something comestible as well."

These chairs and couches looked comfortable enough. The fire crackled by her in orange and reddish glows.

D'Argo, still tense, eyed her and then looked suspiciously at a chair.

He grunted as the ghost drifted away. Aeryn sat down, closed her eyes and allowed herself to unwind.

Grunting, Rygel XVI gave one final shove to the unconscious form of Zhaan's body.

It slipped a little more into the compartment. Odd strands of connectors had already wound around Zhaan, cradling her bleeding head and limp body. He could see pulses of biomedicinal transformation as the pod adapted to fit Zhaan's life-maintenance necessities.

"There! That should keep you!" said Rygel. Carefully, he moved away from Zhaan. Now fully cradled in the pod, she lay still.

With a sigh of relief, Rygel returned and started back to the bridge. Not three steps down the hallway, however, he tripped over one of the DRDs.

"Oof!"

Rygel XVI fell flat on his face. Fortunately, the distance from face to floor was not very great, but the fall left him winded and with a few stars whirling around his head. He sat up, feeling his skull tentatively to make sure the royal noggin was intact.

The DRD he'd tripped over circled around him attentively, eyestalks downcast. Blearily he looked down at it, anger suffusing him.

"Blast and damn you, you clumsy oaf! You have tripped your lord. You have—"

The DRD screeched backward. It twirled around madly, like some jittery bug, then it flopped on its carapace, little wheels whirling.

Sparks crackled. Black smoke twirled upward. The DRD shuddered and was still.

Eyes wide, Rygel got to his feet. The device in his ear began to squeal. He felt for the controls and turned it down. The other DRDs in the area crowded around. Their eyestalks wavered nervously as they surveyed their fallen comrade.

"Rygel! What have you done?" came a voice from above him.

The diminutive Dominar whirled around. "Who said that?"

"It's just me, Rygel: Pilot. I am not projecting my hologram, but I can see what happened."

"It tripped me!" cried Rygel defensively. "And then I yelled at it. Nothing more than it deserved. I swear, I didn't touch it."

"Moya is upset."

"You think I'm not upset?"

"We have allowed you the use of her DRDs on condition that you do not misuse them. What have you done to that unit, Rygel? It appears to have terminally malfunctioned."

Rygel looked at the upturned DRD, its shiny underparts exposed, its wheels now motionless.

"I—I don't know, Pilot I . . . I just yelled at it!"

"Vocal waves cannot short-circuit a DRD—one moment. Moya speaks to me—"

Silence.

Rygel looked down the hallway. The other DRDs were gathered in a circle around him. He felt as if they were accusing him. Even a DRD with a slightly mangled antenna was looking at Rygel as though he were a pile of Argan refuse—and a particularly stinky specimen of it to boot. Or was that just his imagination? By the gods, it had to be! Still, what had happened? Rygel touched the device in his ear. What kind of power had this given him? Rygel had always prided himself on a talent for power—what good was being so gifted unless you enjoyed yourself? But the ability to think something dead would be a little disconcerting—"

"Rygel!"

Rygel thought about just leaping over the ring of DRDs and making a sprint for it. He knew the secret spots and cubbyholes where he could hide. But no: it would be futile to try to hide from Moya. Wherever he hid, after all, he'd still be in Moya. Moya was everywhere.

"I'm here," he said, maintaining an erect posture and regal dignity. He raised an index finger and twirled it in a weak version of a royal signature in the air.

"Moya is very upset with the way you have been treating the DRDs. She has instructed me to examine the short-circuited DRD and report on what happened. Rygel, Moya's DRDs are vital to her maintenance. This kind of misuse can lead to sanctions."

Sanc—He knew what sanctions really meant. It really meant punishment.

"I will return in a short time," said Pilot's voice.

Rygel looked around. The eyestalks of the DRDs wavered accusingly. He looked at the vanquished DRD, upturned and motionless, and thought about what Pilot had said.

Sanctions. Not good. Not good at all!

It was the oddest kiss that John Crichton had ever experienced. It was also the best.

The kiss from the Queen of All Souls—this ghost-woman who looked so much like Zhaan—tasted of cinnamon and lilies. The lips, though cool, were smooth and silky and had an electric bite that sizzled down to dance on the edges of his synapses. Her touch was firm, but gentle enough to make him feel as though all his nerve-endings had been brushed lightly with starlight. Even though she was a ghost, she had substance. She smelled of a musky, erotic perfume. For the moment, spellbound by her kiss, he could do nothing but let her move her soft and rounded curves up against him. Something deep down inside him responded. Despite his better judgement, he could not help but reach out to pull her in closer.

With a tinkling laugh, she pulled away. Spun. Danced. Her robes a swirl of color and smoke, giving brief flashes of pale flesh, she moved away and said, "That was so nice, John."

Crichton's mouth was dry. He realized that he had started to sweat. What kind of enchantment had this strange woman put on him? And how did she know his name? Could she read his mind?

"I can see inside you. Enough to know who you are in many ways."

He felt deeply disturbed on several different levels. She was erotic, and yet she was a ghost. The thinking part of him kicked in, and he realized that, for all her unique sensations, what he'd just experienced was a melding of various sensory experiences from his past: bits and patches of women he had known. Karen's smell, mixed with that Polynesian musk of Aliesha. Rachel's taste combined with the tangy touch of Anna's mouth. Oh God, and all the other fantastic women he'd cared for, wrapped into one, and then somehow transported into seduction squared, all made more potent by his own loneliness and need.

"You . . . you're not human," he objected.

"I am female." Her jewel-like eyes glittered. "Let me more than assure you of that."

As he managed to clear his head, Crichton looked around him. "I'm not sure if I should thank you for that kiss or curse you. I get the feeling that I really don't matter. You're acting as if I'm something special, but if you didn't think you could use me, I'd probably be dead."

She moved toward him again and traced the line of his neck with her finger. "But you are something special," she said. She tilted her head down and looked at him from under half-closed eyelids.

He took a deep breath and tried to steel his thoughts. "I guess Pahl and the others weren't so special, then? Not special enough to live."

She laughed a low, melodic laugh. "No, no, John," she said, putting a cool finger to his lips. "They're not dead. Ghosts can't die—that's why they're ghosts. They'll have reconstituted themselves in less than a day. I merely made them forget themselves for a while, in a manner of speaking."

"That's a pretty drastic kind of forgetting."

The suggestion of a smile crossed her lips. "Perhaps not drastic enough. They will remember too soon for my taste. Here, we are such stuff as dreams are made on."

The line was familiar—and then Crichton remembered that she could see into his mind.

"I am serious, John Crichton. Dreaming is something that all intelligent creatures do—I know. Our data banks have records of millions of intelligent species from many galaxies. All of them dream." She looked at him meaningfully. "All. We're just better at reading dreams. And soon we shall be better at realizing them. The people who brought you here were the Dayfolk. Like all those who live by day, they are slow, blundering, unadventurous. Their lives are daydreams that come to nothing. But you and I shall become acquainted with the night." She ran her hand down his arm, and her touch made him shiver. Her eyes were dark, and in their depths light glittered like stars.

She looked at him with those glittering eyes. "Come with me, John Crichton."

He fought to resist her powerful attraction, and briefly he pulled away, until his curiosity and her smoky seductiveness made him relax. Like Pahl and the others, he thought, I am beginning to forget myself.

"Come with you?" he echoed. "Do I have a choice?"

She smiled slyly. "Choices have led you into trouble, have they not? Let me make the choices now."

He shook his head ruefully. "You want to tell me where you're taking me?"

"Beyond your dreams, John Crichton," she said. "Beyond your dreams." She turned and her train flowed along behind her like velvet fog.

CHAPTER 15

Aeryn, D'Argo and Yanor stood in the turret that rose up from the city of the Dayfolk, rising out of the cavern and giving a view across the peaks of the mountain range. Majestic waterfalls surged and fell among the mountains. A river glittered silver amid the emerald hills. Mists swirled amidst the peaks. In a violet sky, galleons of puff clouds cruised languidly.

"Daytime in the World is beautiful, is it not?" said Yanor. "And some would say the night is equally beautiful."

"How can there be night," said D'Argo, "on the inside of a vessel?"

"We retain the ways of our homeworld," said Yanor. "There must always be night and day—the two elemental forces. The World generated by our ship is as faithful a copy as its makers could manage."

"A copy of your homeworld?"

"A copy of our homeworld." Yanor nodded. "A copy of the way things should be. You have come at a good time. It's late spring now. The weather is sweet."

"Tell us more about this world," D'Argo said.

"There," said Yanor, "off in the mountains to the other side of the crag. You can see a glimpse of the other stronghold of this World: the hold of the Queen of All Souls."

"She opposes you," D'Argo said.

"Violently," said Yanor. "When we set out from our homeworld, uncountable millennia ago, we were of a single mind and purpose: we wanted to explore the universe and map the stars. This we have done."

One of the World's suns had neared the horizon, and the other was sinking lower almost imperceptibly.

"To aid us in our exploration," Yanor continued, "we became 'ghosts'—beings of pure energy who can live forever. But many of us found that eternal life far from home could not satisfy our deepest yearnings. We had seen every world and every star in this galaxy and hundreds of others. What we wanted was the warmth of the sun, the feel of the breeze, the sweet fragrances of growing things and of a living planet. We wanted to live under the warmth of our own suns, not the cold light of distant stars. In this we differ from the Queen and her councillors."

D'Argo put his hands on the stone windowframe of the tower. "Why couldn't the Queen just drop you off back home?"

"To live again on a planet," said Yanor, "we must reassume our fleshly bodies. Each of us retains a small core of flesh, deep in the Hole in the World, for just such a purpose. Except for the Queen. In her quest to live among the stars for ever, she has destroyed her fleshly core. She cannot go back. The other Nightfolk stand with her—they have vowed never to go back either.

"The Dayfolk and the Nightfolk have struggled for millennia. The Dayfolk seek a savior who can enter the Hole in the World—closed to us since our struggles began—and instruct the gems of power to give us fleshly bodies once more. The Nightfolk seek to enter the Hole in the World and destroy our fleshly cores, so that we will wander the dark universe for ever. Thousands of cycles ago, the engines of our ship failed. We have been drifting in space for an uncountable expanse of time. And since we had no engines, we knew our savior, the Promised One, would have to be sent to us. We programmed our sensors to detect him when he came. And he did come to us, and our sensors did approve him. John Crichton is the Promised One—and I honor you as his companions. He will save us from our exile."

They stood in silence, looking out as the shadows of the mountains stretched and lengthened across the plains below.

A ghost in a flowing robe came to the door of the tower and made a sign with his head. Yanor went out to speak to him. When he came back his face was troubled.

"This is terrible news," he said. "We can't travel at night, but we must leave for the Hole in the World at first dawn. Our intelligence informs us that the Queen of All Souls has captured Crichton."

*   *   *

The bed was soft and smelled like attar of roses. Crichton lay in a sea of silk. Behind him were plump, comfortable pillows. Before him was a beautiful room, with candles flickering and platters of exotic fruits. On a golden tray before him lay the remains of the meal he'd just eaten, as delicious as any he'd had on Earth: pheasant and wine and delicate pastries.

"You are feeling better?" asked the Queen of All Souls. Her voice came from the smoky distance.

Crichton sighed. "OK, you cook up a good meal here. But this doesn't distract me from the basic fact that your people have taken us hostage."

Parting from the shadow came a languid form.

"How can you say we have taken you hostage when we treat you so well? I have specially replicated your meal from your memories."

She moved closer, kneeling and moving slowly across the silk sheets like a lithe panther approaching prey. Her lines were sinuous. She had changed her clothing. Before she had been garbed in a cowl and a mantle. Now she wore only wisps of translucent mist. Her hair flowed sensuously, and the look on her face was pure hot passion.

It was very strange to be aroused by a ghost. She was just solid enough to see and touch—and just suggestive enough to be pure fantasy. He realized now why all myths had warned of the succubus. He could not help but fall under her spell. Her soft and sensual lips touched his, just real enough to be felt, and yet a whisper away from a dream. Then she pulled away, her eyes glittering.

"What do you want from me?" he said, mouth dry.

"I need your flesh, John Crichton." She was still smiling.

"You want to kill me?"

"No. I want to possess you. I will take you places I could never reach and you have never dreamed of." The succubus that was the Queen of All Souls struck, her hungry mouth bearing down on his, her arms clasping him.

In an instant her warm flesh was pressed against him, melting into him . . . moving deep inside him.

Rygel kneeled by the fallen DRD.

A wisp of acrid smoke curled up into his nostrils.

Oh dear me, he thought.

The other DRDs were still clicking and clacking. Perhaps they were even preparing some kind of judgement before Moya could get hold of him.

Sanctions, Pilot had said. Punishment.

This was not Rygel's favorite word. At one time the very concept was alien to him, but being imprisoned and tortured by the sadistic captain, Durka, he well understood the meaning of pain and punishment now.

He looked down at the upturned DRD. Its limp eyestalks lay motionless, stretched out on the floor.

Stay calm, fellow, he told himself. Let's not get your eyebrows in a knot.

Rygel poked at the DRD. "Hello! Wake up, acolyte! You can get up now!"

It did not respond, but rocked in place as he poked at it.

"DRD! I, Rygel XVI, Dominar, order you to rise and

take your place," Rygel said in a commanding tone.

The DRD continued to rock, but did not respond.

Rygel fought back panic. What good would panic do now? Rygel's general rule, when stuck between a rock and a hard place, was to glare at them both and declare his superiority. After a rough life, he was still around, so he figured it must be working.

After you'd declared your superiority to that rock and to that hard place, though, you had to do something.

He went over the sequence of events. He'd tripped over the DRD. He'd been angry at it. He had yelled. Most of all, however, he had directed brutal thoughts its way.

Hmm. Could the energy generated in his mind from his rage have been focused directly upon the DRD in such a way as to short the poor little guy out? This certainly appeared to be the situation, as strange as it sounded. The DRD had experienced some kind of overload from Rygel's anger.

But Rygel had been enraged many times in his life, and no one, either physical or mechanical, had keeled over from it—to Rygel's great chagrin. Why would a mere thought do away with this DRD?

Rygel scratched his ear and remembered the furze. Had that somehow allowed him to concentrate his thoughts and direct their power? And if that was the case, could Rygel undo the damage? Well, certainly not with a screwdriver and chewing gum. He was no technician. However, they were all assuming that the DRD was dead. Perhaps it was just in a kind of motorstasis, overwhelmed by Rygel's powerful thoughts.

Rygel kneeled down by the DRD again and placed his hand on the little guy.

OK, Rygel thought. Visualize.

He kept his hand on the DRD. He closed his eyes and pretended he was back on his home planet.

Rygel was in a field. There was the delicate scent of waffa flowers in the air. He could hear the excited chatter of children as they played Bang-Your-Head against the Chuckle Wall.

How Rygel loved the little children! The way he licked them was very popular with the populace, and many a citizen had pictures of Rygel with their infant's head in his mouth, gnawing playfully.

Suddenly there was a scream. Oh dear, what has happened? It seems a youngster has bounced his head against the laughstone too hard and is now unconscious. Oh, great ruler Rygel, come and heal my young one. Make his crushed head better!

"Heal!" said Rygel. "Heal!"

One hand was on the DRD, the other was on the device on his ear. He could feel it growing warm, energy coursing through him, flowing down his hand into the DRD.

"Heal!" said Rygel. "Please?"

The little wheels of the DRD spun. Its eyestalks wobbled.

Rygel opened his eyes to see the DRD, newly alive again, flip itself back onto its wheels. It spun around in a circle, then skittered over towards its fellows, touching eyestalks with them.

Rygel's eyes were wide. At first he only felt vast relief. But when the DRDs grouped around him, eyestalks bowed, as if filled with awe, he began to feel something he seldom felt in these many cycles of exile and pain.

He felt . . . royal.

He'd done it! Him alone!

He felt a surge of energy, and it seemed to come from the DRDs, who were now moving towards him. One reached out with its eyestalk and touched his ankle tentatively. "Yes, my child. It is me!" said Rygel. "More than Rygel XVI, Dominar: Rygel . . . the Healer . . . and . . ."

Dare he say it? Why not!

"Rygel the Messiah. The Glorious One! Deliverer of DRDs from their chains of bondage. Flock, flock, my little ones! Worship me and you shall be saved!"

A voice suddenly broke out from above him. "Rygel, what do you think you're doing?"

He cringed, but then remembered the miracle that had just occurred.

"I am communicating with the DRDs," he said.

"What of the fallen one?" said Pilot. "Moya is getting contradictory information. She is most concerned."

Rygel beamed. "Pilot! I have fixed—I mean healed—the poor little fellow!" He pointed at the DRD, which wiggled its eyestalks enthusiastically.

"My word!" said Pilot. "Yes, he does seem active again. Oh yes, Moya will be most pleased!"

"She's pleased now, and you know it. And you can tell Moya that maybe soon I will be speaking with her directly. I have the power now!" Rygel tapped his head knowingly.

"Remarkable. Excellent. Some sort of projectional

mental powers, in tandem with the energies of the
DRDs. Add the energies of Moya . . . My word! Rygel!
Do you realize what we have here?"

"A new religion! And I'm the Chief Savior!" said
Rygel happily.

"No, I think not. However, with a little work, we
might well have the faculties to communicate with the
alien ship. Rygel, I am very pleased with you, and Moya
is very pleased with you as well!"

"Yes, but do you adore me as your DRDs adore me?"
said Rygel.

"Interpersonal relations is something we will have
time to discuss later, Rygel. In the future, when there
is peace in the galaxy, I believe there will be a great
deal of downtime in which to discuss philosophy,
ethics, aesthetics and the full panoply of issues that confront a self-aware being. In fact, I can positively state
that I, separate from Moya, have been rather melan-
cholically dwelling on certain moral matters that—"

"Shut up, Pilot," said Rygel, feeling rather self-
important and proud after his breakthrough, his return
to greatness after all these weary, awful cycles. "I am
happy to say my days of idleness and humility are over!
With the honor and sanctity and pride that have been
bestowed upon me by my new subjects"—Rygel waved
at the DRDs, who chittered and wavered in unison at
their beloved—"I find myself a new creature. And that
creature"—he leaned over and bowed—"is at the service of you and Moya . . . to get our collective posteri-
ors out of this fix!"

CHAPTER 16

Dawn was breaking, casting a sweet morning light on the rocks and the dew-covered grasses, as Aeryn, D'Argo and Yanor set out from the city of the Dayfolk for the Hole in the World.

The sky was a rich dark hue of blue, the first sun bright. The morning smelled of dew and mist, of fog and campfires, of promise and hope. In a comfortable bed, swaddled by pillowy duvets, Aeryn had slept the best sleep of her life, and she woke up feeling alive and ready to face the challenges ahead of them.

Looking fit and rested, D'Argo took in a huge breath of fresh air and expelled it with great satisfaction, the hale and hearty explorer ready for the new roads of tomorrow. "Ah! This place is to my satisfaction. The air is clean, the scenery is vast and I feel like a true warrior again."

They were now standing on the ground floor of the

city of the Dayfolk, at the mouth of a corridor that led down and away. It seemed the city had turned out to see them go; groups of Nokmadi stood at a respectful distance, silent, with worried looks upon their faces.

Yanor had brought them simple packs with provisions. "We must go on foot," he had explained. "The Queen's scanners can detect mechanical vehicles. We must not use our weapons unless we're in grave danger; her scanners can pick up on the energy from our weapons as well. With Crichton in her hands already, she may have abandoned her pursuit of us, but we will travel in a small group and by roundabout means, so we can avoid detection, just in case."

Aeryn adjusted the strap of her pack, which was digging into her shoulder. "How long will it take us to reach the Hole in the World?"

"It should not take us more than a day. It cannot take us more than a day."

"Why not?"

"Because the night belongs to the Queen of All Souls. If we are caught out at night, she will sweep us into the nightworld."

"What is the nightworld?"

"You have seen the stars?" Yanor asked enigmatically. He swept an arm toward the ceiling, as if to illustrate. "That is the nightworld. Gods willing, we may reach the Hole in the World before nightfall."

"And there?"

"We will try to seize Crichton back from the Queen. We will try to defend the power gems from her wiles— and we will hope it will not cost us dearly."

He turned to make a final bow to the crowd of Nokmadi. They bowed in return, and one cried out, "Blessings upon you, strangers and companions to the Promised One!"

Aeryn cast an uneasy glance at D'Argo. They turned to follow Yanor into the corridor. It had a stone floor and led down and away from the city of the Dayfolk.

"And once we have rescued Crichton and defended the power gems?" she asked.

"Then Crichton will penetrate the Orb of All," said Yanor, his voice echoing off the rocks that now surrounded them. "And we will take on our fleshly forms once more, and return home—not to the city of the Dayfolk, but our real home, the planet Nokmad, which we have not seen for uncountable millennia. And then we will provide you with maps to enable you to go wherever you want to go."

They continued on for a few paces, their journey lit by lamps in the walls of the tunnel.

"Sounds simple when he says it," Aeryn commented.

Eventually the tunnel became cooler and damper, the lights on the walls flickering, the air stale. When the path finally began to ascend, they felt a trickle of warmer air and then saw the dazzle of daylight up ahead. The path slanted sharply upwards. Yanor disappeared into the daylight, then D'Argo and last Aeryn, emerged blinking into the sunshine. They had come through the tunnel into a shallow crevice on a wide plain of tall grasses.

Yanor took a mechanical device from his tunic. He flipped it open and scrutinized its dark face. "We are safe for the time being." He squatted and drew a map in a bare patch of dirt with a stick. "We are in the Plain

Arboreal. Our destination is right in the midst of those mountains." He pointed towards the crags rising at the edge of the horizon. "They're called the Wytchurlds. The Hole in the World is right between Death's Cliffs and the Mountain of Morning. You see we must approach from this direction and traverse the pass here."

Yanor glanced at the sky. "We've made good time. If we can keep up this pace, we'll be just out of danger when night-fall comes."

Crichton!
John Crichton!

He heard his name echoing through the darkness. Swirls of mist and stars glittered around his feet. He could smell jasmine and lilac and hear the breath of distant harps playing.

Crichton!
John Crichton!

Crichton closed his eyes. When he opened them again, he found himself in the bedroom, sprawled among cream-colored sheets.

Then he remembered.

". . . The Queen of All Souls . . ."

Crichton heard his own voice saying those words in his mind, but he did not feel his lips moving. He could feel nothing.

"There you are, darling." It was his voice, and his mouth was moving, he could tell that much—but his voice was not under his own control.

He found himself pushing the sheets aside and rising out of bed. His bare feet touched the floor, but he could not feel if it was warm or cold. He walked to a large oval mirror, its edges worked in filigreed gold and silver, and looked at himself—or rather, whatever was controlling him looked at himself.

The mirror showed Crichton looking back at himself.

But as he stared, he caught a brief glimpse of features superimposed on his face—the features of the Queen of All Souls. Then his features became wholly his own once more.

"You see, John," his mouth, his voice said, with the after-flicker of the Queen's voice, "I needed a body. And yours is a very good one."

My body? he said. For what?

"To do things only a body can do—and the body of the Promised One can do what no other body can do: pass the Orb of All. We must begin our journey."

Journey? Where?

"To the place known as the Hole in the World. I have been waiting for this for a very long time."

Crichton struggled to think what to do. He closed the eyes of his mind, and then opened them again.

The world of mist once more. And in it, another inhabitant!

"Zhaan!" he said.

Zhaan, standing before him in the misty interior world, nodded sadly.

One of the World's twin suns had already set again and the other was low in the sky, casting long shadows down from the crags. The three travellers struggled up the rocky trail to the pass through the Mountain of Morning.

"I can't help thinking," said D'Argo, "that a more

efficient race would have put the Hole in the World in a more accessible location."

They scrambled across the remains of a small landslide. The air was cooler at this elevation, and the sky was turning a deeper blue with the onset of evening.

"The path was made to be inaccessible to enemies," said Yanor without looking back. "Even some Nokmadi do not know exactly where to find it."

"What would enemies want with the Hole in the World?" asked Aeryn.

Yanor leaned on a boulder covered with a carpet of gray lichen. "Our ghostly forms are generated by very powerful gems of quanta-energy," he explained. "These gems have many powers, and many races seek to own them. And not always for good, as you may imagine."

D'Argo narrowed his eyes, thinking. "If the Queen of All Souls wants these gems so much, why doesn't she just go in and get them?"

Yanor nodded his head at the question. "She cannot pass the Orb of All, which reads the minds of all those who seek to enter. With the passing of the millennia, everyone on this ship—both the Dayfolk and the Queen's people, the Nightfolk—have lost the balance necessary to get past the Orb of All. Only an outsider can do it now: an outsider with the perfect mental balance between conflicting desires. That outsider is the Promised One. We have been waiting for the Promised One since your civilizations were young.

"But anyway, it's not the gems themselves that the Queen wants—she wants our fleshly cores stored alongside them. She wishes to destroy the fleshly cores so we will have no choice but to wander space for ever

like her. Our mental and emotional selves—our souls—
are preserved and given form by the power gems. They
will survive the destruction of the flesh, but we will be
ghosts for ever."

Aeryn mused. "Eternal life. That's not the worst fate
I can think of."

A fleeting look of despair crossed Yanor's face, and
he put his hand to his cheek. "I touch my face," he said,
"and yet I feel nothing. The sun sets, yet I can't feel
the coolness in the air as it sinks or the warmth when
it rises again. I cannot feel the touch of any of my
companions, whether it be of comfort or of anger.

"And that's not the worst: should the gems be moved,
I will disappear. In the meantime my mind would be
trapped in the gem, unseeing, uncommunicating, helpless. I am at the mercy of whoever owns the gems. They
are safe now on this ship, but should they be removed,
would the person who moves them put them in their
proper position, so I can assume my ghostly form—or
would my mind be trapped inside for ever, mute and
unseeing?"

Aeryn and D'Argo were silent, thinking over what he
had said. A cool evening breeze had started up in the
mountains. Aeryn pulled the sleeves of her shirt farther
down her arms, but Yanor was oblivious to the chill.

"And yet," Yanor continued, "while the gems are on
this ship, and we are dependent on them for bodily
form, we Dayfolk will be on this World for ever: never
walk our homeland again, never feel or taste or sense.
That is why we want our fleshly forms back: to be free
of being ghosts who cannot feel the wind, free of our

dependence on the power gems—free even of this burden of eternal life."

Aeryn looked at Yanor. "We will help you," she said.

Yanor looked up with renewed energy in his eyes. "You see why our quest is so important to all the Dayfolk. We are very close now. The Hole in the World is just on the other side of the pass."

They started forward again. The mountainside was steep, with fist-sized rocks that came lose and plummeted down as they scrabbled over them. They came to a narrow passage between enormous slabs of rock, stretching out dark and straight ahead of them.

"The pass," said Yanor. There was muted excitement in his voice.

But suddenly they were stopped in their tracks by a savage cry. Ahead of them, in the narrow path, they saw a trembling patch of darkness with two glowing eyes. Another cry came from it: a high desolate shriek that made Aeryn think of all the loneliness in the universe.

"The Queen's nightwraith," said Yanor. There was fear and anger in his voice. He drew a weapon and fired a beam of pulsing yellow light at it.

"But our weapons will alert the Queen—" began Aeryn.

"The Queen has found us already," said D'Argo. He drew his Qualta Rifle and steadied it, then let off a slicing beam.

The patch of darkness wavered and skittered, and then seemed to hover in the pass more darkly.

"Is there another way around?"

"No," said Yanor. "This part must always be traversed on foot—even a dragon cannot go further. It was planned this way, so that no enemy could seize the power gems."

D'Argo shouldered his way forward. "Then I shall go to face this nightwraith, one to one."

Yanor put an arm in front of D'Argo's great chest. "No! It will slice you down to your molecules. But you can see that it does not mean to kill us. It wants only to delay us."

"Delay us? Until when?" cried Aeryn.

A single star winked into being in the cerulean sky overhead.

"Until night comes," said Yanor.

"John?"

"Zhaan?"

Crichton looked around. They seemed to be in a large space, but it was filled with mist and the boundaries of it felt insubstantial. He felt rather than saw illumination. "What is this place? Are we dead?"

"No."

Crichton snapped his fingers—or tried to. "The Queen of All Souls has possessed you as she possessed me!" he exclaimed. "That's why she looks so much like you!"

"She looks like you now," said Zhaan.

"She is me—I mean, she's got my body!" He had a shiver of some sort—but whatever it was, it certainly wasn't somatic. He had a body of his own here in this mist-world, but it didn't feel quite solid. He wished he had a place to sit. He thought about a chair, and suddenly a chair was under him, but when he sat down on it, it felt like sitting on air. He got up again.

"And we seem to be locked in some kind of limbo," said Zhaan, peering around thoughtfully.

"But how did you get here?"

"I managed to engage myself in a rite of meditation that extends the consciousness," explained Zhaan. "I was hoping to learn more about the Nokmadi, or at least do something of value beyond just sitting there with that demented pipsqueak Rygel. Alas, as soon as I found what I was looking for, it found me. I was over-powered—used, as you say, to help the Queen imitate a form appealing to your sexuality and cause you to let down your barriers. Apparently I appear unthreatening to you. And so the Queen combined my body with at-tributes from others who have appealed to you, so she could capture you and, most importantly, your body."

Zhaan apparently thought a chair into being as well; one appeared right behind her, and she settled on it smoothly. She was paler than usual, and her robes weren't quite solid around the edges, as if someone had colored her in incompletely.

"But what I don't understand," she said, "is who ex-actly is the Queen of Souls. She wanted me so she could get to you, but what does she want with you?"

Crichton re-created his own chair and sat down as well. Mist swirled about his feet, and he had to wave it out of the way to keep his hands in view.

"These Nokmadi," said Crichton, "all desperately want to get at certain items, power gems, at the bottom of what they call the Hole in the World. The Dayfolk want to get at these power gems and regain their fleshly bodies and return to their homeworld. And the Queen wants to stop them."

"But if they want these jewels or whatever—why don't they go and take them?"

"There's a device called the Orb of All that stops them. It can't have been created that way originally; it seems that the Nokmadi changed so the Orb no longer recognizes them. Now they think there's only one being that can pass by the Orb of All and get at the power gems. As you might guess, they're under the wild impression that that being is me."

Zhaan sighed, and even though she seemed to have no breath, the sigh was long and unhappy. "If the Queen can't go down there herself, no wonder she wanted your body—if she thinks you can get at the power gems, all she has to do is ride along."

Crichton thought about this. "Wait, do you mean by possessing my body, she can take a ride with it to this bottom of the Hole in the World and use it to get past the Orb of All and get at the power gems?"

"That's precisely what I'm saying, John."

"So the question is: do we want this to happen? Who are the good guys? If I have to be involved in the action, whose side am I on? From what I can see of this Queen of All Souls, she seems a bit suspect to me." He twisted in his chair.

"You didn't enjoy your little seduction, John?"

"You know about that?"

"Sorry. I couldn't help it. I didn't ask to be packed into a body with the Queen of All Souls."

Crichton tried to put his head in his hands, but his head felt insubstantial and his hands felt misty and formless. "So wait a minute—that means we can see what the Queen is doing. How do we get to that state?"

Zhaan settled in her seat, letting her arms fall to her sides, relaxed. "We empty our minds of ourselves and open them to the Queen. Try closing your eyes and opening them again."

Crichton closed his eyes slowly and attempted to empty his mind. Immediately a sensation of motion sickness came upon him, as if he were travelling at great force, being carried somewhere he didn't want to go, at light speed. His mind fought the feeling, and he found himself back in the misty space.

Once more he tried to concentrate, to empty his mind.

He opened his eyes.

"John."

"Zhaan."

"I feel as though I've been a particle in some kind of nuclear accelerator."

"I too had that sensation."

Crichton brought all his concentration to bear on the Queen. He opened his eyes—and looked out of hers. What he saw sent a shock through him.

"I believe, Zhaan," he said, "that we've found the Hole in the World."

CHAPTER 17

It was a grand and glorious thing to be a king. But it was an even more wonderful thing to be a messiah, even if it was only a messiah to DRDs.

"So then. What do you do in my presence when your wonderful savior appears?" Rygel demanded.

"BZZZZZZZZZZZZZZZZ!" replied the drones.

Rygel XVI loved the whoop of audiences, the cheers of crowds, the adulation of the multitude!

Ah yes, even the pitiful little bzzzzings of his acolytes was music to his ears. "DRDs!" pronounced the former Rygel XVI, now Rygel the Great. "DRDs— Diagnostic Repair Drones!"

The little animated creatures buzzed and wobbled at the Great One's words. Rygel the Extremely Great and now Most Holy raised his hand toward the assembled.

"Diagnostic Repair Drones—no longer!"

The DRDs stared at Rygel in total silence. Bewilderment hung in the air.

"You are now—Defending Rapturous . . . er . . . Disciples!"

Again, silence and again, bewilderment.

"Of the Faith, of course! Of the new Faith."

Antennae bent tentatively. The buzzes sounded sceptically. Then, suddenly, they seemed to understand.

He'd contacted them with his Holy Communication Monitor. He could do it at will! There was no limit to his powers, now that he had a troop of obedient and adoring acolytes ready to obey his every unspoken command!

"BZZZZZZZZZZZZZZZZZZ!"

Rygel bowed.

"Rygel!"

The voice sounded down upon him from on high. For just one moment Rygel thought that he had opened up the gates to communication with some ineffable presence even more mighty than he was.

"O Great One, I have found—"

"Oh, Rygel. It's Pilot. What sort of oddness are you about now?"

"I am working on the communication device that I have perfected with my new-found disciples," said Rygel.

"Rygel, you had best be careful with Moya's DRDs. Whatever you are training them to do, you must remember that ultimately they are hers."

Rygel grumbled to himself. The DRDs were helpful to Moya, yes—but she had no grand plans to save the universe. She was merely Moya. But he—he was Rygel the Great, the most magnificent potentate in the known universe, sadly deprived of his full powers just at the moment. But with the DRDs at his command, who knew what could be accomplished?

"Of course," said Rygel with a deliberately penitent look. He climbed onto his ThroneSled and gazed around at the crowd of adoring acolytes. "We're just practicing maneuvers, Pilot. Nothing important."

The ThroneSled took off and the DRDs buzzed along behind it.

The World was not yet wholly dark, but a few stars had appeared, scattered in one corner of the sky.

"It is a good thing we are a party of warriors," said D'Argo. "You know the territory. Where can we best take shelter and prepare to defend ourselves against the dangers of the night?"

Yanor shook his head hopelessly. "There is no shelter near here that can protect us. It will not be merely nightwraiths—next it will be all the harbingers of the night, and then the Queen and all her minions."

"You appear worried," said D'Argo. "But you haven't seen a Luxan fight." He looked at the path ahead; up slightly was a flatter space, a small clearing with a single tree clinging to the rock.

"Nor a Sebacean," said Aeryn, her pulse pistol warm in her hand.

"We will make our stand there," said D'Argo, gesturing to the clearing. "Let us move there while we still have light to see the dangers."

"The nightwraiths will not forget us," said Yanor. "We'll go to the clearing if you wish, but our quest is over. The night will swallow us, and before morning the Queen will have penetrated the Hole in the World."

D'Argo scrambled up the path, scanning the rocks and crags, his Qualta Rifle out before him. "If the Night-folk give up as easily as the Dayfolk, we'll have no trouble fighting off the forces of the Queen." Aeryn followed, stopping every few steps to listen for danger. She heard nothing but the soft whistle of wind in the mountains and the sound of their feet as they scrambled up the rocky path.

Yanor came last, his face clouded with worry.

They sat on the dusty ground of the clearing, listening. Aeryn started to speak, but D'Argo shushed her. He smelled peril in the air, and he wanted to be able to hear it when it descended.

He did not have to wait long.

It came swooping down with talons of steel and dark threatening wings. D'Argo rose up with a lightning spring. The night-thing raced toward him with astonishing speed and a horrid shriek that ratcheted through the gloom.

Instantly judging speed and trajectory, D'Argo thumbed off a pulse from his Qualta Rifle. Energy snapped through the air, sizzling up and slamming into the black chest of winged night. With a shriek, power frizzled around the beast and turned it into a ball of flame. It fell into a sizzling pile of flesh and burning bone, melting into a pyre on the ground.

D'Argo saw the next blur of black, and was already spinning on his heel. But it was Aeryn's gun blast that caught it, snapping off one of its bat-like wings. Spinning, the thing crashed into the pyre with a shriek. As the creatures burned, the stink of sulphur and nastier stuff rose into a black smudge in the gathering night.

Yanor had risen to his feet as well. "Soon she will be here," he said, his voice flat with despair. "Look at the stars."

D'Argo looked up to the top of the sky, where stars were appearing, brighter than he had ever seen.

But there was something darker than the darkness up there, something cubical, and D'Argo's warrior instincts sensed its true design.

"That thing . . ." he said.

"Yes," said Aeryn.

He knew she understood.

"On my mark."

"I'm on it."

"Fire!"

Their bolts met, enveloping the black cube in a hail of disaster. The light from the explosion was so bright that D'Argo had to shield his eyes and look away. A fireball plunged to earth, and then farther down the mountain the fire from the crashed debris of darkness licked at the night.

The night offered no more enemies—for the moment.

He turned to Aeryn and bowed.

"You are a true warrior. I am proud to have fought by your side."

Aeryn smiled wryly. "I'm honored. But I'm sorry that we may have to repeat the experience so soon."

They looked up. The sky was now studded with starlight. A growing sound had begun to rumble out of the mountain passes, like a great wind gathering speed.

They turned to look at Yanor again. He glittered more

vividly in the darkness, as if made of thousands of stars. His outline was more wavery, and his mouth became distorted as he spoke.

"It happens to anyone who is caught outside at night, away from the strongholds," he said, a hopelessness in his voice.

Aeryn glanced up at the gathering brightness of the stars spread across the sky. "What happens?" she said fiercely.

"In the daytime," said Yanor, "the World is imagined by the Dayfolk. Rivers, grass, breeze, soil—it's all our memories. Only the strongholds are real. But the Queen of All Souls is Empress of Night—at night her thoughts take over. All of our world is wiped away." He put his hands over his face.

Aeryn dug the toe of her boot into the dry earth. "Even the ground we're standing on?"

It was as if Yanor had been reduced to a glittering outline. "I can no longer imagine myself," he cried. "Only the Queen imagines me now!" The wind caught at the edges of his form, spinning the points of light around in a vast whirling rotation, pulling him off the ground. It was as if a whirlwind had seized him. With a last cry, he was lifted into the air, now only a great roiling mass of stars like a galaxy in the night sky.

The wind blasted along the side of the mountain. Aeryn felt herself lose her footing; the mountainside was ripped away from under her, but instead of falling down, she fell up. The night was swirling with stars.

"D'Argo!" she called, but she could see him lifted from the face of the mountain as well. He had slung his

Qualta Rifle across his back and had his arms spread wide, as if to grasp the wind.

"The Hole in the World!" he shouted above the roar. "We must . . . get to . . . we must . . . Crichton!" His words were swept away by the wind. His form dipped as if he were fighting his way back to the ground, and then he too was gathered up into the sky.

The ground under Aeryn seemed to melt away into blackness, and she felt herself whipped around into the air. The reassuring solidity of the mountains was gone; there was no tree, no rockface, no D'Argo or Yanor, only a great cold blackness and a swirling mass of stars. She felt light-headed, and then realized she was floating. On all sides there was nothing but inky blackness and the small cold fires of the stars. It was absolutely still.

She was adrift in a universe, a dark object in a black sea twinkling with lights. Now I know what it's like to be Moya, she thought.

Around her, what had been the World was now the seemingly endless expanse of the universe, and she was a dark object floating in a sky of stars. She had entered the kingdom of night.

She felt a moment of exhilaration. It was a kind of freedom, to be able to navigate amidst the stars without space-suit or oxygen. But then she realized that she was cold—bone-deep cold.

She turned slowly in space. Galaxies swirled around her in slow procession; stars were sprinkled through the blackness like glittering confetti. She felt the vastness of the expanse, and it was all cold and terrifyingly lonely.

She tried to maneuver, but she found she could go

no faster than the slow wheeling of the universe. Galaxies turned slowly on their own axes, each scarcely bigger than she was, and there were a hundred, a thousand of them scattered around her. Moving her arms as if she were swimming, she turned to study one nearby. It looked like all the depictions she had seen of her own galaxy. She studied the familiar outlines. Something about it made her look harder, and she realized that this galaxy, glittering and elongated, was Yanor.

She gasped in surprise. His sparkling form was distorted, to be sure; he looked as though he were swimming through space, his arms long and curved and trailing stars, his heart a bright cluster of light. He looked as if he were screaming, but he moved soundlessly overhead.

She searched the blackness for any sign of D'Argo, but there were only the endlessly turning pinwheels of stars. It was time to fight night with fire. She took her pulse pistol from its holster, thumbed up the setting to maximum, held it before her, and fired it into the blackness. The red beam sliced through the darkness, propelling her backward.

She waited, scanning the darkness around her. After some moments, high above her she saw another scarlet beam pierce the sky.

"D'Argo!" she cried, but the words were whipped out of her mouth as if she were standing in a high wind. Aiming below her carefully, she thumbed off another beam. It was as if she were kicked upwards. Aiming carefully, she used the pistol to propel her upwards until at last she could see D'Argo, dim in the starlight, floating amid the galaxies.

"D'Argo!" she said.

Floating like spacemen, they grasped each other's arms.

"Do you understand what's happening?" she asked.

"Clearly the Queen of All Souls is fond of night," he said. "I detect others of the Dayfolk around us; they have been transformed into galaxies. Because they are energy-beings, no doubt they can withstand a night of this, but we, being physical, cannot. Even I am cold. But remember that Yanor said the strongholds of the World are real, and exist even at night. One of these is the Hole in the World, and I have kept careful watch on the place. It is below us—there." He pointed, and Aeryn looked down into darkness. "If we get to it, we may be able to take shelter and start a fire."

"And we can get to it by firing our weapons," Aeryn said.

"Exactly. We must be our own spaceships tonight."

They readied their pistols.

"And when we get down there?" Aeryn asked. "Then what?"

"Then," said D'Argo, "we hold on until dawn."

Dawn had come, rosy along the horizon with a scattering of clouds.

Aeryn and D'Argo had clung to the rocks at the entrance to the Hole in the World for the entire night, overhanging slabs of rock sheltering them from the worst of the cold—and from the view of nightwraiths.

Now the day had returned again, but there was no sign of Yanor.

They stood upon the lip of The Hole in the World and peered down.

The Hole in the World was a large crevasse that plunged into the earth. Its edges were craggy and it seemed more like the opening of some cavern that went straight down into the dark heart of a planet. D'Argo could see a trail ridge that coiled down and disappeared into darkness.

"This is the heart of the ship," he said. "If Yanor was telling the truth, we may be able to restore bodies to the ghosts and end this perpetual conflict."

"And locate Crichton," said Aeryn.

"And find the maps."

"Right," said Aeryn. "Down we go. There's only one thing bothering me."

D'Argo turned to look at her.

"If the machine down there, the Orb of All, only lets the Promised One through—what will it do to us?"

CHAPTER 18

C ommunication," said Rygel XVI, "is vital to life, and particularly vital in keeping the lines of adoration and obedience open between a ruler and his subjects." He pulled his kingly purple robes around him a little more tightly and settled back in his chair, looking out at the DRDs that thronged his chamber.

The DRDs looked back at him with awe.

He smoothed the tufts on his ears and then delicately hooked the furze over his left ear, checking to see that it was in place.

"I have distributed many communiqués in my time as Rygel XVI," he declared stentoriously. "I have given many speeches. I have whispered in hushed tones to leaders of state behind closed doors. I have barked orders to generals. Always I have used my brilliant diction and enunciation. Always I have used language."

He drooped a bit. "Now, it seems, I must use less well-developed faculties."

The DRDs trundled up and touched him comfortingly with their antennae.

"Bless you," said Rygel. "Bless you, my followers."

He waggled his fingers in benediction.

"I am happy to say that all sectors in the esteemed brain-pan are working well. And I am now ready to begin our little effort. I request, however, that you all enter into this mental challenge with every fiber of your beings, with every filigree of your mechanical natures. Are you with me, my children?"

"Bzzzzzzzzz!" answered the DRDs.

"Excellent!" He shifted his weight forward as if this would give his effort extra force. "Now, go away."

The DRDs looked up at him, their ocular sensors unblinking, their eyestalks slightly tilted, as if they were questioning his command.

He squeezed his eyes closed and thought into the furze. *Go away,* he thought. *Disperse. The six to the left, go to the bridge. The ten in front of me, go to the maintenance bay. The eight to the right, go to the primary hallway on tier three. The four over by the wall, go to . . .*

There was a moment of stillness, and then the DRDs began to circle again, slowly, their eyestalks drooping. Rygel concentrated his all on the furze.

"I know," he said aloud, waving the back of his hand at them in a kingly gesture. "It is sorrowful to be away from the presence of a magnificent one such as myself. You will have the memory of my benevolence to sustain you."

And, he thought to them, you will have the furze.

The DRDs began to make their way out of Rygel's chamber, slowly, as if they were dragging their wheels. A bevy of ten scooted straight down the hallway, and another group of eight turned right and disappeared from view. The rest straggled out, whirring to themselves.

Rygel sat back and wiped his brow with the hem of his robe. The first part of the exercise was over. He hadn't done so much heavy thinking since the Hynerian Trivia Brigade had asked him to verify the answers to the Worshipful Majesty section of the Lethal Trivia Combat.

A number of microts passed.

"Pilot?" said Rygel. "Where are the DRDs?"

"You just sent them out of your chamber, Rygel," said Pilot's voice.

The corners of Rygel's mouth turned down in exasperation. "I know that. Where are they now?"

A moment passed. "There are six on the bridge, ten in the maintenance bay, eight on tier three . . ." He enumerated the rest of the DRDs, all in their assigned places.

Rygel allowed a satisfied smile to cross his face briefly. "Thank you, Pilot. Please continue to keep tabs on them."

"I always do," said Pilot. But Rygel had stopped listening. He put a hand to the furze and wrinkled his brow in intense concentration. He thought. He redoubled the intensity of his thought. He squinched his eyes closed and clamped his jaws together and stuck out his ears until the sweat ran down his face and dampened his whiskers.

"Rygel?" enquired Pilot.

Rygel let out his breath in a great exhalation and shook his head, scattering drops of sweat in all directions. "Yes, Pilot?"

"Rygel, is it you who is causing the DRDs to dance in conga lines on the bridge and tier three?"

"Conga lines are a very sophisticated exercise," said Rygel, "especially for mechanical objects. To ask them to do conga lines is to ask for the ultimate in mechanical obedience."

"And then I assume it is you who is causing them to do the Benuvian can-can in the maintenance bay and around the thermal core?"

"Perhaps not such a good idea," admitted Rygel. "I'd forgotten they don't have legs. But their willingness to try is admirable."

"They are kicking with their antennae," said Pilot.

Rygel's eyebrows shot up. "Really!" He narrowed his eyes in satisfaction. "So the furze does work across distances." He put his hand up to his ear and caressed the device. "Thank you, Pilot."

He sat up straight in his chair again, shut his eyes tight, wrinkled his brow, and thought.

My acolytes! he thought. *Let us muster for war!*

The Hole in the World.

From a dizzying height, John Crichton looked down into the heart of darkness. His head spun.

He was perched on a cliff, peering down into a cave that went straight into the ground, down from light into black. A twisting trail wound and coiled along the sides of the hole, spiralling into the depths. It was framed by gnarly roots and smelled like coal and old water and ancient subterranean terror.

"Well?" he said. "Thoughts?"

"I'm not normally a person who minds going underground," said Zhaan. "But this—"

"Yes. My sentiments exactly. And it looks as though we'll be going down by foot."

"And?"

"Well, you're safe, Zhaan. Your real body is back on Moya. If something happened to the Queen, I'm guessing you'd just be thrown back into your real body. But the Queen is an energy-being of some sort, utilizing a host."

"And?"

"Well, I'm the host. I mean, my body is. That's a long way down. The Queen slips . . . oops . . . But she won't really be dead. And you won't really be dead. But as for Mr. Crichton . . ."

"Oh. I see what you mean."

"Yeah. Smooshed in a dimension that was not his own."

There was a silence as they both contemplated this.

"Our only hope," said Zhaan, "is that she'll be careful to keep you alive so she can do—whatever she wants to do with you once you get to the bottom."

Crichton could see out of his eyes, but it was an extremely odd feeling to be viewing his feet moving independent of his will, his hand steadying himself on a rock as he peered down at the precipitous trail.

"How long do you think it's been since the Queen's

had a physical body?" he said. "Do you think she re-
members how to climb down steep paths with it?"

He thought a moment, and then wished that question
hadn't occurred to him.

The Queen was moving Crichton's head to the left.

There, emerging from the pass, were two figures.

"Zhaan, look!"

"Yes, I see them."

"D'Argo! Aeryn!" shouted Crichton. But of course,
his real mouth did not move. He fought to gain control
of his body, but it was like trying to seize mist; he found
himself grappling with nothingness.

"We have to think of a way to override the Queen's
control of my body," said Crichton desperately. If he'd
been able to use his real voice, he would have been
hissing. "Can we distract her? Confuse her? Sabotage
her somehow?"

"These people," said Zhaan, "being energy-beings,
are less stable in their identities than some other creatures. It may be possible to distract her and make her
lose control. The Queen must be using a great deal of
energy to keep you from controlling your own body.
Can you do something to attract her attention?"

Crichton remembered the chair he had thought into
being. He concentrated, and a pair of cymbals appeared
in his hands. He clanged them together noisily until his
arms were reverberating from the effects.

In the mist-world, Crichton's ears were ringing from
the din. In the outer world, the Queen in control of
Crichton's body made his eyes squeeze shut and shook
his head.

He continued to crash the cymbals together, but the

Queen gave no further sign that she heard. Crichton thought the cymbals out of existence again, rethought a chair, and sat down on it with a sigh. He concentrated until he could see out of his physical eyes into the outside world again.

Aeryn and D'Argo were speaking to each other and looking down into the Hole in the World. Just seeing them filled Crichton with hope. He himself—or rather his body, controlled by the Queen—was standing under a jagged cliff, hidden from direct view. It was clear that Aeryn and D'Argo had not noticed him.

"If Aeryn and D'Argo are here, at the Hole in the World," said Zhaan, "they must have talked to some of the Nokmadi. Maybe they're here to do the job the Nokmadi wanted you to do?"

"If that's true," said Crichton, "the Queen will be desperate to stop them."

"She'll have to stay in your body. Clearly she needs it to get what she needs at the bottom of that hole, because no one else can do it for her. When we get to the bottom, maybe it will become clear why she thinks it's you who are the Promised One."

"Yeah," said Crichton wryly. "My Nokmadi job description."

D'Argo and Aeryn were slowly venturing downward along the path that led into the Hole. Crichton willed his arms to move, his voice to cry out, but his physical body remained silent and motionless.

"It's like I'm in a dream," he said. "One of those ones where you're trying to shout but you never make any sound."

"I think that's called a nightmare," said Zhaan.

His feet began to move forward.

"I think—wait . . . We're moving."

The Queen was starting to follow D'Argo and Aeryn down the trail, taking Crichton's body and point of view and Zhaan's soul-essence with her.

"I don't like this," said Crichton. "I don't like this at all. If she wants to, she can just sneak up behind them and push them off."

"She doesn't even need to do that," said Zhaan. "If they see her, she'll appear to be you. They'll welcome her, and then they'll all go down the trail together."

"We know that the Leviathan has no defenses," Captain Sha Sutt told the crew. "However, we also know that this large ship, this thing that may well be a Nokmadi ship, has the Leviathan in its grip. Under the circumstances, it's risky to attack either one. We need more information."

Wariness, like shrewdness, was a strong suit of Sutt's. For some time now she had been assessing the situation. And they had time to be wary. The Leviathan was going nowhere. Sensors showed that the two life forms still upon it were hardly budging—they might even be asleep. The other beings had presumably been taken aboard the gigantic vessel, and they might even be dead soon. It was a nice thought that an alien vessel might do the Peacekeepers' work for them.

The only part that troubled her was that the sensors failed to detect alien life aboard the strange vessel. And the sensors were accurate enough to detect anything larger than a Silurian rat. Did the vessel have no crew?

Or maybe it was abandoned? But if so, why had it enveloped the Leviathan?

Just the idea of an abandoned vessel, floating in space with its power gems free for the taking, made her itch with desire.

The vu-screen still showed the huge alien ship, like a flattened moon, with its grip on the sleek Leviathan.

"Are you certain about the defensive weapons situation upon the alien ship?"

"I've been combing, believe me," said the sensor officer. He punched a button and a sensor-map of the alien ship showed on the vu-screen. Three green dots showed the three life forms aboard, two together. Below them were the golden glinting dots that indicated the power gems. The power gems all seemed to be stored together.

The sensor readout showed the life forms heading downward in the ship, very slowly, toward the power gems. The third life form was at a slight distance, and as the crew on the *DarkWind* watched, it began to inch in the same direction.

"You see," said the officer. "Nothing that remotely relates to any kind of energy or explosive weaponry." That would have shown up red on the screen. The only other color was only a kind of blue static spread across the inside of the ship: the background energy they couldn't identify.

"No explosives—good. But that doesn't mean that they can't defend themselves. Clearly they have their own methods. This ship has done what even Commander Crais hasn't been able to do: capture the Leviathan."

She tapped her finger on her leg. Was there some-

thing she didn't understand? Where were the inhabitants
of the alien ship? Were they just letting the Earth-
creature and his filthy companions walk in and take the
power gems? Or were they dead and the Earth-creature
and his cohort alone on the alien ship?

Clearly in a situation like this, even Crais would step
back and bide his time. Yes, she thought. That would
clearly be the judicious thing to do.

Still, she yearned for the opportunity presented to her.

A last showdown with Aeryn Sun.

"Crew," said Captain Sutt. "Assume attitude of relaxed attention. Utilize de-stress booths now if necessary." A small sardonic smile touched her thin lips.
"We're going to capture the crew of the Leviathan—or,
if they resist, kill them. Let's enjoy the moment."

CHAPTER 19

"How are you faring?" asked D'Argo.

Moving down the trail that coiled down into the Hole in the World, Aeryn kept her grip on the thick, gnarled roots on the walls of the pit. To the other side was a sheer drop, and the trail slanted towards it. Now and again they came across a bit of railing still clinging to the path, leaning vertiginously out into the void. It looked as if the trail had once been even and well-protected, but thousands of cycles of rain and weather and the black wind of night had worn it down to a slanting shelf on the edge of the yawning pit.

"I'm fine!" said Aeryn through gritted teeth.

"I see," said D'Argo.

They completed another loop in the descending spiral. The light was getting dim, and they stopped and lit their energy-torches.

After three loops in the spiral, the trail widened a bit.

It was dry earth, and the sweeping light from their torches revealed few signs that anything had grown here in the millennia this trail had existed. The air grew cooler. Almost below the threshold of hearing there came a dripping sound from the abyss below.

D'Argo increased his lead slightly. The trail still wound downwards at a steep angle, but it had stopped sloping towards the drop-off, and he could maintain a faster pace. The light had become so dim that without his torch the trail ahead disappeared into darkness.

"I am definitely yearning to be out of here," said Aeryn. She hastened her step until she was almost trotting after D'Argo. She raised the torch for a moment to look ahead, and in that moment they came to a patch of even looser soil where a small slide had cast pebbles across the trail.

Aeryn's feet slipped on the pebbles, and with a cry she toppled over the side of the trail.

She felt herself slipping, grasping, desperately scrabbling to stay her fall. Other rocks gave way and cascaded over the edge. Aeryn might have followed them, but her Peacekeeper training had given her lightning-quick reactions, and she found a root embedded in the dirt and gripped it for all her life was worth. Her feet dangled in the abyss, and she kicked, searching for something to give her purchase.

In a flash, D'Argo was down, his hand gripping the back of her shirt.

"Steady," he said. "Steady, my friend."

It was exactly then that the dark figure stepped down from behind them on the trail.

"Greetings," said John Crichton.

*   *   *

"Rygel?" came Pilot's voice from the air above the central table, where Rygel had been absent-mindedly gnawing on a food cube.

"Umm?" said Rygel. He put his hand to the furze, still firmly affixed to his ear. Had the royal attention wandered too greatly? He sent an exploratory command into the ether, and decided not. The DRDs were where they should be.

"Rygel, the DRDs have disappeared. I can only locate three of them, all doing routine tasks in the maintenance bay. I am concerned, as is Moya. Do you know where the rest of the DRDs are?"

"Mmph," said Rygel, stuffing the rest of the food cube in his mouth. "Gone? Mmm, I think I did put them somewhere. Tell Moya not to worry."

There was a slight pause. "Rygel, I'm glad that you feel the DRDs are not in trouble, but I would like to know exactly where you sent them."

"Grrom, grrom," came the noise from Rygel, who was chewing with his mouth open. "It's going to come to me any microt now. Let me see, what did I do with those DRDs?"

"Crichton!" said Aeryn.

There was John Crichton, standing there with a big goofy smile on his face.

He stood stock-still for a moment, as if he were idly thinking over Aeryn's predicament. Then he leaned over toward her.

"Let me help you," he said.

He reached down and grabbed under her other arm.

Then he and D'Argo pulled Aeryn up and over the lip of the cliff and set her down on the trail.

Still trying to catch her breath, Aeryn wheezed, "I don't know what you're doing here, but I'm sure glad to see you."

"As am I," said D'Argo.

"And I am delighted to see you," said Crichton, although he seemed strangely unmoved. D'Argo studied him curiously.

Aeryn brushed her hair back and dusted the dirt off her clothing. "We've been through a lot since we lost you in that room," she began. "Yanor, the Nokmadi who brought us here, said you were being treated well. Are you okay?"

Crichton kept up that smile. "Oh, I'm fine."

"But then he said you'd been captured by the Queen of All Souls," said D'Argo. "How did you escape?"

"Oh, I met the Queen of All Souls," said Crichton. "She's not always as powerful as you might think. It was easy to get away. And the Dayfolk told me you would be going down the Hole in the World, and so I thought, since I've found out so much about this place, I'd better come and help you."

Aeryn gave him a quizzical look, and D'Argo grunted. "The Queen of All Souls—easy to get away? She did her best to have us killed last night."

"I don't doubt it," said Crichton. "She's a pussycat during the day, but she can be mean at night. That's why we'd better hurry, don't you think?" He started down the path ahead of them. Aeryn threw a glance at D'Argo, and D'Argo shrugged. They followed him down the trail into darkness.

"So are we in trouble?" said Aeryn.

"You bet," said Crichton, setting a quick pace. "We've got to get down to the bottom of the Hole in the World, like pronto, and get those gems and help the Dayfolk do what they have to do."

"I take it you know about the gems, then," Aeryn said.

"Yes. Both from the Dayfolk I met and from the Queen herself."

"I, for one, would like to hear about this Queen of All Souls."

"She's the enemy, clearly," said Crichton. "She would like to keep the Dayfolk in perpetual exile. All they want to do is to go home. I, for one, think we should help them, don't you?"

"That's what we're doing right now, Crichton."

They went down and down, deeper into the heart of the Hole in the World. It got colder and time seemed to lose its meaning. The air began to smell not only dank, but faintly sour, as if something was rotting down at the bottom of the pit. They moved in silence, following the bobbing light of the torch.

Crichton's silence bothered Aeryn. Was he keeping something from them? Normally he liked to talk, talk, talk. Still, as they moved down the coiling way, and she watched her feet carefully (rocks rolling off the side, still falling and falling and falling into the dark), she had other things distracting her—like trying to keep from sliding off the slanting trail.

"What's the matter, John?" she asked, trying to keep her mind off the yawning gulf beside the trail. "Don't you have a moo-vee reference for all of this?"

"Moo-vee?" echoed Crichton.

"You really have been through the mill, when you don't have a plot from a moo-vee that's just like our current situation."

"A long plot, with interminable detail," added D'Argo, planting his feet with care as the trail narrowed.

Crichton was silent for a moment. "Certainly, a moo-vee," he said. "Just like this situation. I remember a moo-vee about a trail that went down a hole."

Aeryn grabbed onto a root and a small rush of clods of earth dropped off the trail into the depths. "Not much of a plot. I think I like the one about the Temple of Dune better."

"The Temple of Dune," said Crichton. He sounded a bit absent-minded. "That was certainly a great favorite. I remember that one well."

"And what happened in the moo-vee you saw where they went down a trail into a hole?" said D'Argo.

Crichton negotiated his way past a small wash-out in the trail, putting his foot down cautiously.

"Oh," said Crichton, "in that moo-vee they got to the bottom of the trail and helped the ruler of the place. She turned out to be a very worthwhile ruler. Beautiful, too."

"I guess that's why they call it fiction!" said D'Argo cheerfully, stepping on a pile of loose dirt that cascaded off the path with a scrabbling noise.

"No, indeed," said Crichton. "It was very true to life." He positioned his foot to take his next cautious step.

Aeryn bit her lip thoughtfully and stared at him.

*   *   *

"God, Zhaan! This is kind of like that movie by Joe Dante!"

"Pardon?"

"Yeah, one of my favorite movies from the 1980s. The hero is shrunk and injected into this other guy's head, and he has to help him thwart bad guys. It's kind of a comic version of *Fantastic Voyage*. The real problem, though, is the motor-control issue. You see—"

"Crichton! I understand you love being reminded of your science infarction moo-vees. But please, this is reality."

"Sorry."

They had retreated to the misty land of the Queen's interior nothingness. Before that, they'd peeked out, and were treated to a frightening sight: the Queen, in her John Crichton guise, approaching D'Argo and Aeryn . . . and Aeryn dangling off the side of the cliff! Crichton and Zhaan worked frantically to stop the Queen, to warn Aeryn and D'Argo. They yelled, pounded at the mist, clashed cymbals, threw their insubstantial chairs down onto the insubstantial misty ground. Nothing they did had any effect.

Fortunately, the Queen apparently had other plans, because she had reached over and helped pull Aeryn up. Words were exchanged and then the descent continued. But the experience made Crichton and Zhaan even more desperate to find a way out of their prison of immateriality.

"John," said Zhaan, "as individuals we can do nothing to resist the Queen. But together we may be able to resist her."

"But we are together."

"No. Boundaries are different here. We must meld together into one mind—a mind twice as powerful as that of the Queen."

"I don't know, Zhaan. I kind of like to keep my mind my own, and there've been so many people wandering through it lately, I feel like Grand Central Station at rush hour. If we combined into a single mind-unit, wouldn't that just give the Queen an easier target?"

"I don't think so, John. And—what have we got to lose?"

He had to admit she had a point. When he looked into the outside world he could see his body following Aeryn down the trail, close enough to push her off at any moment. Maybe she didn't want to get into a skirmish on the slippery trail, where the body of the Promised One might sustain some damage and delay her plans. But when they reached the bottom—what then?

"OK," he said. "It's worth a shot."

"Then what I need you to do, John, is very simple. I want you to now visualize yourself as a blank slate."

"And once my mind is a blank slate?"

"Go through it. And I'll be there."

"You mean I get to look into your mind this time?"

"If you like. Of course, if you would care to avert your psychic eyes from certain secrets, I would appreciate it."

"Just like you've done for me, hmmm? I know you've been checking out the old girlfriends. And the barf story. Boy, that will get a laugh around the food cube table on Moya!"

"That was remarkable. But very well. Let us make a pact. I will not share the things I have seen from being

inside your mind. And if you see anything disconcerting
in your mental journeys, then you will hold your tongue.
Are you ready?"

"Yes."

"Come to me."

Crichton stepped forward, moving his incorporeal
form towards Zhaan.

CHAPTER 20

D'Argo, Aeryn and Crichton continued to move down the dark trail, and after a while they caught a glimmer of light from the very bottom of the pit.

D'Argo, in the lead, noticed it first. After his time in the dark night of the Queen of All Souls, his heart leaped at the idea that they might be coming out into light again.

"Look," he said. "At the bottom, there. Just a glimmer." He switched off his torch and they stared downwards.

"I don't see a thing," said Aeryn.

"Yes," said Crichton. "I see it!" His voice was excited.

D'Argo switched on the torch again. "This must mean that we're near the floor of the pit—and the Orb of All."

They descended several more loops of the spiral, and

the light became clearer—luminescent specks of jade, amethyst, and crystal that shone like jewels lit from within, gleaming under the water of a dark pond.

Aeryn said, "Yes, I see them now. Those aren't lights, but reflections of lights. The thing that is casting those reflections is to the side, out of our view."

"Like memory," said D'Argo softly. In truth, the lights opened up memories he had suppressed since leaving his homeworld. His mind travelled back to the Lightsongs of D'Arpath in the C'Narran temples. Each cycle, every Luxan who could made the pilgrimage to see these fabulous gems, to bathe in their radiance and to perform the rites of the True Hearts in Quest.

He remembered the exhilaration of first seeing the lights in the temple, an awesome falling into color and glory, the reflections of a universe so peaceful and radiant that it took his breath away. With these lights in the pit below him turning his memory back, he drew strength from the peaceful lights of home.

Eventually they came to a place where the trail broadened into a kind of road. Soon D'Argo was able to see the floor of the pit, a great pool of oily liquid. The lights were reflected in this lake of darkness.

Only when they had almost reached the bottom of the trail did the canopy of stone give way enough for them to see where the lights were coming from. A great stone archway revealed a vast cave of stalactites and stalagmites, carved into geometrical designs and adorned with rings, apertures, and antennae. Beyond it they could see rows of small crystalline domes set into the rock, each of them glowing like a miniature star. The archway was guarded by an energy-barrier like a shimmering curtain of light, emanating from a shining orb set in the ceiling—the Orb of All.

"What is all this?" said Aeryn, stepping forward to study the array.

"Mineral computers of some sort? The technology is alien to me," said D'Argo.

"You're saying those are machines?" said Aeryn.

"I'm saying it's tech."

"You do mean machines."

"In the sense, perhaps, that Moya is a machine," replied D'Argo. "In many ways we biological creatures are living machines. Machines come in many forms."

"This apparatus is a huge machine," said Crichton, "used by the Nokmadi to give them something like immortality—it was what rendered them into their 'ghost' forms, and what keeps them that way. But now the Dayfolk want to take back their bodies. And the means of doing that is also in there."

They studied the curtain of light guarding the archway.

"Yanor mentioned this barrier," D'Argo told Crichton. "What it does exactly and how we may pass it, we do not yet know."

"I know," said Crichton.

Aeryn looked at him again, eyes narrowed. "How do you know?" she asked.

He gave another of those goofy smiles. "I found out from the Queen. The barrier reads brain patterns: it was designed to let only Nokmadi through. They have a particular brain pattern because of their particular character. The Nokmadi have always been great explorers, but their hunger for the universe was always tempered by a love for their home."

"No longer," D'Argo put in. "The Nokmadi on this ship have become polarized: some want only to stay in space, and others only to go home."

"Exactly," said Crichton. "But the machine has not changed. It will only let someone through who has the old pattern: the love of space, perfectly balanced by a desire for home."

"If that's all it requires, then we can all pass through," said Aeryn. She moved towards the barrier. The light-curtain shimmered, and when she was still several paces away a bolt of energy crackled through the arch.

She retreated a few paces.

"I think," said D'Argo, "that although you have some yearning for a home, Aeryn, you mostly grew up on a spaceship, and you have no home to go to now, and so your mind inclines more towards space. And although I love travelling the galaxy, I miss my home so deeply that my mind is not fully balanced between the two either."

Aeryn nodded. "That's true. And Crichton?"

Crichton shrugged.

"Crichton may have that balance," said D'Argo. "He came out into space, but he yearns for his homeworld."

Aeryn thought for a moment. "And in that room, the 'reality' room—he was thinking about an old legend on Earth, about that mysterious abandoned ship, and it made him homesick. Yet when he was back on Earth, that same legend made him want to explore. When he's here, he wants to be there; when he's there, he wants to be here."

"Story of my life," said Crichton. He walked towards the veil of energy, his right hand outstretched. Again the curtain crackled, bright daggers of light snapping across the entryway like a dazzling storm.

"Crichton!" cried Aeryn.

"But I am supposed to be the Promised One," cried Crichton, and he stepped into the lightning.

Crichton was now fully merged into Zhaan's mind, and the two of them were listening to the conversation between D'Argo, Aeryn, and the Queen of All Souls commanding Crichton's body.

It was strange in Zhaan's mind, but also peaceful, like floating on a lily pond. He wanted to take in the tranquillity before renewing the assault on the Queen, but the thought of someone else controlling his actions—and possibly hurting or killing Aeryn and D'Argo—renewed his focus.

"If we concentrate," said Zhaan.

But then the Queen took Crichton's body through the curtain of energy, and they were shaken as though an earthquake had dislodged the ground from its moorings. Crichton felt as if he had been hit in the face by a fighter jet. Then he was spinning backwards, spinning until he was nothing but a spiral of ghastly intensity, hurtled into a dimension where there was no footing.

Conjured out of mind and memory, he was elsewhere.

Crichton was in the room again, the room with the table, the room with the view of the launchpad, the room with the view of the Old Man.

"Dad!"

"John," said his father. "Johnny Boy!"

His dad was dressed in his old beat-up dark green flannel robe, the one that Mom had given him for John's sixth Christmas. He wore his ratty old moccasin-slippers and his dark hair was mussed, the way it was in the morning before he had a cup of coffee and a shave. Here was a version of Jack Crichton he remembered as a child. He was so unaccountably glad to see him, he almost ran over to hug him. He smelled of pipe tobacco and Old Spice and work. He was big and he was strong and he was Home.

"Dad!"

"Where the hell have you been, Johnny?"

"You remember. I went out aboard the *Farscape I.* I've been in space, far, far out in space."

His father was listening this time. "In space? Well, you can tell me all about it in the car—but we're not going until you clean up your room."

"What?" Crichton was aghast. "Clean up my room?" And then he knew this was no hallucination: his dream-meanderings had segued into memory, and he was eleven years old, and his father was a giant presence, intimidating, infuriating, comforting.

Crichton felt a sudden surge of mingled emotions. Above all he felt relieved to see his father—and as he looked around he saw that now they were in the old split-level house back in Houston, where they'd lived when he was a boy. There was the blue recliner, the cream-colored walls with framed photos of the family, the picture window looking out on the pecan tree, its leaves full. There was the dog-bed for his dog Corky, and Corky's leash hanging by the door. His feelings swelled. Damn if he wasn't really home! When he yearned for Earth and all of Earth's comforting familiarity, wasn't it really his home and his family that he yearned for?

His father continued, and Crichton also recalled why he had wanted to escape from home, explore the unknown where there was excitement and danger—where you made your own world and your own responsibilities.

His father was still talking. "How can you expect to be an astronaut, Johnny, when your room is knee-deep in books and electronics and comics and models of the *Mary Celeste*? I've never seen such a mess in all my born days. And then when I ask you to clean it up, you make more noise than a fox in a two-story chicken house. Scientists have to be organized, Johnny. You'd better clean that up, or we're not going to the movies this afternoon."

The eleven-year-old John squirmed. "I'm too old to go to the movies with my father anyway," he replied. "I'm going out to play spaceships with some guys from school."

Jack Crichton's face fell, and he spun on his heel and turned towards the window. He was silent a moment, and then he turned back toward John and nodded. "OK. I think you better clean your room up anyway, because I'm not kidding when I say that scientists have to know where to find their stuff." He sank into the recliner and sighed. "Do me a favor, eh, John? At least push the piles around a little." He looked away. "Guess you're getting too big to go to the movies with your old dad."

We didn't go to the movies, thought Crichton, but I

did follow him to the stars. And poised between memories of his father and memories of breaking away, a
longing for the stars and a longing for home, Crichton
knew he yearned for both—and the Orb of All let him
pass.

Then there was an enormous rumble and a crack of
energy, and Crichton was through the barrier, and standing next to the great mineral computer.

Pebbles, long embedded in the earthen walls, pelted
down as the rumbling continued. One of the small
stones flew into Aeryn's face, stinging and drawing
blood. More detritus rained down on her back. From the
corner of her eye she could see that D'Argo was still
standing before the archway, staring after Crichton.

"Get down!" she cried.

D'Argo tensed, but in another second the room had
quit shaking.

Aeryn took a few deep breaths and then got up.
"What do you think happened?"

"The barrier read Crichton's neurological patterns
and let him through—but something was not quite
right."

"I've been thinking that for some time," said Aeryn.
She called into the chamber: "Crichton!"

Crichton stood with his back to them. He was studying the array of minerals, wires and lights that made up
the Nokmadi machine. They heard him laugh.

"Crichton, can you find a way to turn the energy-
barrier off?" Aeryn called. He seemed not to hear.

"Crichton!" she yelled. "What's wrong? Can you turn off the barrier and let us through?"

At last Crichton moved towards the machine. He ran his fingers along the alleys and crevasses of the crystalloid mass, exploring the surface. His fingers found something, and he laughed again.

"D'Argo?" said Aeryn.

D'Argo looked at her and nodded. "I'm having the same doubts you're having," he said.

Crichton pressed indentations in the rock, and a series of red lights suddenly came to life. He worked his fingers over another set of indentations, and one of the red lights began to flash like an angry pulse. A humming and tremor arose, followed by a high-frequency beeping.

Then from the rock he pulled a giant switch and in a single motion he flipped it down.

The scarlet pulsing slowed and the machine fell silent. In the rows of domes set into the rock, the glowing dimmed slightly, and then, as they watched, it darkened even more, like the light dwindling as a winter day draws toward evening.

"Crichton!" yelled Aeryn. Crichton turned to face them. The smile on his face this time was calculating and pleased.

"You're not Crichton," said Aeryn, suddenly knowing with an absolute certainty that this creature before her was something entirely other. And who else had kidnapped Crichton and wanted to pass beyond the energy-barrier? "You're the Queen of the Nokmadi!" She drew her pulse pistol and took aim.

"No, no, no," said the Crichton-figure reprovingly,

wagging a finger at her. Even his voice sounded different now: imperious, self-satisfied. "I may not be Crichton," said that voice, "but this is certainly his body, and it can certainly die."

Aeryn lowered her pistol uncertainly.

"What have you done to the machine?" demanded D'Argo.

"I have disabled it," said the Crichton-figure. "In those domed recesses are the fleshly cores that underlie the form of everyone on this World—everyone except me. I have given up my core, and so I shall live forever. Now those fools and cowards, the Dayfolk, are crying to go home. To do that they would need to regain their bodies, because as ghosts they are tied to the power-gems for ever. But flesh must die! I have destroyed their fleshly cores—now they have no bodies, and so they will stay here, with me, and travel through space for eternity."

"You have destroyed them?" cried Aeryn.

The Crichton-figure waved a hand towards the rows of domes, their light dwindling. "See? They are dying. And I—" He seemed to lose his train of thought, and then fixed his eyes on them again. "I shall make sure they cannot be revived." He drew a pistol from his holster, took aim, and sent a bolt of energy slamming into the machine. The rockface exploded in a hail of sparks. With the stony surface blown away, they could see a complicated interior of panels and intersections, now blackened and twisted.

The domes emitted the faintest of glows, dying down even as the three of them watched.

D'Argo had turned pale with anger. Aeryn stared at the destruction before them.

"And now there is one last thing to destroy," said the figure, raising a pistol. Crichton's hand pointed it at Crichton's own temple. "Now I shall destroy Crichton."

CHAPTER 21

The experience of drifting and commingling with the essence of Zhaan had been disjointed, alternately pleasurable and uncomfortable. It smelled and tasted of thoughts, concepts and suggestions that at times were alien. For all that Crichton tried to peer into Zhaan's mysteries, he found that they remained mysteries because there were no microbes here to translate for him. And even if there had been, would these things even be translatable?

Ceremonies, smoky rooms filled with fragrant incense—plants, plants everywhere, vegetable-mind. Worship sunlight, sucking in nitrogen, glory to the water, glory to the blue and the green, chlorophyll heaven, cascading glory and darkness-in-the-roots fibres seeking and attaching . . .

Then the Queen moved his body through the energy-barrier, he was flung away from Zhaan's mind and into his own past. Again he felt an overpowering sadness welling up in him.

"Zhaan?" he called. But she was gone. He was no longer melded with her mind, and even in the mist-world he could not find her. He thought for a moment. It must have been as they theorized on the march down the Hole in the World—something had disrupted the order, and Zhaan had been thrown back into her real body on Moya. Now he was alone, trapped mute inside his own body.

A dangling snake-like shimmer formed before him in the mist. "Now it's just you and me," said the Queen of All Souls. "And soon it will just be me."

"What have you done with Zhaan?" Crichton demanded.

"She is leagues away, back on your pathetic little ship," said the Queen, and there was satisfaction in her velvet voice. "She was useful for a time, keeping you occupied with each other. I hope you won't be bored without her. But you haven't long to be bored, anyway."

"Look—" said Crichton, but the shimmer of the Queen had gone. He was alone in the mist-world once more.

He gave a long sigh and put his head in his hands. The plain wooden chair he had conjured up for himself was hard, so he thought himself a stool upholstered in red and sat down on that.

He and Zhaan had been occupied with each other, the Queen had said. "Useful" had been her word. What had been useful about their talking to each other? Even melding their minds had made no difference. Unless—

unless that had distracted them from other efforts, efforts that might have prevailed.

He remembered the cymbals, and how they had thrown the Queen off her stride for one glorious moment. If cymbals could be distracting, what was more than distracting? He thought back to home, and the music coming out of the West Springfield Vets' Club Polka Nite. Now that had been a distraction. A thought occurred to him. He visualized the interior of the club carefully.

In short order he had conjured up an accordion. He didn't know how to play the accordion, but that was all to the good, because it would make a more obnoxious noise that way. He could bet that on the cultured and far-ranging homeworld of the Nokmadi they had nothing so noisy and blaring as accordions.

He began to push the ends of the accordion together with all the force he could muster. The instrument wheezed like an asthmatic donkey. He pulled the ends out again, and the wheezing was louder. Then he began to play in earnest, disregarding rhythm and tune happily, and singing loudly. He relished being off-key. "Mama's got a squeezebox!" he sang, making up the rest of the words as he went. "She keeps the Nokmadi in at night!"

As he pulled at the accordion, he closed his eyes and concentrated, and he saw out through his physical eyes into the exterior world. Aeryn was speaking. "You have destroyed them?" she was saying, fire in her voice. His heart warmed to see her, angry and resolute.

"Queenie's got a squeezebox!" he sang raucously,

squeezing the accordion so hard it sounded like a herd of sick donkeys.

"See? They are dying," his voice was saying in the external world. "And I—"

He squeezed again, and the accordion brayed.

"I—" his voice was saying. The Queen had lost her train of thought again! He had been able to distract her with the glorious cacophony of discordant Earth music.

"I shall make sure the fleshly cores of the Dayfolk cannot be revived," the Queen finally continued in his voice. He looked down; his mist-world hands were empty.

He concentrated and looked out at the external world, and to his horror he saw his real hand bringing his pistol up to his own temple.

He thought for all his life was worth. The cymbals had distracted the Queen for a moment, the accordion for a fraction longer. He needed something much more powerfully distracting, something that would drive her from his mind like a swarm of bees repelling a bear.

And then he knew he had it.

As he concentrated, a tartan bag appeared under his right arm, with another, smaller bag spilling down in front. His fingers were on the pipe, and he took in a deep breath of air, expanding his chest until his lungs were bursting.

Blowing into the tube, he began to play the bagpipes.

The noise was shrill, ear-splitting. He was badly out of tune, and he couldn't seem to coordinate blowing into the pipe with squeezing the bag under his arm. The blaring that resulted was again like a donkey with a breathing problem, but this one was a cranky beast whose closest relative was a goose, with overtones of a circus full of calliopes and the faintest touch of kazoo.

He took another deep breath and started in on "Country Roads."

Aeryn and D'Argo watched in horror as the Crichton-figure held the pistol up to his temple. "No!" Aeryn shouted. D'Argo began to run, as if he were going to burst through the energy-barrier by sheer force, but when he got within a few paces, sheets of lightning crackled across the archway, snaking out as if to touch him. He stopped, an expression of utter fury on his face.

The lightning died away, and once more they could see the Crichton-figure standing on the other side of the barrier, smiling as his finger tightened on the trigger.

Then the Crichton-figure shook his head quickly, as if trying to rid himself of a noxious buzzing. He looked at the gun blankly. Then he gave a small shudder, as if a tiny animal with a lot of legs had just run quickly down his spine.

"I have—destroyed—the Dayfolk—" said Crichton in a strained, high-pitched voice. "I will—destroy—you—All—I want—is to be—among—the stars— West Virginia—Mountain Mama—take me home—"

Aeryn and D'Argo stared.

Crichton opened his mouth wider. Suddenly a scream escaped him. It was not a human voice: it sounded as though it were ripped from the throat of death itself.

He began to stagger, and his eyes became unfocused. The gun dropped to the ground with a thud. He shook his head again, and his whole body shuddered.

Then he stood composed once more, looking at Aeryn and D'Argo.

"Good," said John Crichton. "She's out of the way. Remind me never to buy K-Tel's *Best Loved Bagpipe Ballads,* OK?"

"Crichton!" called Aeryn. "Is it you? Is she gone?"

"Turn off the energy-barrier and let us through!" said D'Argo.

"It's me, and she's gone," said Crichton. He gave them a wink. "Want me to sing a particularly annoying John Denver tune to prove it to you?"

"I believe it is indeed the real Crichton," said D'Argo.

Crichton turned to the crystalloid machine beside him and scanned it, looking for some way to turn off the energy-barrier. Much of the machine was blasted and blackened by the Queen's attack, and he could see no controls.

"Crichton!" warned Aeryn. "The fleshly cores of the Nokmadi—the Queen turned off the life-supports! You must turn them back on—quickly!"

Crichton looked at the rows of small domes. Lights still gleamed faintly in them, but they were dwindling towards darkness even as he watched. He ran his hand over outcroppings and jagged slices of metal, pressing with his fingers.

"Oh no you don't!" said the Queen of All Souls.

Crichton whirled around. Standing in front of the row of small domes was the glittering, transparent Queen.

"You can eject me from your mind, John Crichton," she said, "but you cannot kill me. I am immortal. I have waited a millennium of cycles for the Promised One to arrive and transport me through the foolish barrier that has kept me from determining the destiny of the Nokmadi. You shall not oppose me now.

"Step back from the machine, O Promised One," she continued, pointing a finger at him. From that finger came the crackling of lightning, slashing across the room towards Crichton. Instinctively he dived out of the way almost before the bolt had left her hand, scrambling behind one of the protrusions of the machine.

"Flesh must die," repeated the Queen. She moved to one of the domes, flipped open the crystal cover, and withdrew the contents. There was a pulsing nub no bigger than a thumb, a perfect tiny sphere of flesh, cradled in the hollow of a power gem.

The power gem was the size of D'Argo's fist, like a cradle of resplendent color. It sparkled from within, as if lightning storms of spectra animated each facet: brilliant white, scarlet, gold, indigo, emerald, spangled with silver-tinged colors.

The Queen held the gem aloft in one hand and gestured at it with the other, sending bolts of energy into its core. The small globe of flesh was vaporized in a sizzle of black smoke.

Then she opened her hand and let the gem fall to the floor. It shattered instantly into a thousand pieces. The glinting energies within it were scattered across the floor in shards and slivers of crystal. With it there came a moan, and for a fraction of a second a wisp appeared in the chamber, a wavering figure a touch away from nothingness, who shivered briefly and then was gathered into oblivion.

Outside the chamber, a flash of sadness came over Aeryn.

"I have the power of life and death over everyone on this ship," said the Queen. "You are thinking I am cruel to let their fleshly bodies die. But what you don't realize is that I am merciful to let them live at all. They shall be ghosts for ever under my rule."

Crichton peered out from behind the stony outcropping, estimating his chances. She was turning back towards the domes, walking down the rows, turning back the coverings, looking in, and replacing the covers again.

"Let me see," she said as if to herself. "Who else has particularly offended my royal presence? Who else deserves to die?"

The light glowing from within the domes was almost gone, and Crichton knew that soon the fleshly globes would be dead for ever: soon the ghosts would be forever tethered to the gems that held their spirits and generated their translucent ghostly forms.

He focused on a single dome in the centre, a dome that was slightly larger than the others, placed slightly higher in the wall of rock.

The Queen had opened another dome and was looking down at the hapless gem within, smiling.

Crichton made a dash. Before the Queen could turn, he had the central dome open and the gem exposed. As he had expected, this gem cradled no fleshly globe. It sparkled with a dark energy. He reached in to touch it.

"No!" screeched the Queen. A look of the wildest panic on her face, she raised her hand to strike at him with all the powers her electrical nature could summon.

But before she could loose her energies, he had the gem out of its socket.

The Queen began to scream.

It was like no other sound Crichton had ever heard. The agony of its expression pierced straight to the centre of his being. Even D'Argo winced at the power of it.

Eyes wide, her body shaking, the Queen raised up her arms, as if those pitiful translucent limbs might shield her from the disruption of her gem.

The Queen of All Souls began to dissolve.

Crichton watched with horror as pieces of her semi-corporeal form dropped from her body. The rapidity of the shuddering increased, and the Queen began to melt and fray, like something blasted away by a driving, relentless sandstorm. Even though she was a ghost, it seemed as though this ghost was not just ectoplasm. There were layers. When the skin shredded off, there was an endoskeleton, with supporting electro-power circuitry. These were frizzling now with an emphatic dissipating rhythm, like a roaring fire, consuming.

Still the scream . . .

The outside of the ghost's face peeled off, showing the ghost skull behind the ghost skin.

Then suddenly the disintegration stopped.

Slowly the ghost began to reassemble, shred by shred, until she was whole.

Again she was a glittering, shimmering form— crouched upon the floor, weeping.

CHAPTER 22

Crichton ran the beam from his pulse pistol over the Orb of All and the Nokmadi circuitry, slicing away its outer shell, leaving it a mass of frizzling innards, fragmenting the already blackened panels into dozens of warped pieces on the floor. The energy-barrier vanished, and D'Argo and Aeryn ran into the chamber. D'Argo slapped Crichton on the back, and Aeryn lowered her eyes when she found herself face to face with the real Crichton once more.

Crichton still had the Queen's gem balanced in his left hand. He tilted it, and the Queen winked out, fading as rapidly as breath disappears from cold glass. When he tilted it in the other direction, she reappeared, now clambering to her feet, still weeping.

"I appear to have you in the palm of my hand," said Crichton.

"I ask for mercy," said the Queen, and she stretched

her arms towards Crichton in an imploring gesture.

"We'll see what mercy you have allowed the Day-folk," said Crichton. "D'Argo, can you make sense of this machine?"

D'Argo was studying the blackened ruins. "I suspect no one will be able to make sense of it now," he said.

Crichton faced the Queen again, tilting her gem ever so slightly. "Tell us how to revive the flesh of the Nok-madi," he commanded.

The Queen sank to her knees. "It cannot be done. The machine has been destroyed beyond our capacity to repair it."

"I think she is right," said D'Argo, fingering a clutch of blackened wires.

"There must be a way!" said Aeryn. She pulled at one of the twisted panels of the machine, which dropped to the ground and shattered into fragments.

"We have—Wait! What new peril is this?" cried D'Argo.

He was looking beyond the archway of the chamber, back into the bottom of the dark pit that was the Hole in the World. Staring at them from the darkness was an army of glowing eyes.

"A military commander always attends the scene of the victory," said Rygel, floating next to the Orb of All on his ThroneSled and fingering the collar of his royal robe self-importantly. "The wisest commanders, such as myself, do not arrive until the foot-soldiers have ensured that it is a victory. Or in this case, I should say wheel-soldiers."

The army of DRDs clustered on the shattered Nokmadi computer like arg-ants on a fallen glikglik. Three dozen extensors were at work on the com lex innards of the machine, and others were pushing panels upright, straightening wires and gathering debris into heaps.

The first thing the DRDs had done, on marching like an army of unstoppable beetles into the chamber, was to restore power to the Nokmadi domes. The lights in those domes had faded until they were scarcely discernible, but within moments they had started to gather strength, and now the lights were glowing as brightly as ever. When Aeryn checked them, it appeared that only one Nokmadi had been lost—the single creature the Queen of All Souls had pulverized. The rest were safe, and the DRDs had already set the enfleshing process in motion. Soon the Nokmadi would be in their bodies again and the power gems could be shut down— all but the Queen's gem, since she had elected to remain a ghost forever.

Rygel had one hand on the furze attached to his ear, the other waving in beneficent greetings. He cocked his head as if listening intently to information no one else could hear. "My, my," he muttered. "Well, yes, fix that too."

"Are the DRDs telling you something?" asked Aeryn.

"Something about faster-than-light," said Rygel. "Seems the drive was broken, so I told them to go ahead and fix it, while they're doing the rest. That should take care of all the problems."

"With one exception," said Crichton. He turned to the Queen of All Souls. Since Crichton had taken hold of the gem that kept her ghostly form stable, she had been slumped in the corner. Even her color had become a mournful smoky gray.

Now she turned her face to the others, an expression of hope upon it. "Faster-than-light!" she said. "The Nokmadi can travel the universe once more!"

Crichton nodded. "I guess so, as long as you can work out who wants to stay on board and who wants to go home. If you asked me, I'd propose some serious negotiation instead of all this warfare and taking over each other's minds. You could start—"

But the Queen had moved into the center of the chamber and was kneeling in a position of obeisance.

"Forgive me! I was wrong!"

"You were wrong?"

"You are not the Promised One!"

"Well, I did tell you that," said Crichton. "Several times."

"No. It is that glorious creature who has restored power and life to the Nokmadi ship! It is he who is called Rygel!" Her ghostly eyes were aglow with religious fervour. "There is hope now, thanks to Rygel! I have met our Savior!"

Rygel wrinkled his face and looked toward the floor with barely disguised gratification. "Yes, yes, people do tend to worship me," he said. He looked almost bashful, if an expression of irrepressible self-satisfaction could be called bashful.

"Rygel?" said Crichton. "Uhmm . . . look. I know Rygel, and I should warn you: this savior could have feet of clay."

"I must approach the hem of his robes! When I am deemed worthy!" said the Queen.

"Whatever," said Crichton. "Listen, we've got a lot going on here. Why don't you just sit down, take a load off?"

"I am in great debt to you, Crichton—Acolyte of Rygel the Splendiferous."

Crichton rolled his eyes. "Does this mean you'll agree to negotiate with the Dayfolk—this, plus the fact that I have your power gem in my hand?"

The Queen bowed her head. "I will negotiate with the heretics."

"And you will free our ship?"

"The blessed ship of Rygel the Incomparable shall go free. You have won, John Crichton."

"I think I'll keep hold of your gem until then, just in case," said Crichton.

"Well, good, it's all solved," said Rygel, looking more than pleased with the proceedings. His Throne-Sled gave a small celebratory dip.

"It's all solved on board this ship, perhaps," said Aeryn.

"You mean there are problems on Moya?" said Crichton. "How do you know?"

"I don't know," said Aeryn. "Yet. All I know is that we've spent two solar days on this ship. And that's two days more for the Peacekeepers to find us."

"Captain! The gems. One of the power gems is moving!"

The words of the sensor-tech pulled Captain Sha Sutt out of an intense puzzle-exercise she had been practising at her station. The compu-link dissolved at the touch of her forefinger and the reality of the *DarkWind*'s bridge took the place of the VirtReal corridors in which she had walked and thought and fought, keeping her wits and reflexes sharp. She'd been expecting this, hoping for this. They would have invaded the alien ship if necessary. How nice, though, that it seemed as though one of the power gems—those energy nodes that would bring her acclaim in the Peacekeeper High Command, and perhaps the deeper regard of Commander Crais— were being hauled out of their position deep within the alien ship. They could make a quick attack on the Leviathan, seize the gem, examine it and, if it were genuine, perhaps use some of its great powers to subdue the Nokmadi before they even realized what was happening to them.

She rose and stepped over to the sensor station, hovering above the work of the tech there. In the schematic of his sensor-screen she could see a three-dimensional representation of the alien ship. The tech was still pressing buttons, bringing up the ship in greater and greater detail. Even as she watched, one of the amber crystalline illuminations representing the power gems inched away from the central core.

"I see only the life forms from the Leviathan on board the alien ship," she said to the tech. "Therefore they must be taking the gem to the Leviathan."

"Indeed, Captain." There was a smile of anticipation on the tech, mirroring the attitude of all on board. This treading of time and space, awaiting the return of the crew of the Leviathan, had not been misspent. The crew was not merely rested, but ready and eager. Captain Sutt had kept it no secret that these power gems would bring them not only promotions, but most likely riches.

"As soon as the beings board the Leviathan," Sutt commanded, "the *DarkWind* will dock there as well. I want a party of eight prepared for boarding. All will bear full inter-ship assault gear and be prepared to kill everyone on board if there is any resistance. We will demand surrender, of course, but I have no patience for lengthy negotiation. Am I understood?"

She was.

The trek out of the Hole in the World was arduous, but the group was buoyed by the exhilaration of having restored control of their destiny to the Nokmadi. Rygel hovered beside the group as they toiled upward, zooming ahead on his ThroneSled whenever the slow pace became tiresome to him. Behind D'Argo, Aeryn, and Crichton came the Queen, deferential to Crichton and his control of her power gem, which he kept firmly in his hand, and still adoring of Rygel. Trailing after them was the army of DRDs, who had set the Nokmadi computers and engines to rights in record time.

When the group emerged from the mountain pass they found Pahl and Leff, having reconstituted themselves, as promised. Each had a dragon to ferry the voyagers and the DRDs back to the edge of the World and the passage back to Moya.

They flew over the lush and beautiful Nokmadi landscape, the strong wings of the dragons beating. As they flew, Aeryn noticed that the shimmering form of Pahl, sitting ahead of her, was gradually growing denser, full of color and life. It was as if color were suffusing a bowl of clear water.

By the time they landed, the Nokmadi were fully enfleshed. Pahl and Leff threw themselves on the ground, feeling the soil, testing the textures of earth and grass and stone, the sheer sensual joy of being alive. Throngs of Nokmadi came to give their thanks, bringing great loads of fruits and delicacies, foods they had cultivated on the ship for millennia, in memory of the homeworld, but which, for all those millennia, they had never been able to taste.

Then the two Nokmadi led the visitors up a set of stone steps and into the sterile corridor that ringed the Nokmadi World. Rygel and the DRDs went ahead to Moya while the rest stayed behind to parley.

"We have restored order to your world," said D'Argo to the two Nokmadi. "Now it is time you fulfilled your end of the bargain. Will you provide us with a map that will lead us to our homeworlds?"

Pahl shook his head sadly. "It is a great tragedy. We no longer have such a map on our ship."

"What?" cried Crichton. "You've spent millennia mapping the universe, and you don't even have a map of this very galaxy?"

"Yanor promised us the map," said Aeryn.

Pahl's face was clouded with sorrow. "Yanor was the map," he said. "Each of us embodies the map of a galaxy. Yanor was the map of your galaxy." In a flash Aeryn remembered him, trailing with stars across the sky of night. "The Queen killed one of our number, and the one she killed was Yanor."

Now Aeryn knew why she had felt a rush of emotion when the Queen had destroyed the gem and the globe of flesh, and why the wisp of ghost that had appeared and faded had brought tears to her eyes. Yanor had read her mind and fashioned his appearance to appeal to her; he had embodied her memories.

"You never made copies of your maps?" Crichton was saying.

"We were made to be immortal, and our maps in us," said Pahl. "We do not have copies aboard this ship, but we have always sent copies back to Nokmad, our homeworld. We will need no maps to return there: the way is imprinted on our hearts."

"May we follow you," asked D'Argo, "and obtain a copy of your maps?"

"We shall be delighted to lead you to Nokmad," said Pahl, folding his hands together in a gesture of honor. "It is the loveliest planet in two thousand galaxies, as you can see from our copy of it here. Now that our engines have been restored, we can be there in less than ten solar days. If you like, I and some other Nokmadi will travel aboard your ship to ensure that you get there without difficulty."

They made ready to return to Moya. At the last moment, Crichton pressed the Queen's power gem into Leff's hand. "Here," he said, "you take it. Keep her in line this time, will you?"

CHAPTER 23

Zhaan, Rygel and the DRDs greeted them when they stepped across the threshold of the Leviathan's docking bay.

"Behold the return of the triumphant voyagers, the companions of Rygel the Magnificent!" announced Rygel, waggling his eyebrows. "Now to the important matter. Did you bring those delicacies they gave us?" The diminutive monarch's fingers fluttered and his nostrils twitched expectantly. He cast a fond look down at his little friends, who gazed up reverently. "And you doubted my powers! Do I not deserve a reward for my efforts?" His eyes gleamed.

"Very well," said D'Argo. The big warrior actually smiled. "Yes, we brought quite a haul, Rygel. Have a look." He towed a hovercart behind him, and pulled up the tarpaulin flung across it, exposing piles of magenta and blue fruits.

Rygel's eyes bulged. He scurried over and dived into the fruits, coming out with two handfuls and chomping away madly. Juice ran down his face and onto his chest. "Oh, excellent! Wonderful! Succulent!"

"The elkaberries alone make me remember how good it was to have an appetite—to say nothing of taste buds," said Pahl. He had brought two other Dayfolk with him, as well as complete coordinates for finding their way to the Nokmadi homeworld.

Crichton oversaw the closure of the docking-bay door, then turned to his companions. "I'd like you to meet our guests," he said. He introduced the Nokmadi first to Zhaan and then to Rygel. When he was finished, the Nokmadi bowed deeply. "Hail to thee, O Promised One!"

Rygel laughed, showing a maw full of bright purple pulp. "There! You see! Someone finally appreciates me."

"We must head back to the bridge now," said D'Argo, "and see about getting Moya into action."

"That's right, Rygel," said Crichton. "We appreciate your excellent efforts on our behalf, to say nothing of your new Promised One status. However, we've got a few of our own promises to deliver on."

The ghosts followed them mutely as they made their way up to the bridge. They examined the interior of the Leviathan coolly; their only reaction was a lift of their eyebrows when, back on the bridge, the holograph of Pilot appeared before them, greeting them on behalf of Moya and himself.

"Moya thanks you for her current good health," said Pilot.

The Nokmadi bowed. Pahl said, "Our greetings to our esteemed fellow-sentients. We are honored that Moya will accompany us Home."

"The detachment of filamental fibres and probes is nearly complete," said Pilot. "The tractor beams, of course, have long since disengaged. However, the strong tensile projections from the hull of your ship—"

"We are safely aboard now," said Pahl. "Retraction has already commenced. If you turn on any screens, I think you will see what you request."

Zhaan strode to her station and turned on the vu-screens. Crichton turned to look at them. Sure enough, even as he watched, the huge tentacle-like projections around Moya began to move, slowly undulating to release their captive. In a very short time, he could hear the hull fall loose of its mooring. Moya was once again free in space.

"Thank you," said Pilot. "All is in order. I am entering the coordinates for the planet Nokmad now."

"If we're taking these creatures to some faraway planet I've never even heard of," said Rygel, hovering at the side of the bridge, "I think we ought to be compensated for the inconvenience. I, for one, feel very inconvenienced. Where did that hovercart go? My DRDs are quite willing to unload more of the foodstuffs, which would be a satisfactory start to my personal compensation."

"Calm down, Rygel. You've had your share for now," said Aeryn.

"But I am the Promised One," retorted Rygel.

"That's all very well in the Nokmadi ship, Rygel,"

said Crichton. "Too bad you couldn't stay on board and soak in some more of the adulation you so enjoy. Now you're just a member of a desperate crew of an escaped prison ship again."

Rygel grumbled to himself.

Moya quickly pushed away from the Nokmadi ship. The vessel loomed large in its screens as Zhaan and Crichton checked all vital signs.

"Right," said Zhaan, turning to the Nokmadi. "We're just about prepared. At last, you're on your way home."

Pilot's image frizzled into view in front of them. "Moya says she's being attacked!"

In retrospect, the undetected approach of an enemy ship seemed like an accident waiting to happen. Desperate to free Moya from the grip of the Nokmadi ship, they had been forced to leave her essentially unguarded, with only Pilot to keep watch. Zhaan had not even returned to her body and emerged from the pod until shortly before the others returned to Moya. They'd all been so busy with everything else, it was no wonder the small vessel had been able to sneak past their visuals and right up to the docking bay, where it had attached itself like a remora to the bottom of a shark.

"Attacked! Who?"

"A Peacekeeper cutter," said Pilot.

"Peacekeepers!" said Rygel, nearly falling off his ThroneSled. "What are Peacekeepers doing here?"

Crichton could not help but turn to Aeryn, as though she might have an explanation.

"As I feared, they must have followed us from the asteroid cluster somehow," said Aeryn. "We are many light-years beyond the boundaries of Peacekeeper space."

"Whatever kept Peacekeepers within boundaries?" snarled D'Argo. In one quick motion, his Qualta Rifle was drawn and he was marching toward the docking bay.

"People called Peacekeepers," said Pahl mildly, "should not be waging war."

"Welcome to the new universe," said Crichton. "This doesn't make sense, Pilot. We StarBurst away from them. How could this have happened? How could they have followed us so quickly?"

"I was just asking myself the same question. Moya is reviewing past impressions—yes, she has something she had not noticed before. There was an anomaly in the last StarBurst. There was an explosion of some type of energy Moya has never encountered before. The Peacekeeper ship must have utilized that energy to travel after us."

"Damn!" said Crichton. "That madman Crais must have sent a ship right up our tailpipe! Peacekeepers. Here!"

"This burst of energy occurred when we StarBurst?" said Aeryn. "That must have been the cutter that was pursuing us, the one that was with Crais when we eluded him. The *DarkWind*." A cloud passed over her face. "I know the commander of the *DarkWind*. We're in a bad situation. I should help D'Argo." She grabbed up her weapon and was gone.

"Will this interfere with our plans to return home?" said Pahl. "Are we in real danger?"

Crichton looked over to Zhaan. "You'd better explain

it to him. And keep things going here. Maybe you and
Pilot can jog Moya's memory on some kind of defensive possibility. I'd better go down and see what I can
do to help D'Argo and Zhaan repel the invaders."

Zhaan nodded.

Crichton grabbed his pulse pistol, took a deep breath
and hurried down to join his crewmates.

When Aeryn reached the cusp of the docking-bay area,
she could already hear the sizzles of weaponfire zinging
through the great hallways of Moya. Cautiously she
peered around a corner, keeping her rifle alert and her
safety off, ready to let go a blast of her own if necessary. Mostly right now what she wanted was to reconnoiter and then decide the best course of action to take.

Sure enough, the Bay had been ratcheted open and
an artificial Peacekeeper boarding door had been inserted. However, the invasive force had clearly run into
D'Argo, because they'd quickly dived down for what
scant cover they could find. From what she could tell
there were around eight of the Peacekeeper invaders,
which sounded about right for a force from a cutter the
size of the *DarkWind*. This was the one positive element
in this mess: the Peacekeeper force here was limited.
And when you had a warrior like D'Argo on your side,
you could bet that things evened out a lot.

Aeryn watched with admiration as the Luxan jumped
out from hiding and used a new angle to blast across a
slew of crates, keeping the Peacekeepers there down.
He dodged a bolt easily and roared, slapping down onto
the floor of the ship and rolling, lifting up his Qualta
Rifle and snapping off a round that wounded one of the

Peacekeepers in the arm. All the while, the big guy was cursing up a storm, sounding more like a herd of stampeding carnivores than a sole warrior.

The Peacekeepers were so intent on bringing down D'Argo that they didn't even notice the arrival of Aeryn. She fully intended to take advantage of this. Carefully, she drew a bead on a foot sticking out from the side of a crate, safe from the position of the Luxan, but not safe from her. She'd always excelled at both artillery and target practice, and her battle nerves were absolutely chilly. She squeezed the trigger, and her bolt connected with the Peacekeeper trooper. There was a howl of pain.

Chalk up one out-of-commission Peacekeeper, thought Aeryn.

D'Argo rolled back to safety, then gave the new arrival a grin. "Our numbers have increased, fools!" he bellowed. "Return to your ship and escape with your lives while you can."

A woman's voice called out, deep and firm and with a sting at its tail. "Impressive display of initial defense, Luxan. But no matter. We are on board now. We have time. You do not. Surrender now, and we may consider showing you mercy."

Aeryn recognized the voice. Yes. It was her. Captain of the *DarkWind*—previous friend, old rival, fierce enemy.

"Private Sutt. You are on a Leviathan. Abandon all hope!" she spat.

"Captain Sutt to you and anyone else, traitor Sun!"

"I am no traitor! I am an excommunicated Peacekeeper!" spat Aeryn back. "Now a Peacekeeper no longer! Commander Crais betrayed me."

"Crais betrays no one," came the answer, the rage in the voice apparent. "If you have what it takes to be a Peacekeeper, then prove your mettle. Kill the Luxan and you shall take your rightful place again."

Instead of glaring at her, as Aeryn had half-expected he might, D'Argo stood back away from any possible fire from the Peacekeepers. He grinned and he puffed out his chest. "I make a handsome target, Aeryn."

Aeryn laughed. "Shut up, you overgrown pukka-monkey. We've got Peacekeepers to kick off our ship!"

"Crais was right!" came the voice of Sutt. "You are a traitor! How easy it is to abandon the glib allegiance you gave to our cause, Aeryn."

D'Argo let go another burst of fire, which almost caught the captain before she ducked lower behind a bulkhead.

None of the other Peacekeepers seemed eager to show themselves. When Crichton arrived a short while later, it was still a standoff.

"Good. Standoff, I see," said Crichton, moving forward to join Aeryn against the wall.

"For now. I can't help but think that they've got other plans that they're going to implement at any moment."

"We've got to keep them preoccupied," said Crichton. "Peacekeepers! This is John Crichton of the planet Earth. I believe it is me that you want. I shall surrender if you promise to leave the others and this ship alone."

"Crichton!" said Aeryn.

"Don't worry. Old Earth diplomatic trick," whispered Crichton. "Stretching the truth."

"It matters not. We shall have you all alive or dead soon enough," returned Sutt.

"Better not!" cried Crichton. "I know for a fact that Crais wants me and he wants me alive."

"Commander Crais will be more than happy to accept you dead, Earthman. And I'm more than happy to make you that way."

"OK, dammit. Then come on and do it!"

Crichton stepped out and blasted.

He dodged a hail of fire and was back soon enough. "That'll show them," Crichton said.

"I'm sure they're very impressed, John," said Aeryn. She nodded toward another crate. "Why don't you take up position there? That'll be about as much crossfire as we're going to be able to manage."

"Right." Crichton scuttled over to take up his place. He dodged enemy fire along the way but made it safely.

Now then, Aeryn thought. We look like we know what we're doing. That's half the battle.

Shortly after Crichton had safely made it over to the crate, things got very quiet amongst the Peacekeepers.

Crichton knew they must be changing tactics. Obviously, though, their placements had been noted—and would be assaulted. It would be up to them to repel all attackers. It was tough travelling through the universe of danger on a ship without any kind of armaments or defenses to protect its crew. Just about anybody who had the engineering and weaponry could board and assault. The trick was staying one step ahead of pursuit—and because of the delay with the Nokmadi ship, Moya obviously hadn't been able to do that this time.

Even as Crichton's head spun with possible plans, something started to move from behind the enemy lines. It was dark and black and spindly. That's all that Crichton could make out before a blast from D'Argo's Qualta Rifle struck it. The black thing shrugged off the fire and moved forward again. As the smoke cleared, Crichton could make out its form. It looked like a tarantula. Barbed legs hauled it along, radiating from a dark bulb of an irregular body.

"A grab-bomb!" said Aeryn.

That didn't sound good. Crichton's immediate reaction was to have a blast at it himself. He let off a spray of fire, but the spidery legs kept moving.

"Save your ammunition," said Aeryn. "It's a close-in fighting device used for just such situations. Frell! We're going to have to retreat."

Crichton didn't have to be told what that meant. This area formed a bottleneck, and the three of them were the cork that kept the marauders from fanning out into the other areas of the ship.

However, knowing the efficacy of Peacekeeper tech, he could pretty much guess what being in the general vicinity of an exploding grab-bomb might do. Peacekeeper tech was anything but gentle.

Then, from behind them, swarmed a group of twenty DRDs. Crichton watched, astonished, as they zoomed past like an angry bunch of beetles. The first to reach the grab-bomb flashed with laser-cutters, prying the thing off the floor. Like a running back in football, another immediately scampered up. Five of the DRDs lifted the grab-bomb up and clamped it down onto the back of the newcomer. The valiant DRD then scurried toward the position where the hull of Moya had been breached.

Before he could even analyze what was going on, Crichton's instincts drew him back for cover. There was an explosion; some DRDs scrambled back and others were hurled back in the wake of the billowing mass of fire and smoke.

"Moya does have defenses!" he cried excitedly. "Kamikazes!"

A voice called out from behind him: "With a little nudge and guidance from a superior military mind!"

There, hovering above his flock of DRDs, was Rygel in his ThroneSled, looking absolutely regal.

"Rygel!" said Aeryn. "I thought you liked to avoid the heat of battle."

"I know the wisdom of proper discretion in certain matters," replied Rygel. "However, I am a Dominar! And even I would rather go out in a blaze of defiance than be imprisoned by Peacekeepers again."

"Good job," said Crichton. He peered around the corner. Four Peacekeeper bodies littered the docking bay. But some of the cutter's crew were still alive and dangerous. Fire sang from behind a bulkhead, glancing off the bottom of Rygel's ThroneSled and blasting down a corridor to sizzle out into Moya's steelskin interior. Rygel toppled off his ThroneSled, thumping onto the floor. A figure bounded past them, blasting. Such was the concentration of blasts now that they all had to duck to save their lives. Such was the figure's speed that by the time they put their head up again, it was already disappearing down the curves of Moya's corridor.

"What or who was that?" said Crichton.

Aeyrn took a breath. "That's Captain Sha Sutt."

And before the others could object, Aeryn ran after her.

CHAPTER 24

"A eryn! What do you think you're doing!" cried the radiovoice in her ear.

Aeryn didn't respond. She was taking care of something she should have taken care of a long time ago, and she'd need to save all her breath and all her energy to do it. She didn't cut off communications because she might need her comrades later. Now, though, what she needed was full concentration on following her nemesis.

It was Sha Sutt, after all, and not only was she Augmented, she seemed to know exactly where she was headed.

As she ran down the corridors of Moya, Aeryn could hear Sutt ahead of her. She seemed to be slowing a bit, probably not expecting anyone to be following her.

As the air rasped through her lungs, Aeryn wondered why Sutt was headed more deeply into Moya. Then the footsteps stopped altogether. Almost gratefully, Aeryn slumped against a wall, fighting to keep her breathing silent. Sha Sutt was around the next bend.

"Leviathan crew." A voice rang over the comm link, and Aeryn recognized the cold, dead tone of Captain Sha Sutt. "You should be informed that I have a device of enormous power embedded on my person. I have now reached a point in the Leviathan directly transactional with a vital life-node transferral artery. In other words, should this device explode, it would kill your ship—and anything on it. You may well point out that it will kill me as well. I am prepared to die. Are you? Throw yourselves on the mercy of the Peacekeepers. Or be destroyed. Here. Now."

During this speech, Aeryn inched along the side of the wall and managed to peer around it. Fortunately, Sha Sutt was facing away from her. Unfortunately, it was obvious that Sutt was not bluffing.

Her right leg—the prosthetic that had replaced the leg she'd lost on those training exercises—was exposed, the fastener down the outside undone all the way up to her hip. Lights and machinery sparkled on that hip: the casing was off. Sutt was punching in numbers on a control panel on her thigh. Aeryn recognized the telltale lumps and nodes of a Concentrate—a particularly nasty explosive device Peacekeepers sometimes planted as booby traps. Yes, indeed, if she pushed the button on that, there was absolutely no doubt it would rip the guts right out of Moya.

Obviously Sutt had no idea that Aeryn was watching her. Aeryn might have been tempted to lift up her gun and blast her, but she well knew that Peacekeeper devices had deadman switches. A blast at Sutt would detonate the explosive. No, there had to be anothe. and Aeryn knew exactly what that was. It was a s. chance, but there was no choice but to take it.

"Sha!" she called. "Sha, it's Aeryn Sun, right behind you."

The Peacekeeper spun around. Aeryn ducked to avoid a blast, but none came.

"You are fast and you are smart, Sun. I should have remembered that," said Sutt. "Now I need a response— or I'm going to blow us all up."

"That will make no one happy, Sutt. Crais and the Peacekeepers will never know what happened. Crais will just keep searching for us—all his life. Peacekeeper goals would be circumvented. You would be doing everyone a disservice. Especially yourself."

"You're just buying time, Sun. Surrender, or you die."

"If you set off that device, you'll die too. You don't want to die, Sutt. You want me to die. And you know what? I'm more than happy to die—if I have a chance to save my friends here."

"Friends? What nonsense is this?"

"I'm not going to explain. I'm just going to make a deal with you—provided my friends, the crew of this Leviathan, agree. And by the way, I'm more than happy to assure them that you not only have the ability to blow yourself and Moya's insides up, but you're insane enough to do it."

"Good. You tell them that."

Aeryn unhooked her comm unit. "You've been listening, I hope," she said to the others.

"Yes, we have, Aeryn," Aeryn heard Zhaan answer. "We are most concerned."

"It's all true. You should be concerned. So let me state my conditions. And explain to you. Sutt has a private vendetta against me, and her most cherished goal is to watch me die. However, if she blows up that bomb of hers she'll die before me—now won't you, Captain Sutt? And you'll have that one thought—what if something went wrong with the bomb? What if it malfunctioned and you died—but I survived?"

"That's nonsense."

"Is it? But you're just like Crais. Too hot-headed to see straight."

"What would you know about Crais?" snarled Sutt.

"You think I don't know about Crais? You think everyone doesn't know? He's known throughout the Captive Worlds for stamping his little foot when he doesn't get his way, isn't that so? And recruiting young female adjutants into his service. But what price do they pay for their blind loyalty? How come they never live long enough to reap their rewards? He uses them to do his dirty work—by whatever means necessary! And if that doesn't kill them, he does it himself—before they become too powerful. He sent you after Crichton, didn't he, Sha? Even though it might kill you and everyone on your ship? And now you're going to blow yourself up for him? Sha! You used to be smart!"

"Lies! Miserable lies!"

"Are they? One thing more. You're not going to be able to take certain revenge on me unless you choose to live—a while longer, anyway."

"Revenge—then you admit it! You did leave me for dead!"

"No, Sha," said Aeryn. "If you had just investigated you'd have found that I was the one who insisted on looking for you. You'd been counted dead by the others."

"Another lie!"

"I'm ready to make a bargain, Sha. Your quarrel is with me. We fight alone. Your friends don't carve up my friends until you and I have had it out—and in turn, my friends will let your friends live a bit longer. Agreed?"

"More than agreed, Sun. Come at me."

"But you've got that leg with a barrel of tricks, haven't you? Let's try it my way. I'm going to put my gun out there in front of you like this." She slowly put her weapon down on the floor and pushed it out for Sutt to have a look at. "I go for it, and you go for me. Is that fair?"

"That sounds just fine, Sun. I'll wait right here for ten microts . . . which is as much time as it takes me to finish setting the device . . ."

Aeryn didn't give her time to finish her sentence. She dived for the gun, grabbed it, and tucked herself into a streamlined gymnast ball, rolling with exercised speed. A blast from Sutt's rifle singed her leg, but she came up and let off a blast from her own weapon.

The bolt missed, but it was enough to slam Sutt against the wall, knocking away her gun. As she slid down, she reached toward her leg to detonate the device.

"No!" cried Aeryn. In a single swift motion she

pulled her laser-pistol from her boot and sliced through Sutt's leg, severing the prosthesis from the living tissue. It fell with a terrible thud on the floor. Now she could shoot Sutt without setting off the device. She levelled her pistol.

"Wait!" cried Sutt. "For friendship's sake! We were friends once."

Aeryn glared at her enemy, her pistol still pointed at her heart.

"For friendship's sake," said Sutt, "I'll tell you that you shouldn't be shooting me, you should be disarming the device—it's set to go off in sixty microts."

Aeryn looked down at the prosthetic leg. In a sliver of a microt, Sutt had pressed a place on her hip, and a new leg, as thin as a spider's and shining with steel, shot out. She hopped to her feet and backhanded Aeryn with a glove that felt as if it were made of iron, sending her sprawling to the ground. "For friendship's sake!" she said, and she scurried like a daddy-long-legs down the corridor. Aeryn had time to fire off a single shot. There was a screech, but Sutt continued down the corridor and around the corner, leaving a thin trail of blood.

"What's happened?" came D'Argo's voice from the comm. "Sutt just went by faster than a Pulbian scuttlespider—she's heading for her ship. While you were occupied, I've done away with the rest of her crew. Should I kill Sutt before she gets aboard her ship and takes off?"

Aeryn felt old. "No," she said wearily. "Let her go." She seized the leg on the floor and studied it. Sure enough, the numerals were clocking down to a detonation. Aeryn knew enough about Peacekeeper equipment to realize that Sutt had not been lying. She wished, though, she knew enough about the tech to turn the damned thing off.

She examined it more closely. If she could just—

D'Argo appeared before her. "The bomb?"

"About twenty microts to go!" Aeryn shot back. She reached over to grab the device. However, unexpectedly, the leg spun around and hopped into a standing position.

"Fifteen microts!" it said. Tiny arms grew from its side. Ocular devices rose up. "Fourteen microts."

The Qualta Rifle fired.

"D'Argo! No!"

Aeryn's warning was too late. The bolt smashed into the detached robot leg and hurled it into the wall. It did not go off. Yet.

"Ten microts," it said.

That was when Pahl arrived.

"These Peacekeepers can be quite troublesome," he said. "I've done an analysis. Having spent millennia as energy-creatures, we are quite familiar with matter and energy."

The Nokmadi moved forward calmly.

"Two microts."

He put his hand into the leg.

"One microt."

There was a buzz.

Aeryn held her breath. The moments passed. It was two microts past the moment of promised detonation, then three, then six: the device was still whole and they were all still alive.

Pahl arose and showed them his hand, glowing a

fierce cherry red. "Yes. I thought I might be of help. I neutralized it. There will be no explosion to harm any of you—or us, come to think of it. Now, can we continue our voyage to the Nokmadi homeworld?"

EPILOGUE

The Nokmadi stood in a row, staring at the vu-screens. They look like zombies, thought Crichton, newly emerged from their graves and not quite knowing what to make of the fact that a great wasteland of nothing lay in front of them.

Silence filled the bridge of Moya, the silence of tragedy, loss—and eternal melancholy.

Crichton took a moment to reflect on the events that had led them to this final confrontation with the truth of the Nokmadi.

A diplomatic council had been held aboard Moya, with the Promised One—Rygel XVI—in charge. Fortunately, Rygel excelled as diplomat as well as savior. His regal tones might have seemed useless before, but when it came to bargaining between two groups who had hated each other for millennia, all that bullying pomposity helped.

After much discussion, Rygel had negotiated a deal: the Nokmadi ship would return the Dayfolk to their homeworld, and those who wished to stay aboard, either as ghosts or as bodily beings, would let them go without hindrance. Then the Queen and her followers could continue their voyage through the universe. The Queen had promptly declared herself High Priestess of the New Cult of Rygel XVI, and vowed she would spread his fame throughout the galaxies, a promise that pleased Rygel so greatly he almost forgot to continue the negotiations.

But the most important thing, of course, was that on their home planet the Nokmadi had copies of the maps that would lead the inhabitants of Moya home.

Moya had arrived at Nokmad, the long-fabled planet of the Nokmadi. The scanners magnified the surface of the planet: cinders, the charred remains of great cities, as though a conflagration had swept over the entire world. Even the seas were gray with ashes.

"Oh my! Some sort of natural disaster?" said Rygel, hovering in his ThroneSled. "Deader than a moon without a planet!"

The Nokmadi, heads bowed, filed away back to their quarters. Pahl lingered behind a moment, as if unable to turn his head away from the planet he had sought for so long. His features were etched with pain and loss. "So the conflagration came," he said. "The core of our planet has always been volatile, and not easily contained. For millennia the Nokmadi have lived with the knowledge that our beloved world might be destroyed by eruptions. Some of us went out to seek the glory of the stars—but others could not bear to leave their home.

And now there is no home for the wanderers to return to."

"We are very sorry," said D'Argo. The Luxan's eyes were filled with tears as well.

"You cannot understand."

"I do understand," said D'Argo.

"I understand as well," said Aeryn.

The Nokmadi nodded. "Thank you. I forgot that now you cannot get the directions that would take you home as well. But at least you have homes. Our—" He lifted a hand and gestured. "Our home is gone, for ever."

Zhaan bowed to him. "We will be happy to do what we can to find you a new home in the galaxy."

Pahl shook his head, heavy with sadness.

"A great tragedy!" reflected Pilot sadly.

Crichton looked up at the figure of Pilot in the halo.

"How is Moya feeling, Pilot?" said Crichton.

"She feels the depths of the loss." Pilot turned his head for a moment. "In fact, she has a message for the Nokmadi."

Pahl looked up at Pilot. "A message for us?"

"From your ship. As you know, your ship is a gigantic plant, modified for space travel millennia ago. She has a very slow metabolism, but she is not entirely unaware. She has been in communication with Moya. Your ship says that you have not lost your real home. Your home is aboard her, the Navigator, in the World you have created, where your memories create your homeworld anew every day."

Pahl's face was still sombre, but his frame looked a little lighter, a little less worn down with grief. "Please convey our deepest gratitude to our ship, which has indeed been our home for so long. We will return to her soon, and resume our travels throughout the universe. I am beginning to miss her green fields already."

"And Crichton?" said Pilot. "Aeryn, Rygel, D'Argo? I know that your goal is to return to your own homes. But for as long as you need to, you have a home here, aboard Moya."

Crichton had to smile. "Thank you for that, Pilot. 'There's no place like Moya.' "

"And in the magnificence of my generosity," said Rygel, "please thank Moya for taking care of my acolytes until they were ready to come into my service. I am prepared to lend them back to her on certain occasions if she promises to—" He was fiddling with his ear, and his voice devolved into a high shriek.

"Rygel!" said D'Argo. "You sound worse than a screamerbird. Whatever is the matter?"

"I've lost it!" Rygel cried. He toppled off his ThroneSled and scurried around peering under things: the consoles, the central table, the chairs. He got himself in a tangle of royal proportions trying to gaze down his own robes. He sat down and began to bang his fists against the floor in frustration.

"Lost what?" said Aeryn.

"The furze!" cried Rygel. "I've lost the furze! My acolytes! Without the furze my acolytes will no longer hear my thought-voice!" He wrinkled his brow and screwed up his eyes until beads of sweat burst out on his cheeks, but nothing happened. "You see? Not a conga line on the whole ship! I've been robbed of an empire a second time—my empire of DRDs! I am going to hold my breath until I turn pink, and then I am going to have a sulk of epic proportions! Epic!"

"I think," announced Crichton, "things are returning to normal."

He thought of exactly how far from normal things sometimes were, and how places that had once seemed so far from home had become more familiar, and even beloved. And then he turned away to get back to his quarters for some Zs.